D0961626

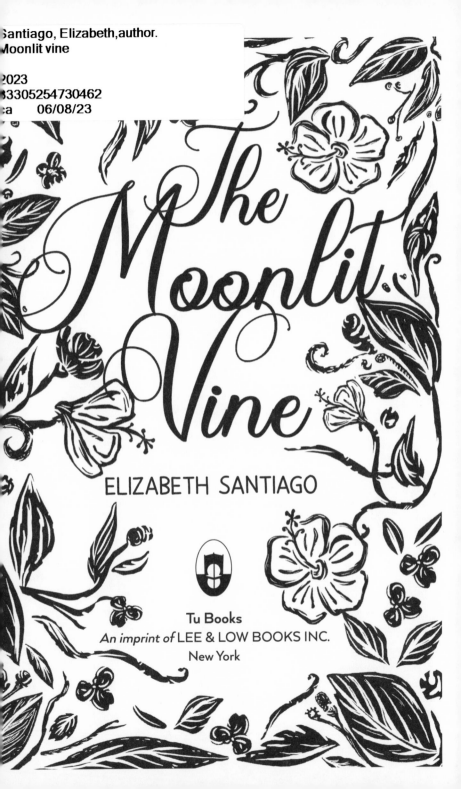

The Moonlit Vine

ELIZABETH SANTIAGO

Tu Books
An imprint of LEE & LOW BOOKS INC.
New York

TU BOOKS, *an imprint of* LEE & LOW BOOKS INC.
95 Madison Avenue
New York, NY 10016
leeandlow.com

Manufactured in the United States of America
Printed on paper from responsible sources

Edited by Elise McMullen-Ciotti
Book design by Sheila Smallwood
Typesetting by ElfElm Publishing
Book production by The Kids at Our House
Interior art by McKenzie Mayle

The text is set in Perpetua and Benton Sans
1 3 5 7 9 10 8 6 4 2
First Edition

Library of Congress Cataloging-in-Publication Data
Names: Santiago, Elizabeth, author.
Title: The moonlit vine / Elizabeth Santiago.
Description: First edition. | New York : Tu Books, an imprint of Lee & Low Books Inc., [2023]
  | Audience: Ages 14-18. | Summary: Told with interstitial historical chapters, fourteen-year-old Taína (Ty)
  must draw from the strength of her Taíno ancestors to bring her family and community hope and healing
  after a devastating incident.
Identifiers: LCCN 2022045938 | ISBN 9781643795805 (hardcover) | ISBN 9781643795812 (ebk)
Subjects: CYAC: Single-parent families—Fiction. | Family problems—Fiction. | Gangs—Fiction. | City
  and town life—Fiction. | High schools—Fiction. | Schools—Fiction. | Puerto Ricans—United States—
  Fiction. | Taino Indians—Fiction.
Classification: LCC PZ7.1.S26353 Mo 2023 | DDC [Fic]—dc23
LC record available at https://lccn.loc.gov/2022045938

This book is dedicated to my mother,
Isaura Gil y Perez de Santiago.
Isaura lost her mother, my grandmother,
Luisa Perez y Aquino de Gil, when she was eight years
old. Even though more than seventy-five years have passed
since my grandmother's death, my mother still grieves her
loss and continues to share her story—her warmth and
struggle—with all nine of her own children. Through this,
my mother taught me selfless love, not just for her children,
but for her mother and grandmother—to respect my elders
and love them as though they are still with us. It is with
deep respect and awe that I dedicate *The Moonlit Vine* to her
and all our mothers who may no longer
physically be with us, but who
will never be forgotten.

Prologue

Jaragua, 1496,
Caribbean Island of Ayiti
(present-day Haiti)

Higüamota stood where the sand met the ocean letting the warmth of the water caress her bare feet. The Moon Goddess would soon make an appearance now that the sun had begun its mysterious descent under the vast blue. Tears fell so freely down her small, innocent face that her people might have mistaken her for Boinayel, the god of rain.

A hand touched her bare shoulder, startling her. She turned to face the dark stare of the most powerful woman in the world, Anacaona. Higüamota wiped her face in vain. She knew her mother had already seen her outward display of emotion. "I'm sorry," Higüamota said. "The sound of the waves lulled me into weeping." It was a feeble explanation, but she hoped her mother would show her empathy, especially today of all days.

"My love," Anacaona said, staring out into the sky and taking in the moon's gradual appearance. "We have no time for grief."

In the waning light, Higüamota thought her mother's face looked like the faces of the elders etched into the cave walls. Anacaona meant "golden flower," and she had always welcomed visitors with a bounty of meat, fish, corn, yucca, yautia, and tobacco. Some thought her to be too generous, too free, but Higüamota had also seen her mother as a fierce warrior, using her spear to spark fear in their enemies. During ceremonial acts, her voice would bring her people swiftly to her side as she performed areítos, songs, and poems that she would recite from memory or improvise on the spot.

Usually, Anacaona would place her favorite flower, the hibiscus, in her thick, long hair. But today, her hair hung unadorned, and red paint was smeared across her face. Red was the color of war and blood, a reminder and a symbol of the murder that had happened earlier in the day. Caonabo, Higüamota's beloved father, had been executed by the strange men who had come from afar.

A sob escaped Higüamota, causing her to look away in shame. "I know, Mother," Higüamota said, anticipating her mother's disapproval. "I simply wanted a moment to honor Father's loss."

"We are not safe out in the open," Anacaona said, turning

from the water and heading back toward their yucayeque, their village. "Let's get back to the protection of the other warriors."

Higüamota skipped to catch up. "Mother, why do they target us?" Higüamota asked. "Do they hate us? What have we done?"

Anacaona continued marching without displaying any indication that she had heard her young daughter's questions. After a time, she replied. "I can't say if they hate us. They are not driven by the same things we are. We welcomed and traded with them, giving them everything we had because we thought they wanted to build on our beautiful land and be our neighbors. Instead, they are driven by greed and will destroy land and life for riches and wealth. They have more powerful weapons and have perfected cunning; therefore, they think they are superior. But they are not better in mind or body. They must use brute force to get what they want. They seek to conquer us, destroy us, but they never will. Do you understand?"

Higüamota was silent.

When they reached the shelter of their bohio, Anacaona stopped, turning to Higüamota, and placing her arms on her daughter's shoulders. They locked eyes. "You have to understand. We will not win this war. We are outnumbered, and they are cruel. It would take us too long to understand their ways, and time is something we do not have. Now listen carefully," she said, kneeling and beckoning her daughter to join her.

Higüamota knelt next to her mother, who pulled two items from a pouch hanging from the belt wrapped around her waist: a zemi and a gold amulet. Zemis, like the one Anacaona held, were carved representations of gods and were sacred objects for their people. This particular zemi was triangular and sculpted to look like a frog, the symbol of fertility. The frog's legs had been chiseled along the sides until they intertwined at one of the points on the triangle. On the opposite side was a face, not a frog's face, but a human face with a large, gaping mouth. The gold amulet sat at the end of a string of small, perfectly round stone beads. On the front of the amulet, the figure of Atabey, the goddess of life, was engraved.

"If you live and are able to pass on your knowledge of who we are, our people will never die." Anacaona handed the zemi to Higüamota. It hummed in her hand and felt like it would rip through her palm. "As soon as they kidnapped Caonabo, I had this made in the likeness of a frog to show fertility, but with a human face to show your father's dignity and wisdom. After he was executed, I went to the shamans and had them incorporate some of my lifeblood into it as a symbol of our struggle."

Anacaona then placed the amulet in her daughter's hands. It felt as if it had a heartbeat. "I know the amulet is a little different, but these are not normal times. There is a way to open it with this little clasp here, but do not open it unless it is necessary. You must promise me that. I had the shamans extract my own strength and that of all the warriors who have come before me to place within the amulet. Keep it safe and pass it on to your daughter. The elders tell me that only my daughters will be able to unleash our protection, but they must do that when there is no other alternative; otherwise, the power will not be as strong."

All Higüamota's efforts to show emotional strength failed her. "How will I know when to use it?" she wailed. "How will they know?"

"You will know," Anacaona responded. "You may not see it now, but one day you will be a grown woman, you will have a daughter, and your daughter will have a daughter. You must be sure that this zemi and amulet are kept safe and passed on to each. They all must learn of our ways, because you and they will have to hide who you are."

Higüamota began to protest. "No—"

Anacaona stopped her. "It's the only way for us to survive now. We must hide, assimilate, learn. We must save our power for when the time is right."

Anacaona closed her eyes, allowing the luminescence of the moon to fill and exalt her features. When she opened her eyes, she fixed them upon her only daughter. A sense of peace filled Higüamota as she absorbed her mother's gaze and the love behind it.

Anacaona placed her fingers on Higüamota's cheek and said, "You tell your daughter that our people are the light that makes the night sky bright. We are the music that warms the heart and blesses the soul. We love proudly and we love fiercely. This is our power. You tell your daughter to never give up this power because one day we will rise and thrive again. Of this I am absolutely sure."

Anacaona grabbed Higüamota and pulled her into her arms. The soft breeze held them and, for a moment, there were no threats, no hatred, no greed: only the love of mother and child who knew their very existence was in their hands and the hands of their future daughters.

Chapter 1

THE MOON DESERTED Ty. She searched for it through her bedroom window, but it was obscured by clouds, only occasionally peeking through to show a glimpse of itself. In all its shapes, colors, and sizes, the moon had always comforted Ty, and she needed that more than ever.

Her father and big brother were gone and, as far as Ty could tell, they weren't coming back, thanks to her mother. Ty wiped the tears running down her face. She hated to cry, and tonight was no exception.

Ty's bedroom door swung open, interrupting her thoughts. Her mother, Esmeralda, stood in the doorway with her small hands on her wide hips, still dressed in her airport security uniform of polyester blazer and tan-colored pants. Her mother's fake badge and leather belt did not impress Ty. She thought her mother wore negativity the way she herself wore glasses.

Crossing her arms against her slim frame, Ty raised an eyebrow and challenged, "What?" It was the same look and stance she'd seen many of the women in her family adopt when they were bothered. It screamed: *Are you kidding me!?* Or it silently asked: *Do you think I'm stupid?* How one interpreted it depended on the situation.

"Don't give me that attitude, Ty," her mother said, inching her way into the bedroom.

Ty loudly sucked the back of her front teeth and rolled her eyes. She had plenty more attitude to give, even though they'd been arguing for an hour.

"Mira, Ty," her mother said, ignoring Ty's not so subtle messages. "I'm not gonna argue about this anymore, okay? Right now, Alex is better off with his father than here with us. Maybe his father can get through to him. He's sixteen now and has to learn that he can't go around getting into fights. Thankfully, he was only suspended, but who knows," she said, throwing her hands in the air. "The school may expel him and maybe they should. Teach him a lesson."

"Are you kidding, Ma?" Ty yelled. She shook her head, causing her thick long brown hair to fall in front of her glasses. She pushed it away, but it fell right back. "Alex was defending himself!" Alex hadn't shared all the details with her yet, but Ty trusted him, and he never got into it with anyone. "You gotta fight this. You can't let them expel Alex for something that wasn't even his fault!"

A faraway voice chimed in, "¡Asi es Taína! You fight for your brother!"

Ty felt the urge to smile but stopped herself. Her grandmother was her champion and Ty appreciated it, but she wasn't ready to smile in front of her mother. That would make her mother think she was not mad at her anymore and Ty was still furious.

Esmeralda rolled her eyes. "Mami!" she yelled toward the voice. "Please, not now." She turned back to her daughter. "Ty, we're done talking about this."

Ty straightened her back. She was a good four inches taller than her mother and enjoyed making her mom tilt her head up to talk to her. "I know you said you didn't believe him, but I don't know why you don't believe him."

"Alex has been cutting classes." Esmeralda paced. "And that's how it starts. Cutting classes, then getting into fights. The next thing you know, he'll be arrested for something. I don't want that here. Your little brother, Luis, needs positive role models, okay? He's only seven!"

Ty felt a little vein throb near her forehead, and she closed her eyes to try to calm herself. Alex had not been cutting classes, like her mother said. He'd cut one class, which was a mistake, and he'd apologized. Now, that's supposed to make him a criminal. Ty couldn't take it.

"So, you send him to Dad?" Ty spat. "Dad, who you still won't forgive!"

Esmeralda immediately stopped pacing and squinted at her daughter. "Watch yourself."

As Ty contemplated whether to pursue the touchy subject of her father, Esmeralda grew silent, looking beyond Ty toward the window.

"He needs us!" Ty shouted, hoping to regain her mother's attention. More tears threatened to appear. The truth was that *she* needed Alex. She couldn't imagine living in the Dent without him. Going to school without him. Taking care of their grandmother and Luis without him.

"You should eat something before you go to bed," Esmeralda said, ending their discussion. "Tomorrow is Friday, and you have school. Remember, you're in high school now. It's a lot more work than middle school." And with that, she walked out of Ty's bedroom. Ty slammed the door behind her. Normally, an action like that would start a new argument, but her mother didn't return.

Back at the window, Ty finally found the moon before it became hidden by a tall building in the distance. But the quick sighting of it gave her little comfort. The only thing that would really bring her peace was Alex standing by her side.

Chapter 2

TY WAS TRANSFIXED by Principal Callahan's continued rocking in his chair. The constant body movements lulled her into a calm she shouldn't be feeling, especially now, but she was tired. She'd had little sleep the night before and had struggled getting to school. Unfortunately, her mother's words about Alex had haunted her all day, and in English class when Ms. Neil had said mean things about one of her classmates, it had been impossible to remain silent. It had felt like she was not only standing up for her classmate but also for Alex, which didn't make perfect sense now, but it had at the time.

Mr. Callahan had just asked Ty to go and apologize to Ms. Neil. He fidgeted, waiting. But Ty was still thinking about it. When Ty turned fourteen in June, Abuela told her that high school was where she would thrive and come into her power. Abuela was rarely wrong. Yet, only six weeks into her freshman year at City Main High School, Ty felt more disempowered than ever before, and she didn't have Alex to help her.

"Okay, Mr. Callahan," she finally said, defeated. "I'll apologize for swearing at Ms. Neil, but I won't apologize for calling her out for telling Beatriz she needed to learn English when she was just pausing to think about her answer. That's not right, and you know it." Ty was pushing it, but she was tired of always being made to feel like she was in the wrong. She needed to know that sometimes she was right.

Mr. Callahan stopped fidgeting and nodded. "Okay," he said, "I will talk to her about that."

This felt like a truce, so Ty also nodded. As she stood to leave, a thought crossed her mind. "Mr. Callahan," Ty said. "Are you going to call my mom to tell her what happened?" She hoped he wouldn't, but she had to know what she would be walking into when she got home.

Mr. Callahan shook his head. "Why don't you go on and apologize to Ms. Neil. If you do that, I don't see a need to tell your mother."

Ty smiled. "Thank you," she said and made her way out of the beige room and into the main office, where she con-templated her next move. There were still several minutes left before the final bell, and she needed that time to prepare for her apology.

A blue flyer on the main office bulletin board caught her eye. On it was a picture of a hand holding a pen and writing in a journal. *I hope it's a writing club*, she thought, pulling it from the board. The flyer described a new after-school program focused on creative writing. It began in two weeks and cost one hundred dollars to participate. But there was a line at the bottom that said that financial aid was available for eligible families. *If there is any family that is eligible for financial aid,* she thought, folding the flyer and putting it in her pocket, *it's mine.*

Chapter 3

T Y HEADED TOWARD the bathroom closest to Ms. Neil's class. The school corridor was flanked by lockers and closed doors to classes that were still in session. The only thing that could be heard were the rubber soles of Ty's sneakers squeaking on the shiny linoleum floor. The walls were light gray, the lockers were dark gray, and the linoleum floors were once either white or some other shade of gray. *City Main High has zero personality*, she thought for the hundredth time. To make matters worse, the overhead lights were never consistently on. Some worked fine while others flickered, giving the corridors a feeling of abandonment.

The gray motif continued into the girls' bathroom. At least the walls were decorated with writing and drawings by girls who wanted to either brighten the place up or leave their mark. There was even a question written in pink and blue letters: "Deena will you go out with me?" Ty always smiled when she saw that. How long it had been there, she didn't know, but she hoped whoever asked this Deena out got their wish.

As Ty walked toward a foggy mirror, a wounded cry came from one of the stalls. She hesitated. Ty didn't want to get into anyone's business, but she hated the idea of lonely sobbing, the kind of bawling that you did by yourself when you thought no one was watching. The kind of crying that's real.

Ty called out, "Hey, are you okay?"

Someone blew their nose. "I'm good," said a muffled voice.

Ty recognized the slight accent and glanced under the door, finding a pair of familiar black high-heeled boots. "Beatriz? Is that you?"

"Taína?" The stall door opened and there stood Beatriz Machado. "Sorry. I was waiting for the bell."

Beatriz was a lot shorter than Ty and the heels gave her extra height, but she wasn't someone who stood out in any way. She rarely spoke out in class, rarely made eye contact with anyone, and generally did not do anything that caused her attention.

"I'm waiting for the bell too," Ty said as Beatriz quickly wiped her face. "Are you crying because of Ms. Neil?" Ty asked, ignoring the fact that Beatriz was desperately trying to compose herself. "Honey, she's not worth it."

"Yo sé," Beatriz said, switching to Spanish.

"She's mad crazy," Ty offered.

"I know. Yo sé," Beatriz repeated. "I was embarrass. She embarrass me." She made her way to the mirror and squinted to see her face in the blur of old, dirty glass.

The bell rang before she could respond, causing a cacophony of sound. Footsteps, loud voices, and laughter filled the air as the door to the bathroom swung open and other girls entered the space. Beatriz quickly walked out of the bathroom, head bowed, and blended quietly into the crowd.

Ty tried to quell her annoyance. *How am I going to get through this?* A memory of her grandmother entered her mind's eye: soft features, thick white afro, big gap-toothed smile. Abuela was nodding with that knowing, shrewd look she often wore and said, *M'ija, sometimes you have to take people's crap to keep the peace, but don't ever let them conquer you. You have too much strength to keep it hidden.* With purpose, Ty exited the bathroom and began to make her way swiftly to Ms. Neil.

As she neared her destination, Ty began to get nervous. Her pace slowed and she leaned against a bank of lockers. *I don't want to do this*, she thought, hanging her head and letting her long, dark hair cover the sides of the glasses she wore.

Strong cologne enveloped her. "Hey, Ty."

Ty looked up to see Vincent Gordon coming toward her. She couldn't help but smile.

"Hey, Vin," she said. "I didn't think I'd see you after school. You usually bounce as soon as the bell rings to find the beautiful Imani." Ty was only half-joking. She and Vin had been tight until Imani, and Ty was deep in her feelings about it. She used to have Vin all to herself until he got shoulder-length locs over the summer and a sword tattoo on his forearm. Then all the neighborhood girls wanted to meet him. Then, Imani showed up, making him too busy to hang out like they used to pre-locs and tattoo.

"Funny," Vin said, pursing his lips. "It's not like we're always together." Ty gave him *the look*. He sucked his teeth. "Fine, we've been together a lot lately." Ty continued with the look. "I know, I know, we always promised we'd be available and I'm kinda not around much."

Ty remained silent, enjoying his discomfort.

Vin swiftly changed the subject. "What happened with Mr. Callahan?" Their class schedules were identical, so he'd been there when Ty had had her outburst in English class.

"I gotta apologize to Ms. Neil and I'd worked up the courage, but now I don't want to do it." Ty shook her head. "How am I supposed tell her I'm sorry when I'm not sorry, you know what I'm saying?"

Vin nodded. "She's always saying something ignorant. Remember the poem?"

How could she forget? The first time she'd been sent to Mr. Callahan's office had been because of a poem Vin wrote in class. Ms. Neil had asked Vin if he'd written the poem himself. Ty couldn't help but ask who else could have written the poem, since Vin had been sitting there the whole time. Ms. Neil had responded that the poem was too good to have come from a student at *this* school. Unable to stop herself, Ty had quickly replied that maybe Ms. Neil should do a better job teaching, then. "Why can't she ever apologize to us for the stupid things she says?" Ty asked.

"Because it don't work like that!" Vin paused. "I wanted so bad to tell her that I could write that poem in English and Spanish."

"That's right," she said, using a head nod to punctuate her words. All those afternoons spent at her house when they were younger had exposed him to Spanish and now he was pretty fluent.

"I wished you didn't get into trouble because of me though," he said.

"Nuh," Ty said, using her hands to dismiss the statement. "Don't even worry about it. I couldn't let that go. Otherwise, they think it's okay to talk to us like that." Ty hated when teachers used their authority against her and students that looked like her. There was only one teacher so far at City Main who she thought was cool, who talked to them like she saw them as good kids, and that was Ms. Carruthers, their history teacher. The thought of Ms. Carruthers reminded Ty of her history project.

"Did you start Ms. Carruthers's history project?" Ty asked. Vin looked at her blankly. "You know, the one she gave us last week about picking a topic that we had only studied a little bit in middle school and going deeper with it."

Vin shook his head, remembering. "Nuh. Not yet. I don't know what to focus on, but I like the idea of the project."

"Me too," Ty agreed. "Ms. Carruthers doesn't treat us like we're cheaters. I wish Ms. Neil was more like her, because usually English is my favorite subject!"

"I know," he said, and returned to the main topic. "Look, all you gotta do is go in there, say sorry, and bounce. That's it."

Ty frowned. "I'm just worried about what else she's going to say, like I'll say something else that will get me in more trouble."

"I feel ya," Vin said. "Like I said, all you need to do is say sorry and bounce. Don't get into a long conversation or anything."

So true, Ty thought. She wished Alex were there.

As if reading her mind, Vin said, "I heard from a couple of kids that Alex was sticking up for Eddie when he got into that fight."

At the mention of Eddie Gonzalez, Alex's best friend, a swarm of butterflies took over her stomach. Before everything had happened with Alex, feelings had been developing for Eddie that she couldn't seem to control. "I don't know," she said a little too loudly.

Vin didn't push the topic. "You around later?" he asked, taming a wayward loc.

Realization hit that it was Friday. Usually, her mother would be home with a massive list of things for Ty to do over the weekend. Ty liked to know what she was in for first before making plans. "Can I get back to you on that? I gotta see what's going on at home."

"Bet." Vin nodded and headed down the hall.

"Wait," Ty said, before he was too far off. "I saw this flyer in the office." She pulled the blue piece of paper out of her pocket and handed it to him. He read it and grinned.

"Dope," he said. "Do you want to sign up together?"

"You know I do," Ty said. "But I don't know if my mom will agree." *Or, if we have the money*, Ty thought.

Vin nodded. "Okay, I can sign up and if you can too, great. It will be like old times when we used to write together."

The most fun Ty ever had at school had been working on a book project with Vin in the fourth grade. It's how they'd become friends.

"Okay," Ty said, realizing she had to get to Ms. Neil's class before she left. "Let me go do this."

"Hit me up later," Vin said before taking off. Ty watched his stocky frame shuffle down the hall. His baggy blue jeans hung low, making it difficult for him to walk gracefully. Ty forced herself to turn around and deal with her destiny— Ms. Neil.

Chapter 4

THE DOOR TO ROOM 121 looked to be sealed shut. *It's like a vault in there*, she thought, grabbing the cold metal handle and yanking the door open. Ms. Neil had her back toward Ty, wiping the whiteboard while humming to herself. Ty couldn't help but feel a little bitter. *Here's Ms. Neil humming away, while Beatriz is somewhere wiping her eyes*. It wasn't fair, but Ty was slowly accepting that teachers were always seen as right, at least in the school building.

Bang! Both Ty and Ms. Neil jumped as the door crashed closed. Ms. Neil clutched her thin gold necklace, but did nothing else to acknowledge that she had a visitor. She quietly resumed the cleaning of the whiteboard.

Ignored, Ty wondered if she should leave, but the sight of a small plastic tub filled with cleaners and disinfectants caught her eye. *Does Ms. Neil stay late every day to disinfect her classroom against the germs of youth?* Ty wondered.

Ty's eyes fixated on a newly hung, plastic-covered poster, describing the classroom rules Ms. Neil chose to prioritize.

Raise your hand before speaking.

Have respect for yourself and for teachers.

Read the classics, and above all, follow the rules.

Next to the poster was another glossy wall-hanging that held a quote:

"Those who fail to learn from history are condemned to repeat it." —*Winston Churchill*

"May I help you?" Ms. Neil asked.

"Ms. Neil," Ty said, inching closer and placing her backpack at her feet. "I wanted to talk to you about what happened today."

Ms. Neil opened the top drawer of her desk, put the whiteboard eraser in it, then locked it with a key. "Sure," she said, gesturing for Ty to sit in one of the chairs near her. Ms. Neil folded her hands across her chest and waited.

Ms. Neil was older than Ty's mother, and looked even older with her lips pursed and her eyes squinting through thick glasses. Her blonde hair was tied back in a severe bun, and she wore no makeup.

Ty blurted, "Um, I really didn't mean to swear at you. I'm sorry about that. It was not the right thing to do." She decided to leave it there, following Vin's advice to simply say sorry and bounce. But Ty had a feeling she wasn't getting out of there anytime soon.

Ms. Neil waited a few moments before replying, "No it wasn't." She pulled invisible lint off the sleeve of her lilac cardigan. "You've not been in school for two months, and I've already had to send you to the principal's office twice. That's not a good way to start the school year."

"I'm not trying to get into trouble," Ty said, hoping honesty would help. "Sometimes I see things that aren't okay, and I have to say something about them, you know what I'm saying?"

"Do I know what you're saying?" Ms. Neil mimicked. "Well, students need to learn when to say something and when not to say something. You will always get into trouble if you yell at teachers or are disrespectful."

Ty nodded slightly to indicate she was listening but wanted so badly to counter that Ms. Neil could be very disrespectful herself. Instead, she inspected her sneakers, noticing the dull shine of the black canvas around the top. She fought the urge to polish them.

"I accept your apology this time, but if you speak out in class again, I'm going to send you right back to Mr. Callahan's office."

"If I speak out at all?" Ty asked.

Ms. Neil tilted her head to one side and blinked, making Ty feel as though she'd asked the most idiotic thing a fourteen-year-old ninth grader could ask a teacher. "I don't want you disrupting the class, Ty-na, so yes, you'll need to keep your opinions to yourself."

Wow, Ty thought. First, her name was not Ty-na, but Taína, pronounced Ty-ee-na, is not that hard. Second, it wasn't like she was shouting out her opinions all the time disrupting class. It was a class, which meant she sometimes needed to provide opinions on class material to show she was learning. Was she supposed to just sit there and say nothing? Maybe she was simply not supposed to ask the types of questions that got Ms. Neil amped, like: Why wouldn't she be able to speak English well?

This is a setup, plain and simple, Ty told herself. She was getting warm, and her heart began thumping rapidly—the telltale signs that she was about to say something others would think was bad. She had to relax. She could not blow up at Ms. Neil again, not after the week she was having.

She closed her eyes and took a deep breath before responding, "Um, I'll try." Then, because her tongue had a mind of its own, she added, "I just wanna make sure I understand. Are you asking me to never speak in class again? Like say nothing at all? What if someone asks me for my opinion? What are the rules?" Ty thought they were reasonable questions, but Ms. Neil shook her head, throwing her hands in the air.

"The rules are the same as always," she said. "Don't speak unless I call on you. Don't share your opinion unless I ask you to. Is that hard to follow?"

Ty gave Ms. Neil the "Are you kidding me?" version of the look—which happened involuntarily, like having to scratch an itch.

Ms. Neil stood and said, "And I don't appreciate that kind of body language or facial expressions either."

Ty's hands, which had been laid out across her thighs, began to ball into fists—which was hard to accomplish with her long, blue acrylic fingernails. Hot tears formed in her eyes, and she found it hard to swallow.

"Fine," Ty said, picking her bag up off the floor. The movement kept her emotions in check. She would rather be suspended right along with her brother Alex than let Ms. Neil see her cry. "No opinions and no body language. Got it."

Both Ty and Ms. Neil stood silently for about ten seconds before Ms. Neil said, "Perfect. You can go now."

Ty bolted out of the room and into the desolate hallway, moving quickly toward the exit. She wished someone would explain all the rules to her, because it wasn't easy to know what was off-limits. Okay, sure, swearing at teachers was always bad, but why was pointing out hurtful words a teacher said to another student the wrong thing to do? Why was it wrong to defend someone? It was almost like she was being asked to accept that some people didn't matter—that she should hold her feelings in secret because she didn't have the right to complain. Ty found it hard to accept that.

Deep in her thoughts, Ty ran out of the school building and hurried along Main Street, where City Main High School was situated. It was about a half mile away from Ty's street, Denton Street, or "the Dent," as it was called. Ty wondered why she was confronted with yet another coffee shop along her route. This one was called *Pour Me* and the words "Grand Opening" were prominently displayed amidst a long line of customers. *Who are these people*, she wondered, *and why do they need to drink so much coffee?* There were already three coffee shops on Main Street as it was!

Just five years ago, mom-and-pop stores such as M&S Discount Furniture, La Botánica Pura, and Super Dollar Heaven lined the street, and she often went to them with her mother and grandmother. Those businesses had been replaced by a paper store, yoga studios, and coffee shops like Pour Me. When these new places appeared, her mother and grandmother stopped shopping on the street. It wasn't that they didn't drink coffee or want to try yoga, it was that they were usually made to feel unwelcome.

People were everywhere on Main, but none of them looked like her or anyone in her family. Instead, there were joggers in neon-colored attire obliviously moving their slim limbs to sounds coming from their headphones; women pushing baby strollers that looked heavier than the electric cars parked in front of meters; and men sipping warm drinks from to-go containers that smelled of roasted coffee and caramel. *Do they know I'm from the Dent?* she wondered. Did they even see her at all? Did it matter? Ty wasn't sure if she even wanted to be welcomed anyway. It all seemed so different than what she was used to in the Dent.

As if to prove that point, a black crow sat on the roof of the new coffee shop near her street. Ty stared at it then quickly looked away. Her grandmother believed certain birds brought news with them, and she had a feeling these crows were not bearers of love and happiness, or creatures that welcomed you into a place. *I didn't want to go in there anyway!* Ty thought.

Ty turned onto the Dent, hoping not to run into the Denton Street Dogs or the Night Crawlers, who ruled Denton Park. Only a mile long, the street felt like a world within a world because once you made the turn onto it, Main Street became a distant memory.

Ty threw her shoulders back. *The Dent isn't all bad.* There were community and a familiarity about the Dent that Ty appreciated. And there was Atabey Market, a Denton Street landmark, which was as far down as outsiders would go. For Ty, Atabey Market was just the beginning. Ty loved hanging out with the owners, José and Hilda, and since she wasn't ready to go home to whatever awaited her, she made her way there instead.

The aroma of fried goodness greeted her before she opened the market door. José and Hilda made the best alcapurrias in the neighborhood. Their outsides made with heavily seasoned green bananas and yautia, and insides filled with meat and potatoes, then the whole thing fried to crispy perfection . . . *Hold up*, she thought. *I have five dollars!* Ty reached into her pocket for the money her uncle had given her. Last time she'd bought alcapurrias they were a dollar apiece—she had enough money for a feast!

Inside the market, she was immediately hit with merengue music and the smell of sazón, a blend of spices that made so many Puerto Rican dishes flavorful and colorful. Ty didn't always appreciate salsa, merengue, and bachata music from the islands, but hearing it played unapologetically made her feel proud. Like she belonged. People standing at the front counter stopped chatting loudly over the rhythms as she made her way inside.

"What?" Ty asked, wondering if she had something on her face or in her hair. Hilda Martinez, the owner, clapped in response.

"Ay, muchacha, ¿qué tal?" she asked from behind the counter. "¿Cómo está la familia?"

Ty passed the onlookers, who resumed their chatter, and leaned onto the counter. "My family is good," she said.

Hilda nodded. "The desk in the back room is clean if you want to use it to do your homework."

Ty smiled in appreciation. Sometimes she or Alex would hang out there to do their homework, but it was usually way too busy to concentrate. Instead, they mostly hung out and ate, listened to their neighbors' chitchat, and, maybe, occasionally glanced at a textbook.

"Thanks, but I came for food," Ty said.

Hilda clapped again, moving to partially reveal a chalkboard behind the counter listing the offerings of the day. Ty scanned it until she saw what she was looking for.

"Yass," Ty screamed. "Cinco alcapurrias, por favor."

"Only five?" Hilda asked. "For you and all your family?" Hilda shook her head. "I'll give you six because you need to eat more than one, honey, you're too skinny—bien flaca."

At that moment, Hilda's husband, José, appeared and said, "Déjala, she doesn't need to gain weight. She's fine."

Hilda dismissed him with her thick hand. "He's always saying the opposite of what I say. I think he just likes to argue with me." She rolled her eyes and added, "Let me get your alcapurrias before I start with him."

José chuckled, rubbing his hands together, like his and Hilda's little argument was about to get good. José and Hilda had opened Atabey Market long before Ty and her family had moved into the neighborhood, cooking up well-loved Puerto Rican treats like empanadas, bacalaítos, and, of course, alcapurrias. Colorful canned goods lined the shelves, and fresh bread from a bakery in another town sat on the counter.

José bent over to pick up something off the floor, giving Ty a full view of the chalkboard. Someone had drawn what looked like a woman with a crown squatting with her legs open. It wasn't offensive, just a little cartoonish. "That's Atabey," José said, following her eyes.

"Oh, who the market is named after?" she asked.

"Yes, the Taíno goddess of life."

"Taíno goddess?" Ty repeated. She was named Taína after the original people on the island of Puerto Rico, the Taíno. But she had never heard of the goddess of life.

Hilda screamed from the kitchen. "¡Ay, me quemé!"

José ran to find her.

"Is everything all right?" one of the men in the front yelled.

In response, Hilda yelled at José, "That's why I don't want you back here!"

"How is this my fault?" José asked, making his way back to the front while the other men started teasing, "You in trouble now, bruh," and, "Just apologize man, save yourself."

José shook his head. "Toma Taína," he said, giving the alcapurrias to Ty. They were in a brown paper bag with oil already seeping through.

Ty held the bag away from her with one hand and gave José the five-dollar bill with the other.

José pushed the money away. "Just take them."

"That's so cool. Thank you!" Ty said. "Hilda's okay, right?" she asked as another customer entered the store.

José smirked. "Of course. She's fine. Just very hot alcapurrias. Let me take care of this guy here." José gave the guy who'd just walked in a big high-five type handshake followed by a side hug, shoulder-bump kind of thing.

Outside, Ty found the guy's car parked in front, windows open, bachata music playing at the highest volume possible, like a mini nightclub. She quickly went around the car and across the street to a row of townhouses that comprised the Denton Street Apartments.

A group of younger kids ran in the opposite direction, entering the park and shouting each other's names and laughing loudly. Ty could see two people, dressed all in black, in the distance. Ty froze, wondering if she should tell the kids to stay out of there, but they came back out on their own, running toward the lower half of Denton Street instead. The Night Crawlers wore all black. Even kids avoided those who only wore that color.

The alcapurrias were leaking even more now, making her hand wet with grease. She had to get moving or she'd get it all over her.

The bachata music from the car continued to play in the distance as Ty unlocked the front door to their apartment. She hung her keys on the hook in their small entryway, then entered the living room. There sat her mother. Face set as if carved in stone and arms folded across her chest. Ty had seen that look many times and it was never good.

"What?" Ty asked.

"I just got off the phone with your teacher, Ms. Neil, and she told me that you were talking back to her. You want to get suspended too?!"

Chapter 5

M R. C ALLAHAN *said he wouldn't call,* Ty fumed. *But Ms. Neil? Like I need a new argument with my mom when we haven't finished the one about Alex!*

Before she could respond, Luis ran in and wrapped his arms around her waist. He was the spitting image of their father and Alex. Dark, thick hair, dark brown eyes, and beyond-cute long eyelashes. He was also brown and slim like them, but Luis had their mother's dimples, which were in full effect as he lifted his face to smile at her. He let go and looked toward the front door as if hoping for Alex to appear, then turned away and disappeared to the bedroom he shared with his older brother.

Alone with the ball of anger sitting on the couch, Ty opted for a food truce. "Alcapurria?" she said, lifting the stained brown paper bag.

"From Atabey?" Esmeralda asked, squinting at the bag as if wanting proof.

Ty nodded, hopeful.

Esmeralda shook her head, not accepting the truce. "Did that Hilda ask a lot of questions? You know how she's always into other people's business." Esmeralda removed the band that held her long, thick black hair, shook it loose, then pulled it back again into a bushy blob on top of her head.

Ty shrugged. "She just asked how everyone was doing, Ma. You know, like normal people do." Ty placed the bag on the living room table.

"Don't put that greasy mess on my table!" Esmeralda said, jumping up, snatching the bag, and then making her way to the kitchen. Ty quickly used her hand to vigorously wipe away any stains that might have been left. She wasn't up for the lecture about how, even though they were poor, they didn't have to have dirty and broken things. Other lectures were surely coming.

Ty eyed her mother through the cut-out window separating the kitchen and the living room, watching her place paper plates on the kitchen table. Ty assumed Abuela was in her bedroom as usual. With the bedroom doors all closed, Ty knew she was on her own. Reluctantly, she joined her mother in the kitchen, quickly grabbing one of her favorite fried treats. "Should I get Luis?" she asked while chewing. She wanted him back as a buffer.

Esmeralda shook her head. "We had pizza already and don't talk with your mouth full. He's probably playing with that *new* iPad his father got him." She waved her small hand in the air as some sort of dismissal when she said the word *new*. Esmeralda was convinced the iPad was stolen, even though Ty had seen her father buy the iPad at the store and told her mom this fact more than once. It didn't seem to matter. Esmeralda was determined to believe the worst about him.

"So," Esmeralda said, tapping her fingers on the kitchen table. "Do you want to tell me what happened this time? Wait," she ordered before Ty could respond. "Let me guess. The teacher said something you didn't agree with, and you felt the need to correct her."

"Ma," Ty said, wiping her hands on her pants. "You make it sound like I'm mad out of control or something. I'm not. At. All."

Esmeralda raised her eyebrows, which in and of itself was a challenge.

"Besides, I spent all day worried about Alex," Ty said, hoping to remind her that there were bigger problems than Ms. Neil. "I was tired, and I just couldn't sit there and let Ms. Neil make fun of Beatriz because English isn't her first language. I can't respect that. You know what I'm saying?" Ty explained the entire incident, including the trip to the principal's office, her apology, and where Mr. Callahan told her there was no need to call her parents if she apologized. "Why would they lie about that?" she wondered aloud.

"Don't worry about them," Esmeralda said. "I would

have been pissed if they didn't call to tell me. I need to know what's up with you at school, Ty. You . . ." She paused, pointing at Ty's face. "You need to worry about yourself."

"But," Ty pleaded, "don't you think it's wrong that I can never defend myself or others? Like . . . like no matter what happens, they're the only ones who get to be right?" Ty was annoyed with herself for stumbling over her words. Ty thought if she could just get the words right, maybe her mother would understand.

"Don't be stupid, m'ija," Esmeralda said. "Nobody wants to hear your opinion or mine even. They just want us to do what we are told and not get in the way. *Hmpf.* If I thought like you, reacted like you, I'd be in fights all day, every day. I can't afford to do that. I need both my security guard jobs."

Ty crossed her arms against her chest. "Ma, if I have to be like that then . . . whatever, why bother?"

Esmeralda shook her head. "You don't understand anything. People like us are on our own. Nobody cares. We all we got. I have to be like this, or else what? We live on the street?"

"Ma, we are not—"

"And you," she continued, "you *will* finish school or you'll end up like me. I quit high school, so now I'm stuck." She paused, picking at an alcapurria. "The office security job is fine I guess, but, man," she said, laughing bitterly. "That airport security job is . . ." She shook her head. "Ty, you don't even know, okay? But I know both you and Alex can do better." Esmeralda stared at the food on her paper plate. "Just go to school, do your work, keep your head down, and that's it. It's not going to kill you to do that."

Maybe it will *kill me*, Ty thought. "Ma, I don't want to be like that, be all invisible. That's not me." Ty paused, hoping the right words would come to her, but they didn't. She simply added, "I'm more like Abuela, you know? She is not afraid to say what she feels—to be her real self."

"*Hmpf*," Esmeralda said. "She's not afraid because she's not in her right mind."

That stung. Ty had had enough. She ran out of the kitchen.

"I didn't mean anything by that!" Esmeralda yelled after her, but it was too late. Ty reached her room and slammed the door as hard as she could.

Ty stood in the middle of her room, staring up at her Bad Bunny poster. "Why do people always say 'I didn't mean anything by that' when they really do mean something?" Bad Bunny didn't respond.

Pulling her phone out of her pocket, Ty texted Alex:

How r u?

Silence. No response.

Ty thought of Eddie. *They were still friends, right?* They had been friends for years when, one day, Ty caught him staring at her, causing her to blush. It was a weird feeling because, as far as she knew, he didn't like her like that. But, after that happened, things with him got awkward, like they both didn't know what to do around one another. Ty had been sorting through her feelings when the fight with Alex happened.

She worked up the courage to text and wrote:

Alex got into a fight and everyone thinks u in it. Hit me up!

After a minute, Eddie wrote:

Sorry.

Immediately Ty responded:

Why u sorry?

Ty waited for five minutes but Eddie didn't answer. She texted Beatriz instead to ask how she was doing, but, again, silence.

Wait. Vin. He'd asked her to hit him up. The call went straight to voicemail. Frustrated, Ty threw the phone across her bed where it landed dangling off the edge as if it were ready to jump.

Her bedroom door creaked. Ty turned to see her grandmother, Isaura Ramos, standing in the doorway, holding an alcapurria in her hand. "Ay, qué rico," she said, taking a bite. Her white afro floated freely above her head like a soft cloud.

"Hi, Abuela," Ty said. "Those aren't going to make you sick, right?"

Isaura swallowed the bite and shook her head. "Mira,

I have problems with my head, not my stomach." Grease dripped down her veiny, thin hand, and she wiped it off with a napkin.

Ty giggled. Her grandmother had been living with them since Ty's grandfather passed away. He had kept Abuela's Alzheimer's diagnosis to himself until he died, but it had soon become evident that Isaura was in the throes of an incurable disease. Even so, Ty appreciated her presence, especially at times like this.

"How are you today?" Ty asked.

Isaura took another bite of her snack, closing the door behind her. "Good," she said, licking her fingers. "I heard a little bit of the fight you were having with your mother. You can't let people walk all over you. Your mother doesn't understand you. She is afraid. Don't be like that, okay?"

"Okay, Abuela," Ty said. "It's just that she thinks I have a big mouth." Ty thought that would get a reaction and it did.

"M'ija," Isaura said, rolling her eyes. "A lot of women in our family had to keep their mouths shut so you could have a big mouth, okay?! The time has come for us to be bold. You will see."

Ty wasn't sure what she meant by "you will see," but Isaura changed the subject. "You know, your mother didn't have the easiest of childhoods," she said, sitting down next to Ty on the bed.

"Really?" Ty said, hoping for some insight. Her mother's life so far had been shrouded in secrecy like a locked treasure.

"Well," Isaura continued, "your mother had a confusing

childhood. We traveled back to Puerto Rico quite a bit when she and your uncle Benito were children. Benito was outgoing and everyone loved him, but your mother was more sensitive. I don't think she ever felt like she belonged anywhere. People on the island didn't accept her because she was quiet, and they said she was muy orgulloso and stuck up. People in the US didn't accept her because she was dark and talked with an accent. She didn't like having to be two people, so over time she became 'no one.'"

Ty made a mental note to write down what her grandmother had just shared. She had been writing her grandmother's stories and sayings in a journal since she was six years old.

"I think she was hoping to be accepted somewhere, but in life, you can't wait for others to accept you. You have to accept yourself first." Isaura patted Ty's hand. "You understand that, Taína. You would rather be yourself than anyone else and that makes you strong. However," she said, becoming more serious, "since you are Puerto Rican, that strength comes with a price. You have to use your strength wisely."

Isaura scanned Ty's room with her eyes as if noticing it for the first time. The fine lines along her face reminded Ty of the myriad of lines on the palms of her own hands.

"Who the hell is that?" Isaura asked, pointing to a poster on the wall.

"That's Bad Bunny," Ty said. "He's a singer I like." She didn't have many posters, some of Rihanna and Cardi B, but her grandmother homed in on a poster of Bad Bunny cut from a magazine. He stood in front of El Morro, a famous Puerto Rican landmark in San Juan.

"Is he Puerto Rican?" Isaura asked.

Ty nodded.

"Puerto Ricans are fighting for so many things . . ." Isaura paused. "You know, I never thought about it like this, but Spanish was the language of our original colonizadores. We are fighting to hold onto it now, because we've been taken over by the United States. We, as a people, have already given up so much, so we fight for our culture and language, as we should."

Ty had never heard her grandmother use the word *colonizadores* before. She assumed it meant colonizers, but she would look it up later because she didn't want to interrupt her.

"M'ija," she said, gazing at Ty with a confused look in her eyes as if she were trying to work out an equation in her mind. "Where is Alejandro, your father?"

Ty's father hadn't lived with them for almost three years, and her grandmother used to know that, but, then again, some memories were better than others.

"Abuela, he doesn't live with us anymore. He lives in another town." Her grandmother still looked perplexed. "Remember, Abuela? He was in prison for two years, then got out last year, and now lives somewhere else."

"Prison? *Hmpf*," Isaura said. "He was always good for nothing."

"Abuela," Ty warned, "he is trying. It's hard to get a job with a prison record."

Isaura was no longer listening, like she had decided to keep only the memory of how Ty's father had been locked up. Ty's memories were more complex. He'd always been the best father he could be. When she had asked him about it, he'd told her he had just needed more money—that his job hadn't been enough. It had not been the right thing to do, but he wasn't a bad person.

"¿Y Alex?" Isaura asked. "I have not seen him all day."

"Alex is staying with Dad until he can go back to school." Ty paused to see if Abuela was listening. It seemed she was. "Remember, Alex got suspended from school for fighting? He's doing okay though," she added.

"Qué ridículo," Isaura spat out. "Alex should be home with his family. He got into a fight because he was sticking up for himself. ¡Qué ridículo!"

One hundred percent facts, Ty thought. She knew whatever reason Alex had for fighting, it had to be good. "I want him to come home too," Ty said.

"Of course you do," Isaura said with conviction. "I am going to talk to your mother now and tell her to bring Alex home. Too much is too much."

Ty grinned. She and Alex loved it when her grandmother said "too much is too much" instead of "enough is enough." And when she said that, you knew it was on.

Isaura got up and walked out of Ty's room. Only to come back a few minutes later with another alcapurria. "Ay, qué rico," she said and disappeared into her own bedroom.

Amoná, 1530
(present-day Isla de la Mona)

*"Goddess, cacique, warrior, mother
a strong beauty like no other
Moon blessed with warmth in her gaze
Welcoming guests with yautia and maze
Open heart and open mind
No greater human, you will find
We worship her in Ayiti and Amoná
The golden flower Anacaona"*

THE AREÍTO Higüamota sang to her granddaughter lulled the little one to sleep as the hammock swung between two palm trees that were swaying in the warm breeze.

Memories of her beloved mother flooded Higüamota's thoughts. She nearly forgot that her only daughter sat next to her until Guanina reached for her hand.

"Mother," Guanina nudged, "will you tell me more stories about Anacaona?"

Over the years, Higüamota had told Guanina how Anacaona had been a cacique, and a warrior who fought for their people. It had been painful for her to share more.

But Guanina was a woman and a mother now. *Is it time for her to know her duty?* Higüamota wondered. She had always kept the amulet and zemi close to her. They made her feel as though her mother was still with her. Maybe it was time to let them go.

Someone drew near.

Both women stood to greet the bronzed figure as he approached. He was thin and broad shouldered; black paint spread across his forehead and eyes.

"Guaybana, I am glad you have come. Can you stay here with Casiguaya?" Higüamota asked, pointing to the infant in the hammock. "I would like to enter the caves with Guanina alone."

Guaybana nodded and sat on the ground by the hammock and leaned against one of the small palm trees that held it.

Higüamota moved gracefully into the cave closest to them, placing her bare feet on the sandy, yet rocky terrain. She was careful not to touch the cave walls she considered sacred even though she could have used the support to balance her moves. Guanina closely followed, holding her arms wide to keep her movements steady.

Higüamota paused at a near imperceptible opening in the cave wall. The shadows made this entrance look like a simple crack in the rock but, as they drew near, it opened into a smaller chamber. Light from an opening in the cave ceiling above revealed it to be a room that others had visited. Drawings etched into the walls told a story.

"These blessed caves," Higüamota began, "have been here

longer than our people and are said to have been made by the ocean and wind. I never told you how we got to this island or what happened to Anacaona, because the loss of my mother and our land was too great a sorrow for me to discuss. But it's time for you to know the truth of who you are."

Higüamota moved deeper into the space and then knelt by a group of carvings on the back wall. When Guanina had joined her, she began. "We are from Jaragua, which was where my mother, your grandmother, Anacaona ruled. She was a fierce warrior and much beloved by her people." Higüamota blinked her tears away as Guanina held her hand.

"She was murdered by the men from the ships—the warmongers we hide from here on this island. I have learned that these devils come from a place called Spain and they want our land and whatever riches they can harvest from our home. Anacaona tried to communicate with them and share what she could of the island's bounty, but they did not see her as leader." Higüamota paused. "I don't really think they even saw her as human, or any of us as human, for that matter. Otherwise, how could they do the things they have done?"

Higüamota laid her hand on the ground, allowing her fingers to play with the roughness of the cave floor beneath them.

"How was she murdered?" Guanina asked.

"She was hung."

Guanina gasped.

"I didn't witness it, thankfully, but as soon as it happened, your father, Guaybana, came and retrieved me and we fled on foot into the vast forest of Ayiti. It felt like many suns and moons had passed before we made it to the other side of the island onto a beach. On that beach were other Taíno who had fashioned canoes and were ready to risk the open waters. Guaybana and I joined them, and we ended up here, on Amoná."

Higüamota shifted her weight in her crouched position and continued, "Guaybana and I found this space here within the caves and hid until we felt we were safe." She sighed. "I don't know if we are ever truly safe, but we seem to be well shielded in this place.

"Sometime afterward, Guaybana and I carved Anacaona's likeness right here." Higüamota traced lines in the rock wall. "We chose this spot because there were other etchings already here that were meaningful to us. Look." Higüamota pointed to a drawing. "Here is a bat. See its wings. And here are some owls. Both creatures are night dwellers, and it is said, if you see an owl or a bat, you are seeing a deceased spirit. The night we arrived, an owl greeted us at the entrance of the cave and when we entered, there was a bat by this opening. When the sun returned the next day, we found this spot and these drawings of bats and owls already here. We took it as an omen and carved Anacaona's likeness here as well."

Guanina stared intently at it. "That is Anacaona, my grandmother?" she asked, pointing at the one carving of what looked to be a human face.

Higüamota nodded. As Guanina continued to study the

portrait, Higüamota reached into a secret pocket within her loincloth and took out the zemi and amulet. "Guanina," Higüamota said. "There is something I must pass on to you. . . ."

Chapter 6

AT ABOUT MIDNIGHT, Ty had grown tired of lying wide awake in her bed, so she sat up and searched for the moon out her window. But the moon was not visible, so she settled for pictures instead. She pulled an old shoebox out from under her bed, where she kept some of her favorite things, including old notebooks and photos.

Ty remembered that she had taken amazing pictures of the moon in Puerto Rico. Four years ago, she and Alex had gone there with their uncle Benny to visit their great-aunt Juana in Mayagüez. It was the only time Ty and Alex had been to Puerto Rico and Ty remembered two things. First, the hammocks Aunt Juana had set up between trees in her yard. They'd looked like big slings, so Alex had tried to cat-apult Ty with one, but Juana had stopped them. They were used for swinging, sleeping, or resting, she'd said. Also, according to Aunt Juana, there was a woman in town who wove them by hand using brilliant-colored rope. It was while she was lying in a hammock that she'd witnessed the second thing—the brightest and biggest full moon she'd ever seen. Ty had been so excited, she'd run inside to get Uncle Benny and ask him to take pictures of it.

Ty found the pictures in her box and gazed at them for a moment, before picking up a nearby book that Miss Mary, the librarian at the library on Main Street, had suggested. It was a book of Greek mythology and Ty remembered it contained the myth of Selene, the Greek goddess of the moon.

Selene reminded Ty of the stories Abuela used to tell about a moon goddess, which was when Ty had first become friendly with the night sky. She wanted to know more, but her grandmother would only share so much. Many of her tales had a fantastical feel to them and she'd shared them with Mary, who'd said they were like other myths and folktales—like the Greek ones she was currently reading.

Ty set the book aside and opened her journal to an entry where she'd recorded all the things her grandmother had shared with her about the moon. There were descriptions like *the moon is magical and all-knowing* and advice like *if you want to know how to solve a problem, ask the moon.* There was even a note about how the Moon Goddess had the power to give and take life.

Ty reached for a pencil and created her own myth:

The Moon Goddess is old, wise, and strong. Each night, before a human or animal takes their last breath, she lifts their soul, elevating it into the sky.

As she gathers a soul, she uses its last breath to expand bigger and brighter until she is full and complete, shining the light of the souls onto the world.

When she is full, she releases the light and exhales breath back into living things on Earth, slowly becoming smaller and smaller until she is just a crescent-shaped sliver.

The Moon Goddess expands again, gathering more souls, more last breaths until full. Then releases again until small.

This is the moon's cycle,

light and dark, life and death.

Satisfied with her myth, Ty set the notebook and pencil aside and reached for the jeans she'd had on earlier, which now lay in a heap on the floor. She pulled the blue flyer from the pocket and reread it. *It would be so cool to be able to join the writing program*, she thought. *Maybe Ma will be okay with me applying for the financial aid?*

She sighed. Her mother never allowed her to ask for financial help, *ever*, so Ty imagined this would be no different.

Once Ty had asked her why. Esmeralda's face had become hard, and then she'd told her about the welfare office.

"I had to swallow my pride when I applied to get an apartment in this affordable housing complex. I only did that because I wanted to take Abuela in and care for her and we didn't have the space in our old apartment, but they made me jump through hoops." Esmeralda shook her head in disgust. "I had to bite my tongue because that social worker who was supposedly there to help us treated us like we weren't even human. She asked us why we couldn't just get more jobs, like we were lazy or something. It pissed me off so bad. I mean I'd explained about Abuela having Alzheimer's and everything, but she made me feel like I had to beg for it. I almost walked out, but I didn't because we needed the apartment." Ty remembered her mother's eyes filling with tears she tried to blink away. "I only put up with it that one time, but when I left, I promised myself I would never be put in a position like that again."

Maybe Uncle Benny? Ty wondered, refolding the paper and setting it aside. But she knew her mother would be angry about that too. Ty loved Uncle Benny. He was always there when she needed him, but her mother refused to take his help. No welfare help. No Uncle Benny help.

Ty lay back, staring at her posters, wishing she could rest. Tomorrow was Saturday and it was going be crazy busy. Without Alex, and with her mother at work, like she always was on Saturdays and Sundays, she would have to take care of Luis and Abuela by herself. She hoped Uncle Benny and her cousin Isabella would come by.

She did sometimes wish she could have a free day. If she

were free, she could go for a walk and maybe bump into Eddie. Ever since she'd caught him staring at her, Ty had started daydreaming about being with him, holding hands with him, hugging him. She never had feelings like that for anyone, so it was unnerving. Lately, it felt as though Eddie had been staying away or avoiding her, but she didn't know if she was being paranoid. The last time she'd seen Eddie, he looked sad and told her he missed her. She'd told him she missed him too, and he gave her a quick hug. He then quickly turned away and she hadn't seen him since.

Soon Ty was lulled to sleep by thoughts of Eddie and the soundless movement and soft breathing of the Moon Goddess.

Chapter 7

TY WAS DREAMING. A car was on top of her, trapping her underneath it. Desperate for a breath, her eyes popped open to find two smiling brown eyes staring down at her and a seven-year-old body flailing wildly on top of her, giggling.

"Oh my God, Luis!" Ty said. "I was dreaming that a car was on top of me and it's you." She hugged the squirmer tightly around his slim waist to get him to stop moving.

"You're crushing me," Luis said as he tried to escape her grip. Ty held on tighter as Luis wriggled and giggled, and the two fell off the bed with a loud thump.

Luis laughed hysterically as Ty rubbed her eyes and

checked the clock. 7:30 A.M. *Who needs an alarm clock when you have a hyperactive younger brother?* she mused.

"I'm hungry," Luis exclaimed, jumping up from the floor and out the door toward the kitchen.

Ty sat on the floor, accepting the fact that the little bit of sleep she'd managed to get was definitely over. Shaking her head to rid herself of the sleep cobwebs, Ty put her glasses on and followed Luis across the apartment and into the kitchen.

As Ty looked for something to make for breakfast, Luis excitedly rambled on about a game he'd seen on YouTube that he needed to show her immediately. "I'll be right back," he said, running toward his bedroom.

Ty wasn't sure how anyone, seven or seventy, could be so talkative first thing in the morning. Her brain was still trying to make out colors and shapes, never mind form complete sentences.

Ty found the last two bagels and popped them in the toaster. As she waited for the bagels to get crispy the way she and Luis liked them, she spotted a note from her mother on the kitchen table. It was a grocery list and a few twenty-dollar bills.

Luis returned and began a show-and-tell about the game he'd discovered. The entire game was about farting. Every time a new fart sound was made, Luis would chuckle, which made her smile despite herself. Time with Luis made Ty miss her dad and Alex even more, but she could never get too melancholy with his dimples smiling at her. After ten minutes of his game playing while they ate, she'd had enough cuteness for one morning.

"Enough farting!" she screamed, cleaning off the table. "Let's get dressed."

Ty followed Luis into his room and stood in the doorway, taking in the sight. Alex had only been gone two nights, but Luis had taken over the room completely. There were hundreds of Legos loosely lying about, as well as books, clothes, papers, and action figures spilling onto the floor from both beds. Ty got serious.

"Luis," she said, scanning the mess. "This room looks like a hurricane hit it! What happened?" It was a rhetorical question that Luis didn't bother to answer. "C'mon," Ty said. "Let's clean up."

She opened the curtains to let in sunlight. A new mural painted on the side of Atabey Market could be seen from the window. Just a month ago, Alex's friend Eric Williams had been caught in the middle of gang crossfire and killed instantly. The loving memorial portrayed a smiling Eric wearing a baseball cap and Malcolm X T-shirt and making the peace sign with his fingers. Elaborate purple, blue, and pink colored wings rose up from behind him and a halo floated over his head. The image made her pause, but something else caught her attention. It was a crow sitting on top of a light post. *Is it the same one from yesterday?* Ty wondered. *What does it want?*

"Why do we have to put them away?" Luis said, sitting on the floor and reaching for an action figure. "I was gonna play with them today."

Ty turned from the window, shaking her head. "Nuh, this can't stay like this." Ty grabbed a green container and began dumping Legos into it. "I'm surprised Ma let this go."

"Ma doesn't care," Luis said sharply, throwing an action figure, causing it to hit the ground with a loud *thunk*.

Uh-oh, Ty thought. *He's mad.* Not that she blamed him or anything.

"When's Alex coming back?" he asked, picking up another action figure and twisting one of its arms around and around.

Ty sat on the floor next to Luis and shrugged. "I don't know, Luis. I hope soon. I miss him too." Ty reached out and touched Luis's hair. He locked eyes with her for a brief second before showing her his dimples. She smiled back as he resumed the launching of items into bins, but this time he made rocket noises as toys propelled into the air.

Less than an hour later, the beds looked like beds, the action figures and Legos were put away, and Luis wore a Minecraft T-shirt and jeans.

The clock by Luis's bed read 9:37 A.M. Time to check on Abuela.

"You can watch the iPad now," she said, raising her hand for a high-five, which he returned while simultaneously snatching the electronic device.

"Yay!" Luis said, looking at the screen.

"What, yay?" Ty asked.

"Alex texted that he's coming over." Luis showed her the message.

"Dope," Ty said, leaving the room as farting noises took over the space. She wondered if Alex had also texted her back after she fell asleep last night. She was tempted to go and check but noticed that the door to her grandmother's room was slightly ajar.

Ty went over and knocked, but there was no response. Ty opened the door fully and stepped in. Her grandmother sat on her doily-adorned bed staring out the window toward Denton Street Park. It was the same view Ty had in her room. Deep in thought, Abuela kept her eyes fixed out the window.

"Abuela," Ty said, fully entering the room, "you hungry?"

Isaura slowly shook her head.

Following her grandmother's gaze, Ty moved closer to the window to see what she was looking at. Maybe a tree? Abuela had once told her that the trees had stories to tell if you let yourself listen. Ty had tried that once, but other sounds interrupted the communication. A car would drive down the street with its wheels whirring as it passed by, or a horn would blare in the distance, or a voice would bellow, making gaining knowledge from the foliage pretty challenging.

An object on the bed grabbed Ty's attention. Next to her grandmother was a strange, ornate box. It was unlike the style of the Virgin Mary statue that stood proudly and welcoming on her grandmother's nightstand, or the large crucifix covering a good portion of the wall above her bed. Instead, it was made of dark, worn wood with something engraved on the top, a face maybe. Ty moved closer for a better look, but Isaura quickly moved the box under her pillow without a word. She was paying more attention than Ty thought.

Okay . . . , she thought. *Abuela wants to be alone.*

Back in her room, Ty was disappointed to find that Alex had only sent the one message that he was coming over to get a few things.

Thanks for getting back to me, Alex, Ty fumed. And no other messages either. *Where are Vin and Eddie?* Ty wondered.

After a quick shower, Ty dressed herself in jeans, a white T-shirt, and high-top sneakers. She wasn't much of a fashion girl, preferring the comfort of her jeans and T-shirts to heeled shoes and dress shirts. She wrapped her hair in a bun on top of her head and shrugged in the mirror. She was as ready as she was gonna be.

Ty's phone buzzed. It was Isabella. Now *she* was a fashionista. Fifteen and obsessed with clothes, jewelry, and makeup. While Ty wasn't a fan of all of that, Ty did like long fingernails, which Isabella did for her. Her cousin had a collection of nail tips and polish that Ty coveted.

"Hallo," Ty answered.

"Hey there, Cuatro," Isabella said, calling her by the family nickname. Most people called her Ty, but her family also called her Cuatro—short for "four-eyes"—thanks to the glasses she'd had to wear since she was three years old.

"Hey, Izzy."

"We on our way, okay?"

Ty smirked. *Do I have a choice?* "Okay," she replied. "Who's coming?" she asked, wanting to be prepared if Izzy's stepmother, Milagros, was also part of the day's entourage.

"All of us," she said. "We will be there in about twenty minutes. See you soon!"

.

Ty held the phone in her hand, watching the screen flash, letting her know the call had ended.

Great, she thought, *the whole gang is coming.* Uncle Benny, her mother's brother, was dope. She enjoyed being around him. Her cousin Izzy, Benny's daughter from his first marriage, was also fine, but Milagros was judgmental and stuck up. When Ty's grandfather had passed away, and they had all learned of Isaura's condition, Benny had offered to take her in because he had a large house in a nearby suburb. Six months later, Benny had told them that Isaura would go missing for hours, taking off from the house and roaming the parks.

Benny thought it was the Alzheimer's, but Ty's mother thought Isaura simply didn't want to be around Milagros. That's when her mother swallowed her pride to apply for the affordable housing unit they were in now. It caused a rift between the families that annoyed Ty to no end. She wanted to scream, *can't we all just get along!*

Ty made her way back into the kitchen, where her grandmother was now looking for something. "¿Y el café? ¿Adónde está?"

Ty had moved the coffeemaker when she pulled the toaster out to make the bagels. Good thing she had, because her mother didn't want Abuela to cook or make anything in the kitchen.

"Sit down, Abuela," Ty said, reaching for the canister of Café Bustelo in the cabinet. "I'll make it for you."

As Ty prepped and then poured the warm, aromatic

drink into a cup for her grandmother, she said, "Uncle Benny is coming with Izzy. They'll be here soon."

"Just those two?" Isaura asked.

"No," Ty responded. "Milagros is coming too."

"Ay Dios," Isaura said. "Do you know that woman microwaves everything? It's a wonder they all don't have extra fingers with all that microwaved food inside of them."

Ty giggled. "No kidding, really?" she said, waiting for more gossip, but Isaura said nothing. Ty unwrapped the Babybel cheese from its red wax container and gave it to her grandmother to have with the coffee. There wasn't any of the bread her abuela liked, but Isaura didn't seem bothered by that. She enjoyed the cheese and coffee in silence.

Suddenly Abuela chuckled. "I remember another time, I heard Milagros tell Isabella that she had good hair." She placed her coffee mug on the table as her body shook with internal amusement. "I sat there quiet, quiet, quiet, you know. They thought I was suffering from the illness, but the truth was that I was listening to everything she said." Abuela shook her head. "She's going on about 'pelo bueno' thinking maybe I can't understand. ¡Qué ridículo! My hearing is fine, and she called my hair bad."

"Abuela," Ty said, smiling. "An afro is good hair too."

"¡Es verdad!" Abuela said, nodding. "But you know she don't think that. Good hair to her is straight hair, anything closer to the colonizadores, right?" Abuela laughed again. "Ay, mira, I let her talk for a while then I yelled, '!Yo tengo pelo bueno tambien!'"

Ty imagined Milagros's horrified look at her abuela yelling *I have good hair too!* "I didn't get the afro," Ty said, touching her own long hair.

Abuela took a last sip of her coffee and smiled. "Your hair is like our other ancestors."

Ty waited for her grandmother to elaborate, but she didn't right away. Isaura got up and placed her cup in the sink and then moved to the doorway. Before exiting, she turned and said, "Puerto Ricans are made up of los colonizadores who came from Europe, los Africanos who came in chains, and los Taíno who were the original people of the island." She paused, smiling. "You look like los Taíno," and left the kitchen to return to her room.

"Abuela," Ty said, following. "What was that box you had on your bed?"

"What box?" Isaura asked.

"I saw a box next to you in your room, and when I tried to look at it, you moved it and kinda hid it under your pillow, like you didn't want me to see it."

Isaura stopped at her bedroom door, her face hardened. "There's no box," she said, moving resolutely into her bedroom and closing the door behind her—leaving Ty alone with only questions.

Chapter 8

"**H**EY," UNCLE BENNY SAID, smiling and hugging Ty as he walked into the living room.

Benny's wife, Milagros, followed in behind him. "Taína! ¿Cómo estás?"

"Bien," Ty responded, trying to maintain light contact but without success. Milagros grabbed on to Ty and held on, so the scent of fruit and vanilla assaulted her nostrils. Ty moved her face toward the open door to get fresh air. Mercifully, the lengthy and awkward embrace was interrupted by Izzy pushing her way through the door. Milagros finally moved inside, allowing Izzy space to enter.

It didn't matter if she had on sneakers or heels, jeans or a dress, Izzy made an entrance wherever she went. "Hey cuz," Izzy said, strutting as if she were on a runway. Izzy was the spitting image of her mother, Benny's first wife, with light skin, hair, and eyes. But even though Benny was darker, there was no mistaking that Benny was Izzy's father due to how alike they were in every other way, from body shape to manner-isms to even voice. They were both tall, lithe, and graceful.

Milagros, on the other hand, was short and stocky. She wore her long, dark hair in a twist on top of her head, which accentuated the big hoop earrings she wore and the elaborate makeup. *It must have taken her hours to mix the six colors she has blended on her eyelids*, Ty thought. Lipstick flawless, eyebrows drawn perfectly symmetrical. Milagros was a hairdresser and makeup artist, and it was clear she was good at her job. *She does look pretty*, Ty hated to admit.

"Where's Luis?" Benny asked. "I have something for him," lifting a bag in his hands. Uncle Benny was the source of many of the toys all over Luis's floor.

"He's in his room," Ty responded. "I'll get him."

"Nuh, I'll go," Izzy said, slinking away. The fact that her cousin Izzy loved Luis's company made Ty forgive the many clueless things she often did and said. Milagros, on the other hand, currently sat examining the living room with what Alex called her "permanent stink face" as if she always smelled something bad.

"How's school?" Benny asked, giving her an excuse to stop examining Milagros.

"Fine," was all she could think to say. The truth was just too complicated. Benny didn't know what had happened with Alex, but before Ty could tell him, Milagros interrupted.

"Aren't there a lot of fights and guns at that school?" Milagros asked as if it were a polite, innocent question.

"There are," Ty responded, sounding serious. "I wear a bulletproof vest now. It's like part of the school uniform."

Milagros wrinkled her brow. "What?" she responded before realization hit that Ty was being sarcastic. "Funny," she said. "I only know what I hear on the news."

"You mean to tell me that Izzy goes to a school in your neighborhood that isn't on the news every day. How boring," Ty countered, making Benny chuckle.

"You always got a comeback," Benny said, taking off his jacket and placing it so it lay neatly folded on the back of the couch. "Just like your grandmother," he added, ignoring Milagros's stink face, which had now become more pronounced. He strolled over to Abuela's old stereo with its knobs, levers, and lights. Benny played with one of the controllers until he found the distant Spanish radio station. It was hard to hear and full of static, but Benny didn't care. He had to have salsa music playing everywhere he went, like theme music.

"How is your mom?" he asked, rubbing his head. He'd also inherited the afro from their ancestors, but his was brown and tight to his head. Ty loved how Benny had this uncomplicated way about him—good-natured and genuine. You never got the sense that he was hiding anything or that he was trying to be something that he wasn't. He was just Benny.

"Ma is the same as always," Ty said. Benny nodded.

"And Alex?" he continued. "Is he out with friends?"

Ty shook her head, then blurted, "He's staying with Dad for a few days."

Milagros's eyebrows shot up in surprise. Before Benny could ask more questions, Izzy and Luis came bounding back.

"Luis showed me a funny farting game," Izzy said, mimicking farting noises with her mouth.

"Ay muchacha," Milagros said. "Don't do that."

Izzy stopped but rolled her eyes in annoyance.

After running into Benny's arms, Luis snatched the bag that contained his gift. Inside, he found a new set of mini-cars and squealed with joy. "Can I go play with them?" he asked, running away before getting a response.

Milagros watched him skip away and asked, "Does he have ADHD or something?"

"What?" Ty retorted, rolling her eyes.

"I love his all-over-the-place, seven-year-old energy." Izzy giggled then quickly got serious. "How's Abuela? Is she forgetting more and more?"

Ty shook her head as if trying to release the question from her mind. "No," she said. "It's not like it gets worse by the day or something. It's kind of like some days are good and some are not."

Unfazed by Ty's tone, Izzy continued, "I'm still learning about that oldtimer's disease," she said, running her fingers through her long light-brown hair. "And it's really bad."

"Girl, are you kidding me?" Ty asked. "It's not oldtimer's

disease. It's Alzheimer's disease, and yeah, it's been bad for a long time." Ty also wanted to ask, *are you just realizing this now?*

"Well, you don't gotta say it like that," Izzy snapped, rapidly blinking her eyes. "I'm just asking." She and Ty gave each other long looks as if they were angry, but then broke into laughter.

"Girl, you are so dramatic," Ty said. As much as Ty enjoyed Izzy, she couldn't help but feel like Izzy got to be ignorant about Abuela while Ty did not have that privilege. She was Abuela's caretaker when her mother was working, which was all the time. Sometimes, Ty wondered what it was like to be Izzy. She was allowed to just be a regular teenager with regular teenage responsibilities while Ty had to take care of others before herself.

"Izzy," Benny said, "why don't we go say hello to Abuela?" He looked at Ty. "Is that okay?"

"Of course it's okay," Milagros asserted. "You're her son, right?" It wasn't really a question, but more of a statement of the obvious. Ty wished she would get credit for the times when she did *not* lose her temper because, right now, she was using all her strength to keep herself from telling Milagros to *eff off* like she had Ms. Neil.

"Milagros," Benny said, turning toward her. "Ty is here with her every day and knows best if it's a good day or not. That's why I asked."

"I think it's okay," Ty replied, wishing she could learn how to handle situations the way he did—calmly. Benny didn't look annoyed or bothered or anything. "She was in a little bit of a weird mood this morning." Ty thought of her hiding the box. "But she's been talking."

Benny nodded as he gestured toward Izzy to join him, leaving Ty with Milagros.

"So," Milagros asked. "Why is Alex staying with his father?"

Wow, she just went right there, Ty thought. "Um, he needed a change," she answered tentatively, looking toward her grandmother's bedroom, wondering if she could escape by joining Benny and Izzy.

Milagros paused, taking in the information. "Is your father working now?" she asked.

"Yeah," Ty said. "He's been working."

"Really?" Milagros nodded slowly and continuously while pursing her perfectly painted red lips. "That's hard to believe. Where?"

Ty wanted to come up with a response that was more like what Uncle Benny might say, but that was taking too long, so she simply asked, "Why is that hard to believe?"

Milagros shrugged. "I didn't mean anything by it," she said, and Ty thought to herself, *here we go again with the "I didn't mean anything by it" lie.*

"I know your dad has been struggling to find a job with his record and everything," Milagros continued. "So, I was surprised. That's all I was trying to say."

"Maybe you should have just said *that* instead," Ty snapped.

Borikén, 1550
(present-day Puerto Rico)

Guanina silently prayed to the supreme goddess who ruled the ocean and the moon to continue to illuminate their path. What they would find when they got to Borikén, she did not know, but the fellow Taíno steering the canoe assured her he would get her there safely. Guanina's gamble had better pay off, because sitting with her were her daughter, Casiguaya, her son, Daguao, and the precious items her mother, Higüamota, had given her long ago. Guanina thought of her husband, Cacimar, who had been murdered on Amoná. Cacimar had tried to lead a quiet life, keeping out of harm's way as much as he was able. All he'd wanted was to ensure the safety of his wife and children. But a month ago, a group of men in tasseled jackets and hats had tried to enslave him. He'd fought back and lost his life in the process.

It will only be a matter of time before they come for me and the children, she thought. Guanina thought of her mother, Higüamota, and her grandmother Anacaona and was propelled by a deep desire to preserve their legacy. The objects were the link to not only their existence, but Cacimar's as well. If the items were destroyed or were not passed on accordingly, the true history of her people could be erased forever.

After Cacimar was murdered, Guanina had heard from her guide and travel companion that there were others like her and her children in the large village of Yagüeca on Borikén who had been resisting the foreigners with some success, and he planned to find them. Guanina had begged to go with him, and, eventually, he'd agreed to take her.

The day before they were to leave, Guanina studied the cave drawing that her mother had carved of Anacaona. She wanted to copy it, so her children and children's children would have the likeness, but with the tools she had at her disposal, she could not think of how to capture it. Instead, she spent every moment she could memorizing how each etch in the stone felt under her long fingers. The face was carved in a circle that tapered at the bottom to show a strong chin. There were two thick gashes where there would have been eyebrows and oval shaped markings where there would have been eyes. As she closed her eyes, she saw the portrait in her mind and knew how it should feel if she ever had the chance to recreate it.

Guanina felt the weight of her circumstance. They were headed into the unknown. She needed Anacaona's strength, help, and guidance. With everyone on the canoe facing forward, eager to glimpse land or catch sight of an enemy, Guanina reached for the zemi, pulled it from a pouch she carried, and placed it on her lap. She then reached for the amulet and mouthed a silent prayer to her grandmother, Anacaona, for protection and guidance. By the time she had learned of Cacimar's death, she had not had time to open the heirloom and call upon her ancestors, but she needed them now more than ever. Gently, she unlocked the amulet and, immediately, she felt calm. Opening her eyes, shadowy clouds separated above them, and the bright moon and what looked like an owl made its way toward them. The owl purposefully flew toward the driver at the helm, caught his attention, and then flew in a slightly different direction. The Taíno steering the canoe adjusted their path to follow it.

Guanina peered forward and saw land in her line of vision. They were close, and her children turned to smile at her. The owl returned, gliding past her once again, and Guanina could see it more clearly under the light of the night sky. It was white and quite possibly the largest she had ever seen. Remembering what her mother had told her that day on Amoná about how an owl had greeted them at the entrance of the cave where she had drawn Anacaona's likeness, Guanina wondered if this white owl was greeting them as they entered

Borikén. The thought comforted her as the canoe neared the shores of a beach. Guanina closed the amulet and returned it and the zemi back to her pouch. "Thank you, mother," she whispered as they all slipped safely into the wild foliage of their new home.

Chapter 9

MILAGROS STOOD, ignoring Ty's comment. "I need a cup of coffee," she said. "I'll make myself one. You do have real coffee, right?"

Ty was about to give another heated reply when Izzy joined them. "Come to Abuela's room," she said, quickly grabbing Ty's arm as Milagros walked toward the kitchen. "Don't get into it with Milagros. It's not worth it, cuz."

"But . . . ," Ty started.

"Let it go, girl," Izzy said, dragging her into Abuela's room.

She heard Izzy but didn't understand why Milagros was being like this with her today. *Hell,* Ty thought, *she was always like this.* Putting Milagros out of her mind, Ty joined them in her grandmother's room.

Abuela was sitting on the bed with her back against the headboard as Benny sat across from her telling her about a seven-alarm fire he had fought. Abuela had seen the blaze on the news and wondered if he'd been there. It had involved three buildings and he was sharing some of the details about it. Benny rarely talked about his work as a firefighter, saying that he'd rather leave the things he'd seen at the firehouse. Ty and Izzy stood by the foot of the bed, listening to the tail end of his story.

"It took hours, but we got it under control before it turned dark, and we helped some families find places to stay," Benny shared, then changed the subject. "You look good, Mami," he said.

"Claro que si," Abuela said, waving her hand in dismissal. "Why wouldn't I?"

Benny laughed then leaned forward, giving her face a lighthearted inspection. "Aunt Juana called me yesterday to say hello."

Isaura made a face.

"I know, Mami," Benny said. "I know you and she haven't been close, but she did ask about you and wanted you to know she is thinking of you."

"If she is thinking of me then she would be here."

"Ma," Benny countered. "You kinda told her never to visit you."

Isaura dismissed the idea with her hand. "I didn't say

that," she insisted. "I said it's a long way here from Puerto Rico, so she should stay where she is. She knows she could visit if she really wanted to." Isaura paused. "You know what?" she continued as if she remembered something important. "I had a dream about her recently. She was standing on the beach with her hands in the air, *asi*"—Abuela lifted her arms to demonstrate and for some reason that made her giggle—"like she was trying to get someone's attention. An owl flew overhead, and she followed it, so I have a feeling she may be coming to visit soon." Ty and Izzy looked at each other in confusion.

"Ma used to tell us that when you see an owl it means movement, change, endings and beginnings, that kind of thing," Benny clarified.

"Just make sure my room is locked so she can't get in and steal anything while she's here," Isaura noted.

Ty and Izzy giggled nervously, but Benny remained serious. "Tía Juana is not a thief, Ma." He was patient in his delivery because he was fond of his aunt and visited her in Puerto Rico almost every year. Benny seemed to want his aunt and mother to have more of a loving, sisterly relationship than they had, but Isaura didn't seem to want or need that.

"*Hmpf.* Friends are like money in your pocket unless there's a hole in it. Family can be worse," Isaura said, nodding firmly to punctuate her proclamation.

This time Izzy and Benny exchanged confused looks while Ty smiled. She enjoyed these moments with her family. She only wished Alex were with them because he would have been cracking jokes in the background, bringing a lighter energy into the room.

The group was startled by a voice in the doorway. "Hola, Isaura," Milagros said. Abuela turned slightly and gave a tight smile. "How much longer, Benny?" Milagros asked, trying to sound lighthearted, but the effort made her seem robotic.

Benny took his mother's hand. "I'll be back later, Mami," he said, kissing her on her forehead and walking out of the bedroom.

"Me voy a descansar un rato," Abuela said, shifting the pillows behind her to comfortably lie down.

"Okay, Abuela," Ty said. "Rest for as long as you want." She watched her grandmother tuck herself under the white quilt decorated with lace and left the room, closing the door behind her.

Back in the living room, everyone was standing as if waiting for orders. Ty refused to acknowledge Milagros, so she turned her back toward her and faced her uncle.

"Izzy and Milagros are going to the mall," Benny said. "Do you want to go with them? I can stay here with Mami and Luis."

There was no way Ty was going anywhere with Milagros. Even if Milagros had offered her front row tickets to a Bad Bunny concert, she would have said no.

"Thanks," Ty said. "But I got things to do, like go to the grocery store. Plus, Alex texted that he was gonna come by, so I want to be here."

Benny nodded. "I'd love to see Alex too," he said. "How

about this, then? How about I drop you," he said, pointing his chin toward Milagros, "and Izzy off at the mall, then I go grocery shopping. I'll take Luis with me. Maybe he and I can go to the park first or something."

Izzy shook her head, "Nuh, I'd rather stay here with Ty." She sat on the arm of the couch then slid off to plop herself onto the seat cushion. "Plus," she said, "I can take Luis to the park. I don't mind."

"Wait," Milagros said. "Now I'm going to the mall by myself? Izzy, I thought we were going to buy shoes?"

Izzy shrugged. "I'm cool, Milagros. I'd rather hang out with Cuatro since I haven't seen her in a minute."

"I'll get the grocery list," Ty said, running to the kitchen to retrieve the list and money her mother had left before Milagros could say anything more about their newly laid plans. When she came back, Benny wouldn't take the cash.

Ty lowered her voice, "Benny, look, you know Ma will be lit if you pay for the groceries, but," Ty paused. She looked back at Izzy and Milagros, who seemed to be engrossed in a shoe conversation, then lowered her voice. "I was gonna ask you for some money to join an after-school creative writing program. You know I wouldn't ask if . . ."

"How much do you need?" Benny pulled out his wallet.

"It's one hundred dollars," Ty said, adding, "I have the flyer in my room, if you want to see it."

Benny shook his head then took the grocery money from Ty and counted it. There were three twenties, so he gave her three more.

"Nuh, that's way too much, Benny," Ty insisted. She could lie to her mother and say the writing program had been free, but if her mother saw her with extra dollars, Esmeralda would wonder where she'd gotten it.

"No, take that just to buy books or whatever. Don't worry about it," he said, smiling and walking over to the stereo before Ty could further protest. He tapped his hands on the table in sync to the music still playing on the radio. Ty grinned.

As soon as Benny and Milagros departed, Ty and Izzy sat together on the couch.

"What's up with you, Cuatro?" Izzy asked. "You look tired."

"I am tired," Ty said. "Izzy, I'm so worried about Alex. He got into this fight at school and I still don't know all the details. Now, Ma's kicked him out of the house." Ty paused as Izzy sat upright as if that would help her listen more intently. "It's only been a few days, but it's not the same here without him."

Izzy looked pensive. "Why'd your mom kick him out? That seems like a lot."

"I don't know." Ty shrugged. "I feel like she's falling apart. Like she's so in her own world that she forgot about us. Like we a burden."

"Nuh," Izzy said. "Don't think like that. When my mom and dad divorced, she moved to Puerto Rico, and I don't see her that much anymore, so I felt like a burden, you know?" Izzy picked at the white nail polish she wore. "Your mom wouldn't do anything like that. She's still here. She's just in a bad place."

She might as well be gone, Ty thought, but didn't voice that opinion out loud. "It is what it is, right?" Ty asked. Izzy continued to pick at her nail polish. "Stop that," Ty said, then held her hand out to Izzy for inspection. "I need you to fix my claws," she said.

"They look okay," Izzy said, examining Ty's fingernails. "You have another week with these nails, I think. Besides, I didn't bring my stuff. I'll bring my kit next weekend. Plus, I'll ask dad to drop me off and take Milagros somewhere else." Izzy laughed. "She can be a handful sometimes."

"Sometimes?" Ty asked rhetorically. "I feel like she has it out for me or something?"

"I don't know," Izzy said. "I see it too, like she don't like you or your mom. I think Milagros got all up in her feelings when Abuela moved here. You know how Abuela is, yo," Izzy said. "She hated the way Milagros did everything from cooking to cleaning to talking to breathing," Izzy smirked, "and she told her that all the time. So when your mother came and got her, Milagros was like angry and started saying all this bad stuff about your mother and that your dad was a loser and that you guys were moving to the ghetto—just crazy things like that."

"Really?" Ty took that in. "Your dad doesn't feel that way, though, right?" she asked before she could help herself.

Izzy shook her head. "No! You know my dad's not like that," she said, facing Ty. "You know that, right? He loves his family. All his family. You see how he still checks in with Tía Juana even though everyone thinks she's crazy."

Ty laughed. "I don't think that! I don't even know her!" she said. "I mean, the last time we visited her I was like ten." Ty smirked. "But . . . my Ma used to say that strange things happened when Aunt Juana was around, like all of a sudden you'd see owls, you know, like in Abuela's dream or bats or something. Or," Ty said, bouncing in her seated position, "they'd see ghosts or weird visions."

"Girl, stop," Izzy said. "You know those stories freak me out. Maybe that's why I always stayed away from her when she visited."

Ty giggled. She understood why Izzy avoided her, but Ty couldn't help but be interested in supernatural things or omens, like the crow who stayed visible in the tree on their street. She had heard her mother and grandmother speak of inexplicable things that had happened mostly in Puerto Rico, like visions of dead people or predictions of the future, and while those stories could make Ty nervous, they also intrigued her. Izzy, on the other hand, wanted nothing to do with them.

Izzy stood and stretched. "I'm gonna go play that fart game with Luis for a bit," Izzy said. "You good?"

"Yeah, I gotta hit the laundry," Ty said, watching Izzy slink away. *Nothing ever seems simple anymore*, Ty thought. When she was a child, things felt so basic. You went to school, you ate, you watched television, you played, and you went to bed. *When did my life start to become part of a patchwork of stories—with backstories, feelings, friends, omens, and ghosts?* she wondered as the abandoned salsa music played heroically in the background.

Chapter 10

Benny grabbed assorted pots and pans from the kitchen cabinets like he was preparing for a feast.

"What are you going to make for lunch?" Ty asked as she reached her hand toward a grocery bag. Benny tapped her hand in a mock slap.

"No," he said. "It's a surprise."

Izzy and Ty exchanged glances. "Girl, I hope you're hungry," Izzy said. "Dad only knows how to cook for a house full of firefighters."

A loud noise from the living room caused Izzy and Ty to investigate. A figurine on an end table was on the floor and

Luis stood over it, watching the porcelain statue like it was going to get up and put itself back on the table. Ty picked it up and examined it.

"It looks fine," she said as Luis threw himself on the floor dramatically.

"I'm bored. We still haven't gone to the park!"

"My bad." Izzy frowned. "We can go now."

"Hold up," Ty said. "Let me check something." Ty ran to her bedroom with Izzy and Luis following close behind. Ty peered out her bedroom window toward the park. If she squinted and pressed her face against the windowpane, she could see as far as the monkey bars. From what she could make out, there were other children there. No young men dressed in black. "Looks good. Let's go."

Outside, as they closed the front door, a voice yelled "por dios, how many times are you going to open and close your door today?!" The trio gazed toward the second floor to see the neighbor, Mrs. Lopez, hanging out her window; the big curlers in her hair matched the color of her light blue terry cloth robe.

"We can open and close our front door as many times as we like, Señora," Ty said, causing Izzy to chuckle. "We live here too."

Mrs. Lopez muttered something unintelligible under her breath and then slammed her window shut.

"Oh my God," Izzy said. "Is she always like that?"

"Girl, you have no idea," Ty said as they walked to the park.

It was a sun-filled October day as they made their way across the street. The sun amplified the reds, browns, and oranges of autumn as stale cigarette smoke and car exhaust moved invisibly around them. Reggaetón also filled the air, but Ty didn't see its source. There were no cars outside Atabey Market entertaining the community today.

"Wait," Izzy said, stopping at the park entrance. "That's my song!"

Izzy wiggled and jiggled, singing at the top of her lungs. Luis joined in and Ty giggled as Luis tried to mimic the moves Alex had taught him. When Alex did the steps, he looked dope. When Luis tried them, he looked like he was getting electrocuted.

Ty stood grounded, though, as she watched them dance. She wasn't about making a fool of herself in public. As she shifted her weight, something went crunch under her foot. It was shattered glass. Ty remembered a time when someone had driven by and thrown a bottle near where she was. She had thought it might have been a stupid prank. It had missed her by an inch and smashed on the ground at her feet. Why the remains of glass were there now, Ty didn't know, but a feeling of urgency washed over her as she turned toward Luis and Izzy, who were still feeling the reggaetón beat, and said, "C'mon."

As they neared the playground, two boys playing on the monkey bars called out to Luis. He bolted away to join them.

"Damn, yo." Izzy laughed. "Luis knows more people than you!"

"Why would I know anyone at a playground?" Ty snapped.

Izzy continued to laugh as she found a bench. Even though there wasn't a cloud in the sky, there was still a cool breeze, and Ty pulled her jacket tighter around her body. Luis and his two friends ran past her at full speed playing some sort of game of tag, and Ty noticed a few other people in the park. Mostly children, but there were a few adults standing around, either speaking loudly on their phones or in deep, one-on-one conversations. Monkey bars, swings, and slides made for good distractions.

"Hey, why didn't you want to go to the mall?" Ty asked as she sat next to Izzy, crossing her feet at her ankles.

Izzy shrugged. "I feel like now that I'm older, Milagros thinks I'm her friend or something. I'm not really. I mean, I appreciate that she's been there for me, you know, but I like to keep my distance sometimes." Izzy paused. "She wants me to tell her about my friends and if I'm seeing anyone, things like that."

"Wait," Ty said, "that's right. What's up with that shorty you were talking to? His name was like David or something?"

Izzy played with the silver ring she was wearing. "I still see David," she said. "He plays baseball on the weekends, so I might see him tomorrow," she added. Ty felt a twinge of something she couldn't identify. It was a flash of feeling that left her speechless. *Why can't I look forward to seeing my boyfriend tomorrow?* she wondered. *Am I jealous?* she asked herself then pushed the feeling away.

"That's dope," Ty said, so that Izzy wouldn't think she had weird feelings.

A child squealed uncontrollably at nothing in particular.

It seemed to come from the joy of running freely on the playground's rubber turf. Ty watched Luis and the other kids play. Only a few years ago, she would have been out there playing with him.

"Are you still friends with Eddie?" Izzy asked. Ty bristled.

"Um, I don't know." She shrugged. "I haven't seen him for a while." Ty was moments away from sharing her feelings about Eddie when Izzy interrupted.

"Oh? Cuz he's right over there," she said, pointing to the other side of the park.

"Don't point." Ty grabbed Izzy's hand and looked in the direction where her finger had been guiding her. There, slightly obscured by monkey bars and bodies flying in the air on swings, stood a young man dressed in a black sweatshirt and jeans. He was leaning against the playground fence, staring in Ty's general direction.

"Izzy," she whispered. "Do I look okay? Is my hair okay?" Ty wished she'd had more time this morning to get her looks together, but all she could do was hope that Izzy would lie.

"You look cute," she said. "Anyway, nothing you can do now since he's coming over."

Before she could ready herself, Eddie Gonzalez was standing in front of them. The last time she'd seen him, he'd been wearing his long hair in a ponytail, but today, he kept it back with four thick braids. He had light brown skin and perfectly straight white teeth. He was muscular and slim, which you couldn't see very well through the baggy jeans and oversized hoodie he was wearing. *Why is he wearing black?* Ty wondered. *He would never join a gang, so why is he dressed like a Night Crawler?*

"Hey, Cuatro," Eddie said, grinning. He crossed his arms against his chest and Ty could see the little tattoo of a broken heart in the space between his index finger and thumb. It was a tattoo someone in the neighborhood had done for him when his brother died.

Ty and Izzy stood up to greet him. "Hey, Eddie," Ty said, trying not to fidget but failing miserably. She couldn't seem to find a comfortable place to put her hands.

"I'm gonna see what Luis is doing. Byeeee," Izzy said, waving her fingers.

"Wow," Eddie said, glancing toward the playground. "Look at little man. He's getting tall, looking like Alex more and more."

All Ty could do was nod in response. *Get yourself together and speak*, she commanded herself, but Eddie continued.

"I'm surprised to see you out here," he said. "You never hang out at the park."

"No," she said, finally finding her voice, "but my cousin Izzy is here, and we wanted to take Luis out to play." *Wow*, she thought, *can I be any more boring?*

"Oh," Eddie said, gazing in Izzy's direction. "That's who that is. I remember meeting her a couple of years ago. She grew up." Slowly, he turned toward Ty, and his eyes lingered on her face. "I guess we're all growing up."

Ty felt the blood rush to her face. There was something about how he said it that made her self-conscious, as though he were looking at her in a different way than he had when they were kids. "What does that mean?" Ty challenged. She hoped that he would finally explain himself, but she was disappointed.

Eddie shrugged. "I didn't mean anything by it," he said quietly.

Ty ignored her "least favorite thing anyone could say" and continued to challenge. "Where have you been lately? We used to talk all the time." Ty hated the way she sounded, but the words came out and she couldn't take them back.

Eddie closed his eyes. Opened them but turned away from Ty. "I know."

The frustration started to build. *So, he knows, so what?* she thought. *And why is he not looking at me? Does he not want to be my friend anymore?*

"Are we still friends?" Ty asked.

"Yeah," Eddie said. "We'll always be friends. I'm just, I just gotta figure some things out," he said, then gazed toward his black sneakers. "You know, since Willie died, I've had to step up at home and, um, it's just not that easy, you feel me?"

Ty felt the hairs on her forearm rise and she rubbed her arm to make them stop. Eddie never talked about his brother who had been killed a few years back. Willie had been older than Eddie, more of a father figure than a brother. Eddie loved and looked up to him, but Willie got into some bad things, selling drugs. He had been in prison a year when he was attacked and killed. The prisoner who did it was given more prison time, but that didn't help anyone cope with the loss. When it happened, Eddie had been distraught, and it seemed like only Ty could comfort him. Then one day, Eddie just stopped talking about Willie—like he wanted to forget Willie ever existed.

Caught off guard, Ty forgot to be angry and said, "I can help."

Eddie reached out to touch her fingers. She gripped his hand without thinking, liking how it felt to hold onto a part of him. He finally looked back up at her, and she saw something in his eyes that she didn't understand before he abruptly let go of her hand. "Be careful out here, okay. This park can be hot."

Ty found herself giving Eddie *the look*. Whereas with Ms. Neil it had meant *do you think I'm stupid*, with Eddie, the look was more *why are you being like this?*

"How's Alex?" Eddie asked, ignoring her body language. Another voice responded.

"Why don't you ask me yourself," Alex said, planting himself in front of Eddie.

Chapter 11

ALEX AND EDDIE stood almost toe-to-toe. Even though they were the same height, Alex had straightened his back and lifted his chin to make himself appear taller. Eddie, on the other hand, shrunk and kept his gaze toward the ground.

"I gotta go," Eddie said, and scurried across the playground. Ty watched Eddie until she couldn't make out his figure anymore.

"Stay away from him, Ty," Alex said, watching her. "He's not worth your time."

Ty examined Alex. He had dark patches under his eyes

and a bruise on his cheek, no doubt a relic from the fight he'd had. His bushy, dark eyebrows were partially hidden by the backward cap he wore.

"What?" Ty snapped. "Since when? Aren't we all friends?!"

"Are you blind, Ty?" Alex demanded. "Look what he's wearing. He's one of them now and I don't want you around him."

No, she thought. *Why would he join the Night Crawlers?*

Ty shook her head. "Alex, you have to talk to me. What's going on? Why did you get into a fight? What does all this mean?"

Suddenly, Luis and Izzy were next to them. Ty watched as Alex lifted Luis high in the air and spun him around. Alex had inherited Abuela's gap-toothed smile, and he was displaying it as he laughed and talked with Izzy and Luis. They were headed back toward her house, but Ty hung back. She could see his weariness. *What is he not saying?* she wondered for the hundredth time. Ty slowly followed the trio, scanning the park hoping to catch a glimpse of Eddie, but he was nowhere to be found. He seemed lost to her in more ways than one.

The strong aroma of pepper, onions, and garlic wafted out of the kitchen and into the entire apartment. It was the kind of smell that would stay on your clothes long after you moved away from it. Ty eyed the giant-sized caldero of orange rice and beans; a pan filled with pork chops; and a large plate of uncooked, cut plantains.

"Milagros is missing out on all this," Ty said.

"I'll bring some leftovers to her later. She wanted to finish all her errands." Benny put a wooden spoon to Ty's lips. "Here, taste," he said, and she gulped a mouthful of rice. "Tiene suficiente sabor?" he asked, watching her intently as she swallowed.

Ty nodded, licking her lips. "It tastes perfect," she said, leaving Benny with his tasks in the kitchen to see what everyone else was up to.

Ty found Luis in his room with Izzy, playing with action figures on the floor. "Where's Alex?" Ty asked.

Izzy shrugged. "Not here."

Ty checked her bedroom to find Alex sitting in her little chair, staring out the window toward the park.

"Alex," Ty said as she closed the door. "Are you okay? You *gotta* tell me something."

Alex gave her a look. "What do you think? Do you think I'm okay?" He leaned his head against the glass window. "I know, sis, I'm sorry. It's not you." Alex was quiet for a second. "I don't see why I can't stay here. You feel me?"

Ty sat on her bed, facing Alex. "It's not the same here without you," she said. "I didn't even get to tell you about what happened at school yesterday with Ms. Neil."

Alex smiled. "My favorite teacher from ninth grade!" he joked. "What's up with her?"

"She asked me to leave her class because I told her to stop

being mean to Beatriz Machado. I can't even with Ms. Neil, but I had to apologize to her anyway."

"Really?" Alex asked, standing to face her. "Did that help?"

"Nuh, not really," Ty answered. "I got in trouble with Ma anyway."

"Well, I guess that makes two of us now." Alex swiveled back to watching the leaves sway in the breeze from the window. "At least Ma didn't kick you out."

"Ma can't kick you out again," Ty asserted. "So, you should just come back. Stay in your room and when she comes home, I'll tell her you're back and that will be that. What she gonna do if you're in there sleeping with Luis? Nothing."

Alex smirked. "No way," he said. "I plan to be out of here before she gets home from work. Dad and I already talked about it. He was like, go get more of your clothes and just stay with me. I might not come back, Ty."

Ty felt her heart drop to the floor. "You have to come back!" She stood as if that would help, but Alex remained silent.

"Sis, I'm sorry," Alex said slowly. "It's not just Ma, you know? I should probably not be in the Dent that much anymore."

"Because of the fight?" Ty asked. Alex nodded. "Tell me what happened."

Alex sat back in the chair and began to explain. "That day of the fight—"

"Taína!" Uncle Benny called from the hallway.

Ty and Alex jumped up, startled, and ran quickly into the hallway.

Benny stood in the doorway of Abuela's room holding a plate of food.

"What happened?" Ty asked.

"I think we should call an ambulance."

Chapter 12

ISAURA WAS BREATHING slow, shallow breaths as if she were in a deep sleep, but her eyes were open and fixed on the wall opposite her bed. Around her stood Ty, Benny, and Alex.

"Mami," Benny called, but she did not respond. Ty drew closer and took her pulse. It felt a little sluggish but followed a regular pattern.

"She's fine," Ty snapped without thinking. But when she glanced over at Benny and Alex they both looked worried, so she added, "I mean, why do you want to call an ambulance?"

Benny stared at Isaura for a few seconds. "She looks a little lifeless, don't you think?" Benny asked. "And she was talking earlier, so I thought, I don't know, I got nervous."

"She *was* talking earlier," Ty confirmed, "but maybe she just doesn't want to talk now." There were so many times when Abuela would be talking then she would just stop. That was another joke Alex and Ty would make. When Abuela would not respond, they would say, *Grandma is done with you. She don't want to hear your voice anymore.*

As if remembering the same joke, Alex said, "Yeah, she gets like this sometimes."

Benny peered at his mother, then bent over and kissed her on the forehead. "How often is she like this?" he asked.

"Not often," Ty lied. "I told you she was acting some kind of way this morning, so maybe she just needs rest."

Benny watched his mother in silence as Ty slowly backed out of the room. She thought he might want some time alone, but he followed quickly behind her.

"I'm putting all the food out, so give me a few minutes," he said, forcing a smile.

As Benny went back to the kitchen, Ty motioned for Alex to return to her bedroom.

"So what happened?" Ty asked when they were alone again.

Alex gazed toward her posters and stopped at the one of Rihanna. "She's so pretty," he said.

Still staring at the poster, Alex asked, "Remember when we were little? And we all went to that amusement park— you know the one that's right near the exit, but you have to wait like an hour before you can get off at the exit?"

Ty nodded, remembering how she rode with Luis on a flying caterpillar ride.

"It was one of the happiest times of my life. Ma and Dad were good. You knew they still loved each other. Luis was a happy baby and you and I got to ride on every ride." Alex paused. "But then everything changed so fast. Grandpa died, Abuela became sick, Dad got arrested, and Ma went into zombie-robot mode." Alex laughed. "I know we never had money or nothing, but then we moved here. After that, it was like a new level of bad. There were all these problems with gangs and kids killing other kids and nobody seems to care or do anything about it. And it's like we can just walk to Main Street, right, and get away from all this stuff, but we ain't wanted there. We don't belong there. We belong here, but what does that mean? Does that mean we deserve to be treated like we nothing? Or does that mean I forget about school? It's not like that school is for us anyway, you feel me?"

"No, don't quit school, Alex," Ty said, even though she had said something similar to her mother just the day before.

"You think I want to do that?" Alex asked, turning to face her. "I got suspended and that's like another level of bad. It makes me feel like all of the things they say about Puerto Ricans or poor kids are true. We like a stereotype, Ty, but what else can we do? It's like this is my destiny, you know?"

Ty shook her head. "Nuh, nope, negative. Don't let what people say get into your head. There's nothing wrong with us. We just in a situation."

"I don't know, Cuatro. I don't know," Alex replied.

"What don't you know?" Ty asked. "I mean, you are still my brother, and you are not a bad person. You just got into a stupid fight, and everyone is acting like you killed someone. A fight doesn't mean anything."

Alex began to pace then abruptly stopped and blurted out, "Eddie is a Night Crawler now, Ty, and the fight was about him."

Chapter 13

*T*HERE IT IS. Ty thought. *Eddie is a Night Crawler.* "How long did you know that?" Ty asked.

"Well, you know Jayden is a Night Crawler?" Alex asked.

Ty nodded. She hadn't thought of Jayden Feliciano for years. There was a time when Alex, Eddie, and Jayden had been friends. Much to Ty's annoyance, because Jayden was a pain to deal with. Ty remembered one time he purposefully put bubble gum in her hair, which resulted in a haircut and her retaliating by pouring water over his head when he wasn't expecting it. Last year, Jayden stopped hanging around with them and joined the Night Crawlers.

"What's that punk Jayden up to now?" Ty asked.

"Ty, Jayden is not that same kid you used to fight. You know he had a lot of problems growing up, so I used to give him a pass, you know? He's . . ." Alex paused and sighed. "He's into bad stuff now."

"Is Eddie running with Jayden?" Ty asked, trying to make sense of what Jayden had to do with all of this.

Alex nodded. "They've been hanging out for a few weeks. I didn't think anything of it at first, but then I felt like Eddie was avoiding me, so I confronted him, and we got into it."

"And?" Ty asked, wanting to know more details. "What else? I mean you got into a fight with Eddie, right? Was Jayden there?"

Before Alex could answer, the door to the room opened and there stood Benny with a ketchup-stained fork in his hand. "C'mon, dinner is ready," he said, opening the door wide and walking back toward the kitchen.

Alex followed Benny before Ty could stop him. Ty threw up her hands. *Are you kidding me?* she thought. She still had so many questions. *Is Alex in trouble with the Night Crawlers? Is he coming back home? Is he going back to school? And, finally, am I wrong for still liking Eddie?*

Ty had often wished she were a superhero who had the power to transform people. She daydreamed about snapping her fingers and changing someone's attitude or situation. With a snap, people would go from sad to happy or from angry to loving. If she had that power, she could snap, and Alex would be home again and in school. Her grandmother would be well. Her parents would be together and . . . Ty felt a lump form in the back of her throat and tried to breathe it away. She hadn't hoped her parents would get back together for at least two years and was surprised to find herself wishing that now.

She sat on her bed and placed her head in her hands. There wasn't any time for fantasies. There was some real stuff going on and, as much as she wished it to be true, she didn't have superpowers. She had to face it that this was her reality, and no amount of daydreaming would change that.

"Ty!" Uncle Benny called from the kitchen. Jumping up, she hurried to the kitchen.

Ty sat in the empty chair next to Benny. Alex, Luis, and Izzy already had their plates full and were getting ready to eat. *What I wouldn't give to have a nice family meal without worry*, Ty thought. The aroma of sazón did nothing to lighten Ty's mood as she listened to silverware clanging and mouths chomping.

"Everyone's so quiet huh," Benny said, playing off a classic family joke that the only time the family was quiet was when they were eating.

"We eating," Luis said, causing granules of rice to become projectiles.

"See," Izzy said, swallowing. "That's why we don't talk when we eat! Food be flying out your mouth like bees."

For some reason Luis thought that was the funniest thing he had heard and laughed uncontrollably, causing most everyone at the table to giggle. Ty was the odd one out. She kept eating, ignoring the jovial tone, until she couldn't eat anymore. She remained silent until everyone was done eating and sitting back in their chairs, feeling the food comas.

The doorbell allowed her to have an excuse to leave the table. Ty ran to the front door to find her father standing there.

"Dad," she said, collapsing into his arms.

Alejandro held his daughter close to him and kissed her head while her face was buried in his chest. "You okay?" he asked, realizing that she hadn't let go as quickly as was usual.

Ty nodded against his shirt then released him, giving him space to enter the apartment. The tall, dark-haired man stepped into the living room and stopped. *Why does he always pause before entering like that?* Ty thought. Ty noticed he was wearing a massive new set of keys, attached to a belt loop on his pants, which jangled with each purposeful stride as he made his way toward the kitchen.

"Dad," Luis screamed, duplicating Ty's behavior moments before. Alejandro held his youngest son in his arms while simultaneously greeting Benny and Izzy. Ty hung back in the living room, fiddling with the radio to see if she could get the Spanish music station to come in better.

"What's up, sis?" Alex asked.

Ty hadn't realized he'd joined her, so she swiveled, startled. All she could do was shrug. The truth was that she couldn't be around them acting like a big happy family.

Her father came back into the living room. "You aren't hungry?" Ty asked.

He shook his head. "Nuh. I can grab something later.

That food is for you all. Besides, Benny was already clean-ing it up and putting it away." Alejandro looked behind him at the sofa, then carefully lowered himself onto it. "How are you, Ty?" He was sitting very still on the couch, as if he were afraid any movement would make a mess. Alex, on the other hand, plopped himself on the couch, causing a framed picture on an end table to fall over. He didn't fix it.

"I'm good, Dad," Ty said, pushing Alex over and sitting next to her dad. "I heard you have a new job. Do you like it?"

Deep lines around his eyes appeared as he formed a smile. "It pays the bills," he said, standing and readjusting the frame that fell over.

"Is that what all those keys are for?"

Alex sat upright, chuckling. "Dad wears those keys every-where. I can even hear them while he's taking a shower!"

Alejandro shook his head. "Alex loves to joke about the keys," he said, giving Alex a playful push. Ty joined in on the laughter at first but then became silent, suddenly real-izing they were on borrowed time. They would soon be leaving her.

Benny, Izzy, and Luis joined them in the living room. "The kitchen is clean," Benny said. "Your mother will never know I cooked anything," he said.

Except for the smell and the piles of leftovers, Ty thought.

"It's also getting late," Benny continued. "So we better get going." Benny had brought his own Tupperware for Milagros's leftovers and packed the food into a plastic bag. He and Izzy grabbed their jackets.

Izzy stopped Ty as they all headed to the door. "You know you can text me any time?" Izzy whispered. "We only live a town away. I'm not that far."

"Yeah," Ty said, realizing that reaching out to Izzy rarely crossed her mind. Ty saw her most weekends and their lives felt so different, but Izzy was cool. "I know, Iz. And next week, my nails," Ty said, waving her fingers in the air.

"I got you," Izzy said, following her father out the front door.

"Well, we should go too," Alejandro said.

"But you just got here!" Ty screeched.

"Yea, but Ma will be home soon," Alex said. "So, it's better to bounce before she gets here."

Alejandro gave both Ty and Luis a hug before he and Alex headed out the door. Alex didn't say another word, and Ty watched as two people she loved were leaving her. A minute passed before she realized Luis was clinging to her side. Facing him, she said, "Do you want to teach *me* that farting game?"

He smiled and took off running toward his bedroom.

Chapter 14

THE MOON was just a little more visible tonight than it had been the previous night and Ty couldn't help but think of her made-up Moon Goddess getting fuller and fuller. Every time she closed her eyes, snapshots of the day's events appeared, keeping her weary mind at attention.

Her mother had come home shortly after everyone had left. She noticed the food but didn't eat any or comment on it when Ty came out to let her know that Benny had visited and cooked. Her mother didn't seem to be interested in hearing about Alex's visit and didn't want to know about her estranged husband's new job. She asked about Abuela, who was still listless, then went into her own hideaway of a bedroom. She only came out to say good night and make sure all the curtains were drawn and the lights were out, then she went away again.

Ty wondered what she could do to help her mother not do her "robot thing," as Alex put it. She was also thinking about Alex. They hadn't had another chance to talk about the details of the fight, and she was worried that Alex might be in deeper trouble with the Night Crawlers than he'd shared. *How can my life be any worse?* she thought.

Eddie flashed before her mind's eye. Closing her eyes, she imagined him smiling and then laughing loudly, like he used to do when Alex made a joke. *Why would he join the Night Crawlers?* Ty wondered. *And how could I have missed it? Maybe if I'd noticed, I could have stopped it. Do I still have a chance to stop it?*

It was late, but she wondered if she called Eddie, would he answer? And, if he answered, would he listen to her? Could she help him get out of this situation? Ty reached for her phone when suddenly her bedroom door swung open, and she swirled around in fear of what or who might be there.

Standing in the doorway was Abuela. Gone was the frail, faraway look she had worn hours before. Instead, she looked strong, almost regal. She cast her gaze toward the moon through the window, as if transfixed by its essence. For a moment, Ty was reminded of a younger, more vibrant version of her grandmother—the one that used to play with her when she was a little girl. She felt a pang of sadness at the memory of this beautiful woman, carefree and fun, teaching her to dance and correcting her Spanish.

Ty swiftly moved to her grandmother's side. "Abuela," she said. "Are you okay? What's happening?"

Ty took her grandmother's arm to steer her back to her own bedroom, but Isaura Ramos stayed firmly planted in the doorway. Ty released her arm, backed away, and waited. It was then that she noticed her grandmother was holding something in her hands.

Isaura pushed past Ty and into the bedroom. She sat on the bed and placed the item she had been holding next to her. Ty could now see that it was the box her grandmother had hidden from her earlier that morning. The box she had said didn't exist. Mesmerized by it once again, Ty instinctively knew it was important.

"M'ija," Abuela said. "I need to talk to you, and you have to listen carefully. It's a long story, and I don't know how much time we have, but I will tell you all I can. You have to promise to listen with respect."

Ty was shocked because her grandmother had seemed unable to communicate just a few hours ago and now she was speaking clearly and confidently. And she had never been disrespectful to her grandmother. She wasn't sure why her grandmother felt the need to remind her to be respectful, but she wasn't about to waste time arguing, so she nodded and sat next to her on the bed.

"We are descendants from the last great caciques, Anacaona and Caonabo," she stated.

Ty was confused. "Caciques?" she interrupted. "What's that?"

"That's the Taíno word for ruler," Abuela continued. "Our ancestors were rulers, kings, and queens in the Caribbean before the Spanish came. They were slaughtered by the Spanish colonizadores under Columbus's rule. We are the descendants of great people."

Ty had a bit of an understanding of the word *Taíno* because of her name and because she had asked her grandmother once why Puerto Ricans referred to themselves as Borinqueños. Abuela had explained that Borikén, or Borinquén, was the name the Taíno had given to the island of Puerto Rico. Ty watched her warily. *Would Alzheimer's make her tell mad crazy stories like this?* she wondered. *Probably not. Maybe she's hallucinating*, Ty thought. The counselors who came to visit them had mentioned that sometimes people with Alzheimer's hallucinate, and that it was best to reassure them.

"Abuela," Ty started. "Everything is going to be okay. You might be having a hallucination."

"Ay Dios," Abuela snapped. "Don't be stupid. This is why I said you need to listen with respect. Listen to my story, then you can talk to me about hallucinations, okay?"

Ty looked away in embarrassment. She peeked at the box between them and saw it was made of wood and had a design on the top that she couldn't make out.

"Columbus killed Caonabo," Abuela continued, "who was our great-great-great-"—she swept her hand in the air indicating that there were more greats to say—"grandfather.

Caonabo was married to Anacaona, who was our great-great-grandmother. When he died, Anacaona, along with great spiritual leaders, placed their powers magically into this zemi." Her grandmother reached into the pocket of her housecoat and handed a thick stone object to Ty.

Ty hesitated. She didn't want to touch the thing, unsure of what it was going to do. But Abuela insisted she take it, and she finally did.

The zemi was almost as big as her hand and, as she held it, she could feel its presence. It was made from a heavy, thick stone that had been crafted somehow into the shape of a triangle. Carved into it were frog legs folded around the lower half of its body. The face, however, was a human skull that had a gaping mouth. It was simultaneously the ugliest and most fascinating thing Ty had ever seen, and, as odd looking as it was, it inexplicably felt like it belonged to her.

Abuela took something else out of the other pocket of her housecoat. It looked like a beaded necklace with a gold pendant at the end. "Anacaona also gave strength to this amuleto," she said, holding the amulet and looking at it solemnly. The pendant part of the chain was etched into a weird human-looking shape as well. The design looked familiar, but Ty couldn't place it.

"Carved onto the front is the Divine Goddess of Life and Creation," Abuela continued. "There is a way to open it here, see," she said, pointing to the lock mechanism. "What I've been told is that when the time is right for it to be opened—when Anacaona's daughters and daughters' daughters need her, the holder will know." She placed the amulet into Ty's small hands then covered them with her own frail and thin ones, holding them as she spoke. "I am now passing these on to you and only you. You have to keep them to yourself. This is not something you share with anyone, do you understand?" Abuela paused to caress Ty's hair. "Pass these objects along to your daughter or granddaughter like I have done."

Ty extricated herself from her grandmother's grip. *I am only fourteen years old!* she thought. *I am not thinking about daughters or sons or anything like that!* She stared at the strange items now sitting on her lap and felt a surreal sense of awakening, like she could feel every bit of air and could hear every silent sound. She also felt a weird sense of déjà vu because she had just imagined a Moon Goddess who elevated young souls and this story was just as out there as the one she'd made up.

"And the box?" she asked, feeling it next to her leg.

Abuela caressed the wood lovingly. "In the box is a list of the women in our family who kept these heirlooms safe over the last five hundred years. You will find that I am listed here and now so are you." Abuela made this statement matter-of-factly, as if five-hundred-year-old artifacts were typically handed over to fourteen-year-old girls living in affordable housing units.

Darkness now engulfed the room as the moon became obscured by trees. *Was this all some memory gone crazy?*

Ty moved the objects from her lap to her side. "What you are telling me is that our family comes from rulers who were murdered, and these things come from them. And they have been passed down to the women in our family for over five hundred years."

Abuela stared, nodding slightly to acknowledge Ty's recap.

Ty took that in. "Why me?" she asked. "Why didn't you give these to Mami?"

Abuela grinned. "I knew the day you were born that I would pass these on to you. Your mother named you Taína for a reason. She thought it was a beautiful name, but I took it as a sign that you would one day know yourself and our ancestors." She paused. "Your mother, on the other hand, I'm not sure she will ever understand."

Maybe I'm the one having a hallucination. Ty thought. *I have to be, right?* Ty reached out to touch her grandmother's face to see if she were real or some hologram her mind had created. Soft skin and underlying bone greeted her tentative fingers, and Ty fell to the floor on her knees as the enormity of the situation hit her. She let the emotions of the last two days come crashing to the forefront. Isaura guided her back onto the bed and put her arms around her.

"I'm sorry, Abuela," Ty said between sobs, "but I feel like you're saying goodbye."

"Taína," Abuela whispered. "There is no time for tears. You must remember that you are a warrior, a fighter just like Anacaona. Our people, the Taíno people, are the light that makes the night sky bright. We are the music that warms the heart and blesses the soul. We love proudly and freely. This is our power. Our ancestors had to hide to survive, but our power never died. It's been inside of us all this time."

Ty looked at her grandmother's face. "This must be a dream or something because I've got no power, Abuela," Ty countered, "and every time I fight for anything, I lose."

Abuela hugged her. "You have power, m'ija. Our people sacrificed everything to get you these items, so that their existence, our existence, would not be forgotten. These objects and the knowledge of your birthright are your power now.

"But I'm sorry that I have to pass these on to you like this," she said. "I tried to wait as long as I could, but I can't wait anymore." Abuela stood and looked down on Ty, lifting her chin so their eyes would meet. "Remember, you are an amazing young woman who comes from a long line of amazing women. My time is over, but your time is just beginning." Before Ty could respond, her grandmother exhaled a long breath, hugged her with a ferocity Ty had not known she still had, and walked out of the room. Ty wanted to follow but was paralyzed.

Even though there was only a sliver of light illuminating the space Abuela had occupied, Ty could see the box, the zemi, and the amulet clearly on the bed. She was tempted to open the wooden contraption and look inside, but then she wasn't sure if she could take any more surprises this evening. Instead, she reached for the shoebox under her bed and fit the wooden box inside it.

Once again, she heard her door creak open and jumped, thinking her grandmother had come back to tell her more. But it wasn't her grandmother; Luis stood there waiting to be invited in.

"Can I stay in here with you tonight?" he asked. She reached out her hand and Luis ran into the room and onto the bed. Sleeping with him in her twin bed was always cramped, but tonight she didn't care. She didn't want to be alone either. She lay next to his warmth as he put his head on her shoulder and fell asleep. She finally dozed off herself, repeating her grandmother's words so she could write them down later: *We are the light that makes the night sky bright. We are the music that warms the heart and blesses the soul. We love proudly and freely. This is our power.*

Yagüeca, 1634
(present-day Mayagüez)

Guaynata was dying, but she wasn't going to tell her granddaughter, Antonia, that on her wedding day. Instead, she sat and watched as Antonia carefully laid out her wedding clothes on the bed. Antonia had a slim yet curvaceous body, long dark hair, and light brown skin. While that was the look of many of the women in this region, Antonia also radiated grace and kindness. Those qualities came from her ancestors, Guaynata noted. Antonia bore the exact likeness of Guaynata's mother's mother, Casiguaya—from beauty to spirit.

Guaynata watched the palm trees swaying in the warm

breeze. She recognized the beauty surrounding her, but the pain she endured in her lifetime overshadowed much. The one thing that still made Guaynata appreciate Borikén, or Puerto Rico as the others called it, was how the moon reflected onto the ocean waves, making the light ripple with life. It would bring her great joy to live her last days on the shores swaying with the bouncing light from the night sky.

At that moment Guaynata's son, Mateo, and his wife, Quiteria, walked into the room. Quiteria took one look at her daughter and started sobbing, going on about how God and Mary had blessed their family with such a beautiful daughter. Guaynata did not yet fully understand the god and saints Quiteria worshipped. Her mother, Tinima, had tried to keep the Taíno beliefs she learned from her own mother, Casiguaya, alive. Guaynata feared she might be the last one to know about their ancestors' ways, so she was eager for her son's cow of a wife to leave, so she could be alone with Antonia.

"Mother," Antonia said. "I will be ready soon, I promise." She gave her grandmother a quick side glance then said, "I'd like to have a moment with Abuela, please. It may be my last time alone with her for quite a while."

To that request, Quiteria's face completely changed. The tears were immediately replaced with a scowl, and she turned to face Guaynata.

"Fine," she said. "But don't use this opportunity to fill Antonia's head with nonsense. We are not savages. We are God-fearing citizens in a tropical paradise."

Thankfully, Mateo took Quiteria by the arm and led her out quickly. He gave his mother a quick, apologetic smile before they left, but Guaynata shook her head. "¡Estúpidos!" she exclaimed, to Antonia's pleasure.

"Abuela," Antonia laughed. "My mother only wants what's best."

"Hmpf," Guaynata said, instead of saying what she really wanted to say about Quiteria. That woman acted as though her god had anointed her to a position of superiority over others who believed differently. "Well," Guaynata continued, "I guess marrying you off to that skinny, silly-looking Hernán is best in her eyes."

"¡Abuela!" Antonia scolded then giggled. "Hernán will be a good husband, I think."

Guaynata would pray to any god if it meant that he would be a good man. Please, Atabey and Jesús, make him a good husband, she pleaded. Let him not be like my late husband, who tried to force me to forget my ancestors. Guaynata shook her head, as if the movement would solidify her prayer.

"Antonia," she said. "There is something I need to share with you before it is too late."

Antonia situated herself next to her grandmother and became attentive. "Of course," she said. "Anything you wish."

Guaynata started, "For many years, I have been telling you about your heritage. It's very important that you remember where you come from and that your ancestors were warriors and caciques."

"I know," Antonia assured her. "I was sad to learn that

great-great-grandmother Guanina and great-great-grand-
father Cacimar were murdered resisting the Spanish,"
she said.

"Yes, that was a terrible day," Guaynata said. "I was only
thirteen, but I remember it like it happened yesterday. The
majority of the Taíno in that hidden village were either killed
or enslaved. My mother, Tinima, and I survived but were
forced to assimilate in order to keep our lives. My mother
became Jimena, and I became Maria, but I still prefer to be
called Guaynata." She felt as though Maria was a character
she was emulating, but Guaynata was her true being. She
had accepted long ago that she would never be Guaynata in
public again.

"Before my mother died," Guaynata continued, "she
passed on these objects to me." Guaynata presented the
objects to Antonia, scanning the area to be sure they were
still alone. She explained what the sacred objects were, but
she also had a wooden box.

"I remember the day my mother took me to a place
hidden in the mountains. In that place, etched into a large
rock, was the image of Anacaona. From what I was told, her
grandmother, Guanina, had carved the picture along with
some markings to show the lineage. First Anacaona then
Higüamota then Guanina then Casiguaya then Tinima then,
eventually, me. It wasn't until I learned to read and write the
colonizers' language that I was able to copy the illustrations
onto a piece of cloth that I kept hidden." Guaynata paused
to scan the area once more. Satisfied they were still alone,
she continued.

"Your father told me that he wanted to make something special for me. You know how he loves to carve things out of wood." Antonia nodded as Guaynata continued. "Well, I immediately knew what I wanted. I gave him the cloth and asked him to carve Anacaona's likeness first, then surround her with something that depicted growth, nature, strength, and beauty—he chose vines." Guaynata ran her fingers over the box. "It's beautifully carved, isn't it?"

Once again, Antonia nodded. "These are all lovely," she said, as she continued to examine the box and the amulet. "But what do I do with them?" she asked.

"Never let anyone know about them," Guaynata said. "Do what you must to ensure their safety."

Antonia gently touched the zemi and glanced nervously at her grandmother. "I will have to keep secrets from my husband. What if that becomes too difficult?" she asked.

Guaynata could not help but laugh. It was not a happy sound, but a bitter, telling laugh that caused Antonia to grimace.

"M'ija," Guaynata said. "I'm sorry that I'm asking you to do this, but please understand that this is important. The Taíno, our people, keep dwindling in numbers because the settlers who have come here want to dominate. They don't want us here and they want to erase our history. I can't say why that is, but it's the situation we are in. I'm afraid that if they see these items and the box, they will destroy them." Guaynata inhaled, realizing she had forgotten to breathe.

"Of course, Abuela," Antonia said, vigorously nodding. "You can trust me."

"Good," Guaynata said, hugging her granddaughter. "Now, put them away and remember that you can call upon your ancestors when you are in great need." Guaynata stood to give Antonia a handkerchief to wipe her tears. "When you are ready, pass them on to your daughter or granddaughter. Make sure to choose someone who respects the elders and can keep this a secret. Make sure you tell her that our people are the light that makes the night sky bright. We are the music that warms the heart and blesses the soul. We love proudly and fiercely. This is our power."

Antonia promised.

That day turned out to be one of Guaynata's best. It was a perfect end to the mostly painful existence she had experienced there. After Antonia left to be with Hernán, and Mateo and Quiteria went back to their life in town, Guaynata was finally alone. While she didn't know exactly what illness she had, she felt that the end of her days was upon her. She chose to spend each night of her last nights on the shores of Yagüeca, allowing the vibrations from the moon to fill her until the supreme goddess was ready to take her. On the last night of her life, Guaynata swore she heard the ocean call to her, Guaynata, come home, Guaynata . . .

Chapter 15

THE NEXT MORNING, Ty lay on her back in her bed, staring at the ceiling. Luis was curled up against her side, his head buried under her arm, giving her warmth. She rubbed her eyes as the events from the previous evening came rushing back. Gently disentangling herself from Luis so as not to wake him, she pulled the box out from under her bed. Opening it, she found the small wooden chest sitting inside. As she lifted it, she realized she had been hoping that it all had been an elaborate dream and that the old shoebox would only contain her journals and pictures. But it was real, and she knew the amulet and a carved stone object would be there as well.

She glanced toward the door, wondering if she should go see her grandmother, but then decided against it. She wanted to give her abuela space, and she honestly wasn't sure if she was ready for another lesson in her Taíno ancestry. Instead, she picked up a journal and pencil and wrote:

We are the light that makes the night sky bright. We are the music that warms the heart and blesses the soul. We love proudly and freely. This is our power.

Ty homed in on the word *power*. Did she or they really have power? *What power did they have exactly?* It didn't make sense. Ty closed up everything in the shoebox and pushed it back under her bed.

Ty made her way into the kitchen to make breakfast. Her mother's keys were gone, signaling that her mother had already left for work. Pulling the milk from the refrigerator, she heard footsteps behind her. "Hey, big head," Ty joked.

"Hey, big nose!" Luis yelled, like his insult was the funniest thing in the world.

"Here's your cereal," she said, as Luis settled into a seat at the table. "Do you want a banana?" Luis gave her a thumbs-up. She cut the banana into pieces, and then sat next to him in a stupor. She wondered if she should tell Alex about what happened the night before, but where would she begin? If she understood correctly, the items were passed down for many years in secret to girls and women in their family. She wasn't sure if she would be breaking tradition by telling

Alex, or anyone for that matter. Did her mother know about the items? She doubted it because her grandmother had said her mother wasn't ready for them, or *I'm not sure she will ever understand*, to be exact. *Izzy then*, she thought. *Maybe she could talk to Izzy about it?* Deep in her thoughts, she didn't notice as her cereal began to get soggy.

"I'm going to fart all over you."

"What?" Ty asked, realizing Luis had been talking to her.

"I said, I'm gonna fart all over you because you not listening to me," he said, grinning widely and revealing two big front teeth that had recently grown in.

Ty laughed. "Oh damn, is that the punishment for not listening? Because that's nasty as hell."

"I'm going to get dressed and play my game," Luis said definitively and then ran into his room, leaving a bowl pretty much licked clean.

She quickly ate her limp cereal, put away their dishes, and pulled out the coffeemaker to make Abuela's Café Bustelo. Once that was set, Ty strode toward her grandmother's room. *Will she remember what happened last night?* she wondered.

Ty knocked a few times on the door before letting herself in. Abuela was lying faceup on the bed with her hands crossed over her chest like Egyptian mummies in their sarcophaguses. Abuela's position gave Ty pause. As she stood at the foot of her grandmother's bed, Ty immediately knew that Abuela was dead before she even checked her pulse or looked at her face.

Heart pounding rapidly, Ty stumbled her way back to her room and sat, putting her head between her legs like she'd seen in a movie once, trying to keep herself from fainting. *What to do, what to do?* she asked herself. *Alex.* She quickly dialed his number, but he didn't answer. *C'mon, Alex, answer the damned phone!* Quickly disconnecting, she dialed Benny.

"Ty?"

Ty couldn't speak.

"Taína, is that you?" A few moments passed in silence. "I'm on my way," Benny said, ending the call and leaving her to stare at the device settled in her hand. *What to do next?*

Ty stood but then sat back down, feeling lightheaded. *Ma,* she thought. Ty knew her mother couldn't take calls at work, so they had a system to text only if there was an emergency. Ty texted "911." In about three minutes, the phone buzzed.

"Ma?" Ty sobbed.

"What's wrong?" Esmeralda asked.

"You need to come home," was all Ty could get out before ending the call.

She dressed while thinking about what to say to Luis. She found him in his room, also dressed, but engrossed in something on his iPad. "Luis," she said. He didn't look up. "Listen, please," she said more urgently, and he finally focused on her. "Benny and Mom are on their way. Abuela is not feeling good."

"What's wrong with her?" he asked.

"I'll tell you later, okay? Just keep watching that as long as you want."

Luis resumed his video as the doorbell rang. She sprinted across the living room to open the door. Benny stood there alone. Seeing him, Ty let out a sob. Benny put his arms around her and held her as Ty pointed toward her grandmother's room. Benny then took off in that direction.

Ty stayed by the door, frozen in place, hoping that Benny would come back and tell her that she'd been mistaken—that Abuela was talking and laughing. But the muffled cries coming from the bedroom told her it was real. Ty felt a rising sense of dread, as if she had done something wrong. *Did I cause Abuela's death?* she wondered.

Suddenly, her mother opened the door, almost knocking into her. Seeing her face, Esmeralda dashed to join Benny. The cries were no longer muffled but in stereo. Alex had said that when they moved to the Dent, it had brought a new level of bad into their lives and that when he got suspended, it was another level. Ty remained frozen, wondering what new level of bad this would bring.

Chapter 16

Ty and Alex sat in the living room. They'd been staring at the walls surrounding them for at least twenty minutes. While there was so much to say, neither said anything. Ty didn't know what to make of Abuela's visit the night before. *She looked perfectly healthy and strong*, Ty thought. Alex leaned forward to say something, but then sat back in silence.

The whole family was there, along with Abuela's doctor and EMTs. Esmeralda and Benny were speaking in hushed tones outside Abuela's bedroom. Ty had never seen them in intimate conversation and wondered what they were discussing. Her father, Alejandro, stood with them, leaning against the sliver of a wall between Ty and Abuela's bedrooms, arms crossed against his chest, head bowed. Milagros was crying in the kitchen, more like hollering and screeching, inconsolable, even with Izzy tending to her.

In Abuela's room, the EMTs were prepping to take her to the hospital to determine the time and cause of death. Luis was still in his room. No one had really explained to him what was going on. He had peeked out to see strange people go into Abuela's bedroom but then returned to his room and his iPad—his safe space. No questions or comments. Ty envied him. She'd much rather be in her room than listening to Milagros's over-the-top hysterics. *Why am I sitting here?* she wondered, finally getting up and passing through the family outside Abuela's bedroom to get to her room. Alex followed.

"You okay, sis?" he asked, finding words.

"Um yeah," Ty said. "Best day of my life." Ty closed the door behind them then whispered. "What is Milagros doing? I mean all that fake-ass crying and screaming like she lost someone she loved like crazy. She didn't love Abuela, and you *know* Abuela didn't like her."

"Damn," Alex said. "She is putting on a good show." He then shrugged. "I don't know. Maybe she did care about Abuela."

"*Hmpf*," was all Ty said in response. "I know Abuela passed away, but it's weird to see everyone together, trying to get along. Like did she really need to die for them to act like a family?"

Ty paced while Alex watched. She'd been sad but was now getting angry. *Why Abuela?* she wondered.

"And you," Ty said. "I can't believe you didn't respond to me. I called you three times and you didn't answer." Ty faced Alex, hands on hips, giving him the special look she saved for people acting dumb.

Alex sighed. "I'm sorry," he said. "I didn't know it was an emergency."

It was the wrong thing to say. Ty stepped closer and said, "How would you know it was an emergency if you didn't take my call?! I shouldn't have to text you 911 to reach you, you know what I'm saying? Like I have to do for Ma just to respond to me."

Alex moved away from Ty and toward the window. "You're right," he said, then added, "I'm sorry, okay? I can't change what happened. I can't. I messed up, again. I'm always messing up, Cuatro."

Ty didn't respond.

"It's a little weird, isn't it?" Alex continued. "Everybody here and Abuela's not." Alex paused. "I mean, I know we all knew that this day would come, but, like, that didn't keep it from feeling bad as hell." Alex coughed then added, "I hope she's with Abuelo now, telling jokes, dancing, and eating good food." His voice crumbled as he held back tears. She couldn't remember a time when she'd seen Alex cry, not even when he was twelve and had fallen trying to jump over a fence. He'd walked into their apartment, showed his deformed index finger, and said, "I think it's broken." *Alex is hurting too*, she thought, and it made her feel less angry, well, at least with him.

One of Luis's plushies sat on the floor, and she thought of his little face with the dimples. "Do you think we should get Luis?" she asked, picking up the purple animal and holding it. "I mean, I don't think he really understands what's going on."

Alex nodded. "Lemme go get him." But as soon as Alex made for the door, it opened. Luis stood there, iPad in hand, looking perplexed.

"Luis, you okay?" Ty asked, bringing him inside the room, shutting the door, and hugging him. Luis's response was muffled by Ty's embrace. "What?" she asked, breaking the hug. "What did you say?"

"I said," Luis lifted his face, "before they left, I heard one of those men out there say that Abuela prolly died sometime yesterday like ten or eleven at night, but that don't make sense because she was in your room at like twelve thirty, cuz I seen the clock when I came in."

Ty stiffened. She glanced at Alex, who had a questioning look on his face. "Abuela was in your room last night?" he asked. "How? I mean, she wasn't moving when I left yesterday."

"Yeah," Ty answered. "And so was Luis, but it's a long story, okay?" she said, turning her attention on Luis. "You saw her come into my room?"

Luis nodded. "Was she a ghost?" he asked, glancing toward Alex then back to Ty.

Ty hesitated. What could she say? She gazed down at Luis's earnest face and then up at Alex's confused one and decided to tell the truth as she knew it at that moment. "Maybe," Ty said as she reached out and hugged Luis again. Alex joined them in a group hug. But the comfort and love didn't last. Arguing had begun in the living room.

"I just want to help," Benny said as Alex, Ty, and Luis made their way to the rest of the family. Ty lingered in the hallway, peeking into Abuela's room. It was empty. *They've taken her*, Ty thought, as her stomach twisted and turned like she was falling. *Was that it? Will I never see Abuela again?* Ty finally joined everyone in the living room.

"I don't need your help," Esmeralda snapped at Benny. "My God," she continued. "She just died! Can we leave the room alone for one freakin' day?"

"We don't have to yell," came a weepy, loud voice. Milagros had joined them as well, tissue in hand. Izzy followed close behind.

"No, no, no," Esmeralda snapped at Milagros. "You go back into the kitchen or wherever you came from and mind your business." Esmeralda faced her, daring her to respond.

Milagros took a step toward Esmeralda, her face hard. "Mira—"

"Wait," Benny said, holding up his hands between them. "We are not going to fight. Not now. It's disrespectful!" He yelled to no one and everyone.

Esmeralda opened her mouth to respond, but then closed her eyes to gather herself and walked out of the living room. Everyone heard the sound of her bedroom door slamming shut.

"What was that about?" Alex asked.

"I offered to help clean out the bedroom, that's all," Benny said, wiping his eyes. "It was stupid timing on my part. I should have known better, but I feel like I need to do something, you know?" He turned and went into Abuela's room, closing the door. Milagros was about to follow when Alejandro came forward.

"Why don't you leave him," he said. "He might need a minute."

If looks could cause damage, well, Alejandro would have doubled over in pain. "Excuse me," Milagros said. "Who the hell do you think you are, telling me what to do?" Alejandro stepped back, letting Milagros pass. She bolted down the hall to join Benny in Abuela's room, slamming the door behind her.

Izzy shook her head in disbelief. "Wow," she said. "Everyone is out of control."

"It's okay," Alejandro said, playing with the keys that hung at his waist. "Everyone is upset. People act how they act when they are hurting."

You got that right, Ty thought. What was it that one of the counselors in middle school had said? Hurt people, *hurt* people? When her father was arrested, Ty had been hurt and acted out in class. Her anger had needed an outlet, and she'd had more outbursts during that time than she wanted to remember. She was learning how to better control her hurt, but sometimes it was too hard to do by yourself.

"Will you stay tonight, Dad?" Ty asked almost in a whisper, hopeful that she could have his company for longer than today.

"I'm sorry, Ty," he said as tears filled his eyes. "You know I can't." He reached for Luis and said, "Hey, you want to play for a bit? I can stay until dinnertime." Luis nodded and the two went back to Luis's room.

Ty headed to her room as well. When Alex and Izzy tried to join her, she faced them and shook her head. They nodded slowly in acceptance and stayed behind in the living room.

Once in her room, door closed, Ty cried. *So much loss*, she thought. Her father, her mother, Alex, and even Eddie, but how would she ever get through losing her abuela?

Ty pulled out her special journal that had all the sayings, comments, and words of wisdom from her grandmother and opened it to a random page. The first quote she saw was "¡Esta gente son del diablo!" which made her smile through the tears. She had written the English translation under it. "These people are from the devil!" It was about people in general, but that day, it reminded Ty of her family and how they were all so angry with each other. Ty moved to the last entry. "We love proudly and freely." She wondered if that meant she would love her family regardless.

She pulled out the mysterious artifacts and sat on her bed, thinking about Abuela's words. The zemi and amulet were real, tangible things. As much as she didn't understand fully what they meant, knowing they existed and that they were given to her by Abuela were comforting.

How are we all going to manage without Abuela? Ty asked herself, sitting on the edge of her bed. She was the reason Benny and Izzy visited so frequently. She was why her family lived in the Dent, and she was, Ty felt, the only adult in her family who understood her and championed her. How could she love her family without Abuela? Throwing her journal to the side, Ty laid in her bed, feeling fear and sadness envelop her and lull her into a nap.

Chapter 17

THAT AFTERNOON, Ty stood at the entrance of Denton Park staring aimlessly toward the playground. Children were running, jumping, and swinging, but she remained motionless. She needed air and a break from all the family stress and awkwardness that ramped back up when Benny returned to discuss funeral arrangements. Funeral. *Funeral.* The word echoed in her mind.

Luis had stayed behind to play with Alex in their room. She didn't blame him. She missed Alex too, but she still needed a moment away from the apartment that was now full of family yet empty of Abuela.

"Ty."

Ty turned to the voice. It was Vincent. She immediately hugged him, feeling his cool cheek against hers.

"Thanks for coming out," Ty said. She'd texted Vin when things had become too much at home. They'd used to meet up at Denton Park all the time when they were in middle school, but the park had become less and less inviting over the past year, with more and more Night Crawlers using it as their hangout.

"Of course," Vin said. "I'm so sorry about your grandmother. I remember when my grandmother passed away. It was kinda overwhelming."

"*Hmpf*," Ty snorted. "You got that right. Do you know that the funeral is already gonna be Wednesday? Wednesday!" Ty watched a game of tag in the distance.

"Why so soon?" Vin asked.

"My abuela didn't want to be embalmed, so everything has to happen faster than usual." Ty remembered her grandfather had made the same request. His funeral had also been three days after his death.

"Talk to me about something normal," Ty said after a moment of silence. "What did you do yesterday?"

Vin shrugged. "I played video games, wrote a little bit, and broke up with Imani."

"What?" Ty was surprised. "Why?"

"Well, she stopped talking to me and, well, I just made it official." He smiled. "It's okay though. More time available for my friend."

"Until the next one comes around," Ty joked, and Vincent playfully shoved her shoulder. Her father's car turned the corner from Main Street onto Denton and parked near where they were standing.

"Look, there's my dad," Ty said. "He went to get pizza. Want to come in and join us?"

"You should be with your family, Ty, but call me later? I'm only a few blocks away."

Ty nodded and ran toward Alejandro.

Soon the family was crowded in the kitchen—Ty, her mom and dad, Benny, Luis, and Alex. Ty's father hadn't eaten dinner with them in years, and she was glad he was. She wished her grandmother hadn't had to die for them to be able to sit down as a family to eat, but she was trying her best not to be angry, since they all seemed to be getting along. Ty had even convinced her mother to let Alex stay until the funeral and she agreed, which was a small, needed victory.

"Okay," Esmeralda said, standing nearby and watching everyone eat, but not eating herself. "I'll call your schools tomorrow to let them know we will be off through Wednesday, when we have the funeral. I already called my jobs."

"No school Monday, Tuesday, *and* Wednesday," Luis clarified, smiling.

"Shh, little man," Alex said, before anyone could reprimand Luis's enthusiasm.

"I can only take one day from work," Alejandro said.

"So, I'll come on Wednesday for the funeral, then I can take Alex back after that." Alejandro looked at Esmeralda as he spoke, as if looking for approval from her for the plan. She gave a little nod but nothing more.

"Where are you doing maintenance work, Dad?" Ty asked, mostly for her mother's benefit, hoping it would soften her and lighten the mood.

"It's maintenance for an apartment building," Alejandro said, absentmindedly fingering the keys on his belt. "It's only been a few weeks now," Alejandro continued, "so you know I gotta do everything by the book."

Ty glanced in her mother's direction, hoping to see a sign of something other than annoyance, but her mother remained rooted and quiet. Alejandro's words hung like low-hanging grapes on a vine, something to ingest, but Esmeralda wasn't biting.

"You should eat too," Alejandro said, handing a slice of pizza to Esmeralda and breaking the awkward silence. Ty held her breath, waiting to see if her mother would take it or be rude. After staring at the pizza for a few seconds, Esmeralda nodded, took it, and said, "thank you," then turned and left the kitchen. Ty let out an involuntary squeal of joy, but then tried to cover it up with a cough. It was a minuscule moment of joy because she and Alex wouldn't see their mother again that night.

After Alejandro had gone and Luis was in bed, Ty and Alex finally had some time alone to talk.

"Don't let Ma see you with your feet on the table like

that," Ty said, sitting on the couch while Alex sat across from her.

Alex sucked his teeth and quickly lowered his feet to the floor. "I know, right? She already thinks I'm a loser, but the feet on the table will really put her over the edge."

Ty shook her head. "She doesn't think you're a loser, Alex," she said. "She didn't argue with you or nothing today." *And for our mother that was huge*, Ty thought.

"She was in shock, yo," Alex said, grinning. "She was even being nice to Dad. You know she was out of her mind on that one."

Ty giggled. "Wait! Don't make me laugh! First, the way Ma treats Dad is not cute or funny, and Abuela passed away. I feel bad joking around."

"Don't be, Ty," Alex said. "Abuela wouldn't really like it if we were sad and depressed." He paused, putting his feet back on the table. "I'm gonna miss her." He took his feet off the table again. "Why did Abuela go into your room? Luis said he saw her go in and you said you would tell me why later."

Ty lowered her head and watched her toes work their way through the fabric of the area rug under the living room table. "How about this . . . you tell me all the details of what happened with Eddie, and I'll tell you why Abuela came into my room."

"Okay, cool," he said, and they made their way back to Ty's room.

Alex plopped himself on Ty's bed, lying back, as she sat in the chair by the window. The night was still. The trees stood stoically instead of waving like they usually did. *Maybe they are mourning Abuela's death too*, Ty thought.

"So, tell me, how did you and Eddie actually get into a fight?" Ty asked. "It seems kinda crazy to me, cuz we all are friends."

Alex sat up. "Okay, it was like this. On the morning of the fight, I was hanging out in front of that Pour Me place near school when I saw Eddie. He was wearing a black hoodie, and I asked him if he was a Night Crawler now and he said yeah."

Ty interrupted. "Just like that?" she asked. "He admitted it?"

"Yup," Alex said nodding. "And I was like, 'That's messed up. Why you doing that?' And he told me he felt forced to because he needed money and had taken money from Jayden."

Ty placed her head in her hands. "He needed money that bad?" This was more a rhetorical question, because you'd need money in a real way to take it from a known drug dealer and gang member.

"You know his mother can't work and his father hasn't helped them in a long time." Alex shrugged. "Anyway, I told him that I thought he was whacked to take Jayden's money. Then he said he was desperate and owed Jayden so much money that there's no way to pay him back. That's why he felt forced to join the Crawlers."

What kind of friend am I? I didn't know any of this! Ty berated herself.

As if reading her mind, Alex continued. "I wish we woulda known, then maybe we could have helped or something, but it was kinda late. Eddie told me that Jayden and this other guy, Ernie, were forcing him to beat up John Miller that day at school to prove he was tough."

"John Miller?" Ty was surprised. "That skinny kid that doesn't talk to anyone?"

"Yeah," Alex confirmed. "It was wrong as hell. Eddie could have really hurt that kid, and for what? Eddie told me this plan, and I wasn't gonna let it happen, so I went into school and waited for John outside of class and told John what Eddie was up to. John told me that Eddie asked him to meet him in that area behind the cafeteria. You know that back door that's not alarmed?" Ty nodded. "Yeah, well, John left early that day and I showed up instead. I found Eddie waiting with Jayden and Ernie and told him to fight me instead."

Ty exhaled in such a way that her lips vibrated. "Wow," she said. "I can't believe you did that! You know Eddie's not gonna fight you."

"Well, that's what happened," Alex said. "He wouldn't fight me, but Ernie and Jayden were egging him on like 'Eddie, man up, you betta fight, yo.' Things like that." Alex shook his head. "Eddie looked like he had seen a ghost, because he was paralyzed in one spot. So, I said to Jayden and Ernie that I wasn't gonna fight Eddie, but if they wanted to fight, I was ready. Two against one, but, you know, Dad has taught me a lot of boxing moves over the years and I did okay. I beat them pretty good, but that's when Mr. Callahan came with the police to break it up."

So many jumbled thoughts passed through Ty's mind.

Alex stood and said, "I think this may be dying down, because I haven't heard from Eddie or seen Jayden and his crew."

Ty wasn't convinced. All she could do was hope that her uneasy feeling was nothing more than a result of everything that had happened in the last few days.

"Whoa!" Alex said, standing at the window. "Look at that!" Alex pointed. Ty joined him at the window. Across the street, something was perched on the fence surrounding Denton Street Park. Ty squinted to get a closer look. A flickering of light from a broken streetlamp revealed a large, white owl with piercing eyes that seemed to stare in her direction. Ty gasped because she had never seen an owl before, not even in the zoo, yet here one was as plain as night.

"Is that an owl?" Alex asked.

"Alex," a voice called from behind them. Esmeralda stood in the doorway, staring at them with a tired and glassy gaze. "It's late. You all need to get to bed."

"But, Ma," Ty said. "There's an . . ." Ty turned to point to the owl, but it had disappeared.

"I think it's gone," Alex said. "I'm gonna go to bed. Talk more tomorrow?"

Ty nodded as Alex and her mother left the room, and closed the door behind them. Ty turned off the light, so her mother wouldn't come back. Even in the dark, she couldn't stop herself from continuously peering out the window in the hope she would see the creature again. But it didn't come back . . . not that night anyway.

Chapter 18

O<small>N</small> M<small>ONDAY</small>, Ty sat in the living room ruminating while Benny and her mother flipped through old photos of their parents on the coffee table, trying to select the perfect ones to share with family and friends in remembrance. Images of her own flashed through Ty's mind. Mostly of Abuela, Eddie, and Alex, and occasionally the objects Abuela had given her as her inheritance—but the image of the owl dominated the most. Ty also remembered the crow that had been perched on the corner of Main Street and Denton Street a few days ago. *Did they both have something to do with Abuela?* Ty kept staring down the hallway toward Abuela's bedroom.

"You should go down there and visit her room," Benny said, startling Ty.

"Leave her," Esmeralda said before she could answer. "She'll go in when she wants to."

Ty had been actually thinking about the bird omens, but she didn't want to mention that, so she let them believe what they wanted.

"I know," Benny continued. "But your tía Juana is flying in today from Puerto Rico." Benny looked at his watch. "I'm gonna get her in about an hour and you know she's gonna go through the room to maybe keep something to remember her sister."

"You're bringing Tía Juana here?" Esmeralda snapped. "I thought you were taking her to your house."

Benny rubbed his forehead. "Well, I thought she'd want to see you and the kids, see Mami's room, you know, visit like people do when family passes on."

Esmeralda gave Benny a shrewd look and said, "But they weren't even that close. You know they didn't talk that much." Esmeralda hated pretense of any kind. If two people didn't care for each other when they were living, why would death change that? Benny had a different opinion.

"She's probably upset that they really weren't close," Benny said in a slightly higher pitch. "Imagine knowing that you will never be able to talk to your sister again," Benny added, dropping some pictures on the coffee table.

Esmeralda stood. She was wearing her at-home uniform of oversized worn sweatpants, droopy sweatshirt, no makeup, and hair in her famous messy bun. "Damn," she said. "Tía Juana is a wacko, and I'm telling you, dead people follow her. I hated being alone with her. It was like weird noises and like sightings of things that you never seen before."

Ty was alert. *Sightings of things you never seen before. Like owls? Whoa, wait a minute!* she thought. *Abuela mentioned a dream she'd had of Aunt Juana waving her arms as if trying to get someone's attention, but all that was there was a white owl—an owl like Alex and I saw last night.* Now she was creeped out.

Benny threw up his hands. "She's still our family. And I have never experienced any of that with her, and I visit her the most."

Esmeralda looked unconvinced but didn't respond. She pulled her sweatpants up before they fell off her and marched to the kitchen.

Benny glanced at Ty as if to ask, "What?" Ty didn't respond, so he went to the stereo and started to fiddle with the Spanish music stations. "Maybe I should play those old cumbias that Mami liked," he said. At that moment, Alex came into the living room and sat with them.

"It's a nice day," Benny said. "Maybe you all should go out or something." Benny put his jacket on. "I'm going to get Tía Juana. Do you guys want a ride somewhere?"

"You know," Ty said. "I'd like to go to the library and research some stuff." She was still not sure if the history her grandmother had shared about their ancestors was true, so she wanted to see what she could find on Anacaona and Caonabo. She hoped Alex would join her, because she had wanted to tell him about the artifacts and hadn't had the opportunity. "Want to come with me, Alex?" Ty asked.

Alex got up from the couch. "Sure," he said, stretching.

But Esmeralda came storming back into the living room, having heard everything from the kitchen. She pointed to Ty. "You can go, but not you," she said, directing her chin toward Alex.

"It's just down the street," Benny said, but Esmeralda snapped her head around toward Benny and stared at him. "What?" Benny asked innocently. "I don't see why he can't go."

Esmeralda ignored Benny and glared at Alex. "Alex, I don't want you out there getting into trouble or getting into more fights." She shook her head. "No, you're staying here."

"Ma," Ty started to come to Alex's defense, but Alex cut her off.

"Nuh, let it go," he said calmly. "I'd rather play with Luis anyway. We're making a cool city out of Legos." Then Alex walked slowly past Ty, whispered, "See, she's back to thinking I'm a loser," and was out of sight.

Ty stared intently at her mother. "Don't start with me, Taína," Esmeralda said. "You're lucky I'm letting you go out, since you are in trouble at school too." Ty couldn't believe she would bring that up now of all times.

"Don't think I forgot about that," Esmeralda said, then turned to Benny. "She likes to swear at teachers." Benny looked shocked. "They have to learn to respect other people," she said, heading down the hall and disappearing into her bedroom.

"What happened at school?" Benny asked.

"Give me a ride to the library and I'll tell you," Ty said, grabbing her jacket.

In the car, Ty told Benny the whole story of Ms. Neil and Mr. Callahan. Benny found a parking spot in front of the old library building and got out to talk to Ty on the sidewalk.

"Look, Ty," he said, "don't think I don't know how it is. I once had a teacher ask me if I had just come off the boat."

Ty looked shocked. "What?"

"Yeah, I didn't even know what that meant, so I said, 'I don't have a boat.'" Benny chuckled at the memory. "The kids in the class laughed and the teacher got mad. She thought I was being fresh with her, so she sent me to the principal's office. Can you believe that?" Ty shook her head.

"When Abuela found out, she wasn't having it. She went to the school and raised hell, but I still had to apologize to the teacher." Benny was silent, looking away as if he could picture the past in the distance. "Anyway, teachers control a lot, so you have to be respectful, then when you get home or are with your friends, complain."

The advice was the same as what her mother had given, and Ty was surprised because her mother and Benny rarely agreed on anything. She gave her uncle a quick hug and said "thanks" before heading up the steps toward the library doors.

Ty was eager to lose herself within the majesty of the library and put aside thoughts of teachers and their rules. She felt like she was walking into an old castle, since two seated lions framed the entranceway. Inside the lobby, behind the front desk, stood Mary, the head librarian.

"Taína!" Mary exclaimed. "How are you?"

Ty had first met Mary when she'd moved to the Dent five years ago. Not only was Mary the head librarian, but she was also a neighbor. She lived on Denton Street, a few blocks from where Ty lived. Mary was what her mother called a stereotypical-looking librarian. In fact, her mother had once said that if you looked up "librarian" in the dictionary, you would see a picture of Mary. She had graying blonde hair that she wore in a tight bun, glasses fastened to a gold chain that hung around her neck, and a long-sleeved shirt with a big silver ornamental pin on the collar. Little wrinkles formed at the corners of her eyes, and Ty thought that was because she smiled so much.

"A little sad," Ty said, setting her bag on Mary's desk. "My grandmother died." The words sounded hollow, like they were just echoes exiting her mouth, versus messages with meaning.

Mary came quickly toward her and offered a hug. "I'm so sorry," she said. "Your grandmother was such a lovely lady." Mary squeezed her tight, and then stepped back, locking eyes with Ty. "As long as you are around, your grandmother will never be gone. You are so much like her. Wise, strong, and beautiful."

Ty held back tears. "Thanks," Ty said, hoping they weren't making too much of a scene in the middle of the library entrance. Mary made her way back behind the desk.

"Are you here for something specific or just looking to lose yourself for a bit?" Mary asked. *Why can't all adults be kind like Mary?* Ty wondered. It didn't take much to be kind, but it seemed so hard for some people, especially when they had to be kind to people that resembled Ty.

"I need to do some research," Ty replied. "Is there a computer in the back somewhere or are the ones you have out front the only ones?" she asked, pointing to the three computers that were all currently occupied by the front desk.

"There is one in the kids' section," Mary said. "Oh," she continued, "I have a new work-study student from Canvas College who I think you'll like. She's from the Dominican Republic and used to live on Denton Street, I don't know, maybe fifteen years ago. I'll send her your way to help."

Ty watched Mary walk away then headed to the children's section. Since it was Monday morning, there was no children's programming currently running, but there was a little puppet stage set up right next to the one available computer. The rest of the library was pretty busy. People were reading, participating in one-on-one tutoring sessions, and working on their own laptops. While Main Street was becoming pretty White, the people in the library seemed to be every shade of every color. It's one of the many reasons Ty liked the library.

As Ty was waiting for the computer to start, she saw a young woman walking toward her. She had golden brown skin and thick, curly black hair—what Ty imagined her grandmother's hair would have looked like before it turned gray. That was the only resemblance though. This woman wore a nose ring, and Ty was sure her grandmother never had one of those.

"Hi, Taína," she said, smiling. "Mary sent me over here. Said you might need help with the computer." As she talked, Ty detected a slight accent.

"I'm just waiting for it to start," Ty said, realizing that these computers were probably older than she was and took a long while to get going.

"I'm Sofia," the young woman said, introducing herself. "Mary thought you and I would get along," she said, as she raised her eyebrows in a knowing look.

"I guess because we are both Latinas, right?" Ty said as Sofia smirked. Ty couldn't help but chuckle. Mary was cool and all that, but Ty knew that some people thought all people from Spanish-speaking backgrounds knew each other or would get along just because they had surnames like Martinez or Benitez.

"You go to Canvas?" Ty asked.

"Yeah," Sofia confirmed. "I grew up around here but moved when I was little." Sofia held her hand up to her waist as if to show just how little. Ty noticed that she had a tattoo of a hibiscus on her wrist. "I want to be a journalist," Sofia continued. "And Canvas has a good journalism program."

"That's so dope," Ty said, sizing her up. "I love writing myself." Sofia smiled and Ty thought of other things she wanted to ask Sofia, but the computer was now displaying the library's website, so she turned her attention toward it.

She navigated to Google's search page and, even though she remembered the name Anacaona, she didn't know how to spell it—*Ana-cona* or *Ana-ca-ona*—so she typed what she could remember. Before she hit enter, she heard Sofia say, "Anacaona? Are you interested in Anacaona?"

Mayagüez, 1760

CRISTINA WATCHED. Everyone was occupied in the festivities, and she had a rare, free moment to observe and wonder. In her sixty-five years on the island of Puerto Rico, she had never seen such a celebration. Nuestra Señora de la Candelaria de Mayagüez was now an official town. Although no one called it by that long name. Everyone simply referred to the city as Mayagüez, which made her proud. That was the name her Taíno ancestors had given the rivers in the area, and it stuck.

Cristina's husband, Juan, sat behind a large, wooden drum, striking the top of it with his bare hands. The deep, hollow pounding joined the soft playing of musical strings and the rhythmic scratching of metal on gourd. They were the melodies of the guitar, an instrument introduced by the Spaniards, and the güiro, an instrument created by the Taíno, and all three sounds intermingled and filled the air.

Juan's father had come to the island from Africa, enslaved to work in the sugarcane and tobacco fields. When Juan was still a young man, his father passed away, leaving Juan to fend for himself. Even though Juan was enslaved, he was given some freedoms, including the ability to choose who he wanted to marry, and he chose Cristina. Cristina had little say in the matter, but she was one of the lucky ones, because over time she'd grown to love Juan. Juan eventually bought his freedom but continued to work in the fields to earn a living.

Cristina watched Juan proudly bang the drum as the partygoers laughed and danced. One would think everything was harmonious and everyone considered equal, but Cristina knew better. There were dark-skinned men and women also observing the crowd quietly. She wondered whether they were as distrustful of this moment of celebration as she was.

"Mami." Cristina turned to find her eldest daughter, Rosa, by her side. "Where did all these people come from?" Rosa asked, staring at the large crowd. Cristina shrugged.

"I don't know," Cristina said. "But let's be careful. Sometimes too much drink brings out the worst in people. Where are Maria and Luisa?" Cristina asked, suddenly realizing she could not see her granddaughters.

"They are at the farm with Magdalena," Rosa said.

Cristina was relieved. Her youngest daughter, Magdalena, had children of her own and was a fierce protector. She would keep them all out of harm's way. Cristina took one last look at the crowd and whispered to Rosa, "Come with me. I want to talk with you alone while we have this opportunity."

Cristina walked purposefully toward an opening between a row of palm trees that led to Mayagüez Bay, letting the bottom of her long, frilly, white dress glide along the ground. At her age, she was not able to walk as quickly or as far as she once used to, so she chose a quiet place close enough to the festivities to still hear what was going on, but far enough to have privacy. As the two women walked toward the sand near the beach, the music became fainter and the singing of the coquí, a little frog that can only be found on Puerto Rico, became much louder.

"Mami," Rosa called. "Are you sure we should be out here?" Rosa looked behind her to as if to determine if anyone had followed. "They will miss us."

Cristina stopped walking once she hit the sand. She watched the waves as they made their continuous reach for the shoreline. She closed her eyes to take in its lullaby.

"Ay muchacha," Cristina finally said. "They won't miss us while they dance and drink. Let's take a moment to celebrate in our own way—by honoring the past and preparing for the future."

Rosa nodded, then stared off into the distance while Cristina observed her beautiful daughter's profile. Brown skin, oval-shaped eyes, thick black hair. She looked like a Taíno cacique and African royalty. Cristina was proud of her. She knew this was her chance to share the items that her mother, Ines, had shared with her. She recalled the lineage in her mind: Ines's mother was Luisa, Luisa's mother was Antonia, Antonia's grandmother was Guaynata, and so forth and so on. It was an honor and a privilege to know this lineage. Now it was time to share all her knowledge with Rosa.

"You know, I heard stories from my mother and her mother about how our ancestors traveled to these shores from La Isla de la Mona to settle here. Whenever I come to this spot on the beach, I get a strong feeling that this is where they entered."

"You are speaking about our Taíno family, right?"

Cristina nodded. "Listen," she urged, "do you hear that? That's the güiro and it is Taíno. The hammock we sleep in comes from our people, and the understanding of how the land, trees, sand, water, plants, and soil all work together to give sustenance and life is all ours."

Rosa nodded respectfully.

"The world is changing," Cristina continued. "Our island is changing. Can you feel it? We are losing the old ways. We are mixing with all the cultures and people that are here now, but we mustn't forget that the Taíno were here first and are still here!"

Cristina reached into a pouch sewn into the folds of her dress and retrieved the amulet and the zemi. "I carry these with me always and now I pass them on to you."

Rosa reached for the objects, fixating her gaze upon them. Without touching them, she whispered, "What are these, Mami? Where did you get them?"

Cristina grabbed Rosa's hands and placed the items into them. "They come from our ancestors. There is also a wooden box that holds the names of the women in our family who held these before me. All of these are yours now." As the two women held the treasures between their hands, they felt powerful and calm.

"It's a long story," Cristina started. "Let me begin. We are the light that makes the night sky bright . . ." Cristina shared what she knew and what she had been told as the combined sounds of the coquí, güiro, guitar, and drum serenaded them from a distance.

Chapter 19

"**D**O YOU KNOW who that is?" Ty asked, staring intently at Sofia's dark eyes.

Sofia nodded as she pulled another chair toward Ty and sat down next to her. "Yes, somewhat," she answered. "I'm Dominican, and Anacaona is a historical figure from Haiti and Dominican Republic because she was a Taíno leader. The Taíno were the Native people of both the Dominican Republic and Haiti."

Ty thought about that new bit of information. Dominican Republic and Haiti were also in the Caribbean, where Puerto Rico was. "My family is from Mayagüez, Puerto Rico," Ty shared. "Would she also be a part of Puerto Rican history?"

Sofia shrugged. "It makes sense. You know Mayagüez is on the western side of Puerto Rico, so close to Dominican Republic and Haiti. I mean she was a cacique or leader of the Taíno people, who were the Native people of a lot of the Caribbean islands, so, yeah, I guess we are all connected."

Cacique, Ty remembered. That was the other word her grandmother had used. *Cacique means leader*, Taína realized. Ty had heard about the Taíno people, but they had always seemed like these mythical people—not really real. "Do you know what happened to Ana-ca-ona?" Ty asked, hoping her pronunciation of the name was okay.

Sofia shrugged. "Well, not really. I mean she was killed by the Spaniards who took over some of the islands in the Caribbean, but no one really knows much more than that."

"Do you know if she had children or other family?" Ty asked.

Sofia smiled politely. "I mean I don't know a lot. I do know she was married to another cacique named Caonabo." Sofia paused. "Is this for a project for school or something?" she asked.

Ty nodded, because that was easier than the truth, but then remembered she did have a school project for Ms. Carruthers's history class. She was supposed to pick a topic she studied in middle school and go deeper with it. *We did study colonization in seventh grade*, she remembered. Maybe she could focus on the people who were actually colonized. "Yeah, I am doing a project for my history class and trying to learn all I can."

"Well, let's see what else we can find out," Sofia said, pointing to the computer.

They turned their attention to the computer screen where Ty had already typed her ancestor's name in a search box. Sofia corrected the spelling from "anacona" to "anacaona" and Ty hit enter.

"Wow," Ty said. "There's all this stuff on her?"

Ty scrolled to see what was on the list. Lost in her own thoughts, she barely heard Sofia say, "I'm sure we have some books on her too. Let me see if I can find one that you can take out of the library."

Ty was too engrossed to acknowledge Sofia's departure. Instead, she clicked on the first link and read:

Anacaona was an important Taíno cacique. Her brother, Bohechío, was the chief of Jaragua, a large territory that was located on the island that we now know as Haiti. When Bohechío died, she became leader. She married another cacique named Caonabo, who ruled Maguana, a neighboring territory, and the two ruled together. Caonabo was murdered by Columbus's men, so Anacaona was one of the few Taíno rulers who remained.

Anacaona was an excellent diplomat who worked with her oppressors in order to keep her people safe. She was known not only for her diplomacy skills, but also her beauty and talent as a poet, musician, and dancer. John Williams III wrote of Anacaona in his work, *The Conquest of the Americas: The Discoveries of Christopher Columbus*:

[She was] a beautiful warrior who was adored by her subjects. It was almost as if she held power over them, so winning her over was important in the complete conquest of the Americas. She naively believed that the Spaniards would be true to their word, so did not expect a war to be initiated by the Spanish. She showed the Spaniards every kindness and is said to have composed areítos, or legendary ballads, that held not only the Taíno people under her spell, but also kept the Spaniards enthralled. Eventually the Spanish decided she was a threat and had her killed.

Spanish records indicate that Anacaona and Caonabo had one daughter, Higüamota, but she is lost to history.

"Here," Sofia said when she returned. Ty blinked, realizing that she had had her face practically against the screen.

"I found a book for you," Sofia said, putting it on the table with the computer. "It's called *Anacaona: The Life and Times of a Taíno Cacique.*" There was a drawing on the front cover of what looked to be a mystical, magical princess. She had a large headdress on and what looked like a bikini bottom with long strips of fabric coming from her hips, touching the floor. She was holding a large walking stick and looking off into the distance. Ty ran her fingers across the cover to feel the embossed design. When Ty lifted her fingers, there was dust all over them.

"Thank you," Ty said, wiping the book cover vigorously with her sleeve, getting rid of the evidence that the book hadn't been touched in ages.

"No need to check it out," Sofia said. "Mary knows who you are, and she checked it out for you."

Ty was silent, thinking about what she had just read. *Was this Anacaona really my ancestor?* she wondered. *How could that be?*

"Can I ask you a question?" she asked.

Sofia nodded.

"Does the word *oppressors* mean people who keep other people down?"

Sofia exhaled and made a sound as the air escaped her mouth. "Yeah, and oppressors usually have power in some way, whether it's money, position, or weapons of some kind, and they use those things to keep others from getting rich or having status."

Ty considered that for a moment. "So, when it says here," Ty pointed to the computer screen, "that *Anacaona worked with her oppressors* that means she tried to change their minds or that she tried to get them to leave her and her people alone?"

"Good question," Sofia said thoughtfully. "It probably means both of those things." Sofia paused, deep in thought. "I mean," she continued after a time, "she was a ruler, a queen. She didn't want her people to be oppressed. She probably wanted them to live free and happy lives."

"She didn't want the Spanish to kill her people?" Ty asked plainly. "Oppression also means killing people, right?"

Sofia paused then simply said, "Yes, sometimes that's what it means. Other times it could be long and drawn out, like those people in power continuously making a group of people feel like they are not as good as another group of people. Because if one group feels that way about themselves, they are less likely to do anything when bad things happen to them."

"Because they feel like they deserve it or they feel like it's their *destiny* to be treated that way?" Ty asked pointedly, but Sofia didn't respond right away. It seemed to be more of a statement than a question.

"Wow," Sofia said, grinning. "What kind of project is this?" Sofia seemed to be trying to lighten the mood. Ty was okay with that, because she was starting to get overwhelmed.

"Thank you, Sofia," Ty said, standing.

"Of course," Sofia said. "Anytime. And I'm serious. You'll have to tell me more about the project you are working on one day. I'm here a few days a week until the end of the year."

Ty thanked her again.

As she made her way to the front entrance, she waved goodbye to Mary, who was busy talking to someone at the front desk. Before exiting, Ty saw a sign for a meeting of the Anti-Gentrification League that would be happening that night. She paused to inspect the details. It said:

Gentrification is what happens when profit-hungry real estate enthusiasts and private developers from outside a community buy up homes and drive up the cost of living—transforming a neighborhood's racial and economic makeup and forcing poorer residents out of their homes and communities. The new residents are more often

moderate- to upper-income White people who often do
not preserve, support, or value the community culture or
residents that they have uprooted.

Ty read the description three times before she walked out
of the library and onto Main Street. Gentrification sounded a
lot like what her ancestors had been through, losing their land
and having to hide their culture to live. *Is that how Anacaona
worked with her oppressors?* Ty wondered. *Did she try to make them
respect who she was and who the Taíno were?*

As Ty continued down Main Street, she overheard two
women talking:

Woman 1: I like this neighborhood.

Woman 2: Yeah, it's definitely up and coming.

Ty shook her head. "Up-and-coming" and "gentrification"
meant the same thing as far as Ty understood, but "up-and-
coming" made things sound positive, like people from the
Dent were in on the secret of a blossoming, undiscovered
neighborhood. Remembering her ancestors' struggles, Ty
realized that it all felt like a case of history repeating itself.
Once certain people discovered the neighborhood, they
didn't want anything to do with the people who had already
been living there. It was like they wanted to move in, take
over, and pretend that they had been there all along. Ty pre-
ferred the term from the poster, "gentrification." It reminded
her of the word "colonization," which felt closer to what
these new folks were doing.

As she neared the corner of Main Street and Denton

Street, a little red car zoomed past her and turned the corner onto Denton, causing her to jump.

"Slow down! You almost hit me," Ty yelled through the remnants of exhaust smoke, but the car fled, leaving her standing on the corner clutching the book on Anacaona close to her chest.

"Honey," a woman called from across the street. "You have to be careful because people around here drive like they the only ones in the world."

Ty watched the woman turn away from the road and face the mural of Eric Williams that adorned Atabey Market. "Mrs. Williams?" Ty asked as she safely made her way to the mural. She suspected it was Eric's mother but had never officially met her. The woman gave a tight smile and nodded, never moving her gaze from the mural.

"I'm sorry about Eric," Ty said.

Mrs. Williams touched the painted likeness of her son and Ty noticed there were fresh flowers in front of the mural.

"Did you know him?" she asked.

"Yes," Ty said. "He's my brother Alex's age and they used to hang out at school."

"You all need to be careful, okay?" Mrs. Williams said. "I wish I'd understood how dangerous it could be out here, but we hope for the best, you know? We hope nothing bad will happen to our children or our neighbors' children, but they do. When they do, though, we should make sure they never happen again."

A loud car horn made them turn away from the mural

and toward the noise. It was a black truck parked across the street from where they were. Three men stood outside the car while the driver inside held his hand on the horn. Why, Ty could not tell, but it seemed to be amusing the men standing outside the car, because they were laughing and talking loudly.

"I guess life goes on," Mrs. Williams said, inching slowly toward Denton Park.

Ty watched her walk away. She moved swiftly yet slowly at the same time. It was a mechanical gait, no joy but full of purpose, and Ty couldn't help but think of her parting words, "I guess life goes on." *Does it though?* Ty wondered. *Does it really? Sure, we remain here when others have passed on, but we are forever changed by the loss.* Ty realized she would never be the same now that Abuela was gone, and Mrs. Williams would also be different.

With her head bowed, Ty crossed the street to go home. The red car was still there, but the honking had stopped. The inhabitants of the car were still standing around it but had now quieted down. They seemed immersed in a discussion and less amused by the sounds the vehicle made. Closer to her home, people were standing on the sidewalk talking, children were playing on adjacent porches, and a young man was working on his car while listening to reggae. All this life going on, yet Ty felt strangely separated from it.

When Ty got inside, everyone was in the living room, including Benny. Alex was sitting silently on the couch and Luis was sitting on the floor playing with a minicar. Pacing back and forth, making Ty's eyes dance, was her mother. "What's up?" Ty asked.

Alex simply pointed to Abuela's bedroom door.

Chapter 20

"Tía Juana is here," Benny said, sitting on the couch with Luis and Alex as Esmeralda paced around the living room. "She is looking around." Ty glanced down the hall at the closed door. "And your mother is having a moment."

"Funny," Esmeralda said. "You know that woman gives me the heebie jeebies," she said, shaking her hands as if to make the creepiness go away. "It's like she's investigating or something. I don't know what she's looking for."

"Why are you always so paranoid?" Benny asked.

"It's just a feeling I have," Esmeralda said, pausing to place her hands on her hips. "Besides, I was talking to Ty." Benny got up to turn the volume up on the radio and started to sing along with the merengue song that had caught his attention. "Oh Jesus," Esmeralda said, resuming her marching. "That sounds like two cats fighting against a blackboard."

"Hey, I can sing," Benny said, to which Luis laughed, head back, eyes closed, holding his stomach.

The door to Abuela's room suddenly opened, and they all froze. Tía Juana exited, joining them. She had a slightly larger frame than Ty's grandmother had had, but otherwise she was a carbon copy, with graying thick hair, tan skin, and gold-rimmed glasses. Gold had been her thing for as long as Ty could remember, and she wore lots of it. A thick gold crucifix hung from her neck. Shiny gold bangles adorned her wrists and gold rings were on every finger. She wore a long, loose-fitting white shirt and baggy black pants along with multi-colored Crocs. For a moment, she simply stood, scanning the room, then focused in right on Ty.

"Taína," she said. "Ven acá." She extended her arms and Ty went to her. She smelled of fried food, coffee, and saltwater.

"Let me look at you!" she exclaimed, touching Ty's hair. "Wow, you are so big now. The last time I saw you, you were about six years old and up to here." She motioned with her hand toward her hips just as Sofia had done earlier.

"Hola, Tía Juana," Ty said. "Nice Crocs."

"Ah gracias." Juana beamed. "Milagros sent them to me."

Esmeralda made a face. *She either has a problem with Milagros or the Crocs, or both*, Ty thought. Feeling Juana's eyes tearing into her, Ty tried to fill the silence. "I remember visiting you in the winter once to see the farm that Abuela grew up on. You still live there, right?"

"Yes I do. I liked when you all came, but we haven't seen you for a while," Tía Juana said. "Now, it's a little different than when you were children." She paused. "Remember that shed that was in the back where you used to play house?"

Ty nodded.

"Well, that's gone now because of Hurricane Maria. It wiped out a lot of homes, but our house is okay. Electricity still goes out from time to time though."

"I thought it had gotten better," Benny said. "It's been a while since the hurricane."

Tía Juana sighed. "You know the island doesn't have a lot of money," she said matter-of-factly, never taking her eyes off Ty.

"But," Ty said, "aren't we part of America? Why wouldn't things like that get fixed right away?"

"*Hmpf*," Tía Juana grunted in response. She sounded so much like Abuela that Ty became a little disoriented and looked away. "We are second-class citizens," Tía Juana said. "It's like they wanted the land but didn't want the people."

"Tía Juana, do you want to go to my house and rest a bit?" Benny asked, turning the radio off. "Milagros wants to see you and is cooking a nice dinner."

"I would like to stay here tonight, Benito," Juana said, slowly moving her eyes away from Ty. "I will come with you for dinner, but I'd like to stay here in Isaura's room."

"I guess," Benny said slowly, answering on his sister's behalf. "We have a room ready for you at our house, but . . ."

"Bueno," she said. "I'll go with Benny and be back later."

Benny tried to get his sister's attention, but Esmeralda was now kneeling on the floor playing with Luis's minicar. "Does anyone else want to come?" he asked. Everyone shook their heads, so Benny and Juana left.

Esmeralda waited a few seconds, got up, walked over to the front door, pulled back an inch of the curtain covering the glass windows that made up half of the door, and watched them drive away. "Don't you think that's creepy that she wants to sleep in there?" she said, not addressing her comment to any one person. "I mean, damn, we haven't even had the funeral yet. What's up with that?" She turned toward her children, who were all quietly watching her.

"Abuela's really not coming back?" Luis asked, breaking the silence.

Esmeralda slumped and exhaled. "Sorry," she said. "Let's not talk about this anymore." She walked over to Luis and asked, "You want to help me make cookies?"

Luis, Ty, and Alex found each other's confused eyes. *My mother, bake cookies?* Ty thought. *Since when?!*

Luis seemed unsure what to do, but Alex intervened, pointing to a bag of M&M'S on the table. "Didn't Tio Benny give you M&M'S?" he asked. Luis nodded. "You can put them in the cookies."

Luis jumped and said, "Yes!" as he ran off into the kitchen clutching the M&M'S. Esmeralda followed but turned to give Alex and Ty a look that Ty couldn't decipher.

Ty joined Alex on the couch and whispered, "What was that look?"

Alex shrugged. "I'm surprised she remembers how to make cookies. You watch. She's going to be asking us to take over soon, you know what I'm saying?" Alex glanced toward the kitchen to make sure his mother and Luis were busy, then pulled his phone out from the back pocket of his pants. "I didn't want Ma to see the phone," he said. "She knows I have it, but I'm afraid she'll take it if she actually sees it."

Ty nodded. "Alex, I really need to talk to you."

Alex nodded absentmindedly and Ty looked over his shoulder at his phone. "Who are all of those texts from?" she asked, pointing to the screen.

"Eddie," Alex said.

"What does he want?" Ty asked.

Alex shrugged. "Me to call him. I'm sure it's all good."

Ty gave him *the look*. "How can it be good with everything going on?"

"I don't know, but I can't worry about it right now. It's gonna be fine. Everything is gonna be fine."

Chapter 21

IT WASN'T UNTIL LATER that night that Ty was able to skim
the book she'd checked out of the library. She was glad
for the alone time in her bedroom because the family had
had a disastrous evening together. Ty had had to finish
making the cookies, as Alex had predicted, then they'd all
decided to play cards. It had been a while since the four of
them had sat down to do anything together and it was like
they had forgotten how to interact with one another. Luis
hadn't wanted to sit still. He'd kept jumping and running
around the apartment. Alex had been wordless and sullen.
He had tried to call and text Eddie but didn't get a response.

Their mother had remained in a foul mood, snapping at them and continually making snide comments about Milagros, Tía Juana, and their father, anticipating their return. No one had been enjoying themselves, so they each had escaped to find solace in solitude.

Ty was beginning to understand more about the Taíno and even had a lot of notes to use for her school project. So far, from the book, Ty learned the Taíno were generous and loving people who enjoyed cassava and lounging on hammocks, which they'd invented. They loved music and poetry—they called their poems areítos and they could often recite them from memory. They believed bats and owls were symbols of the dead and they believed the dead walked among the living. That was the good. The bad happened when the Spanish encountered them and seemed to think they would make excellent servants. The Spanish did everything they could to make them slaves but killed many in the process. What was still unclear to her, though, was why? She got that the island had riches like gold that the Spanish wanted, but what she specifically wanted to know was what gave the Spanish the right to enslave and kill other people? And a bigger question was: Why had she never learned about any of this history before?

Ty had found a section in the book about zemis and had become excited. She read that zemis were common in Taíno culture and usually represented a spirit or a god. The pictures she saw were those from museums and she excitedly acknowledged that she had a real zemi in her possession that belonged to her family. Reading these historical details finally pushed Ty to bring out the carved wooden box. As she reached for it, she glanced toward her closed door. All seemed quiet, so she touched the box, still feeling a little apprehensive about opening it.

Ty ran her hand over the carving of a woman's face that adorned its top. She reached for the book on Anacaona and thumbed through to where there were pictures of cave drawings—amazing pictorials left by the Taíno— that were found on an island between Dominican Republic and Puerto Rico called Isla de la Mona. Ty recognized some of the drawings as owls and bats, but then one of the pictures looked familiar. The picture's caption said the image was a carving of a Taíno woman. Ty studied the etching on the box once more and thought the cave drawing and the etching were the same. *Who was this woman?* Ty wondered.

With a renewed sense of purpose, Ty finally opened the mysterious mini treasure chest. Immediately, she pulled the zemi out along with the amulet. Underneath, she noticed a thick piece of white folded paper. Underneath it was more paper and underneath that was a folded, brownish cloth. Ty removed everything and placed the items in front of her.

On the cloth was a faded list of names. She brought the delicate fabric closer to get a better view. Ty gasped because the first name was Anacaona and there was a faint sketch of her that was identical to what was on the cover of the box and in the picture of the cave drawing taken from La Isla de la Mona. She analyzed the picture on the cover of the book of Anacaona. The published image didn't look like the faded drawing on the piece of fabric or the carving on the box. It was clear that the book took liberties, imagining what Anacaona might have looked like. Someone else had taken the time to carve a likeness in a cave then transfer it onto the box.

Ty reviewed the next name, and it was *Higüamota*. That name, *Higüamota*. Ty remembered that name had come up on the website she was reading. She was Anacaona's daughter, who was supposedly lost to history. Only, she wasn't lost. She was on this list of names, which meant she'd survived and made her way to Borikén, to Puerto Rico.

The third, *Guanina*. The fourth, *Casiguaya*. The list continued like this, *Guaynata 1567, Antonia 1615, Luisa 1638, Ines 1665, Cristina 1695*, and on and on and on until it got to the present day. Ty found her grandmother's name, *Isaura 1950*, which meant the dates were birth years. Underneath her grandmother's name, Ty saw her name, *Taína 2004*.

Realization hit Ty. These were the names of the entire female lineage of Anacaona and she, Taína, was on it! Even though her grandmother told her what she would find in the box, it felt more abstract until she saw it for herself. *These women, my ancestors*, thought Ty, *kept these items hidden for hundreds of years as they fought their oppressors. My ancestors must have been badass!*

She held the cloth with the drawing of Anacaona to re-examine it. Ty wished she could ask her things like, what was it like to be a ruler? How did she pass these items onto her daughter, Higüamota? How did Higüamota survive? Are these objects ones that Anacaona actually held in her own hands? Ty was so immersed that she barely heard the knocking. Once she realized that someone was at her door, she tried to hide everything, but it was too late. The door swung open and there stood Tía Juana.

Juana took in the scene and grinned. "I had a feeling Isaura gave these to you," she said.

Chapter 22

"**D**ON'T WORRY, M'IJA," Juana said. "I will never tell anyone about these. They belong to you now and don't you let anyone take them." Juana glanced toward the objects. "Can I look at them?" she asked. When Ty moved to allow Juana room on the bed, Juana sat next to Ty and caressed the items lovingly in her elegant hands, saying things like, "Dios mío," and "Ay bendito," as she placed each item gently back where she found it. As she read the record of their ancestors, she became emotional. "Do you know what all of this is?" she asked, wiping her eyes.

"Just what Abuela told me," Ty responded, "but how do you know about them? Abuela told me they were a secret."

Juana looked pensive. "There were a lot of things in our house that were supposed to be a secret, but nothing was, really." Juana reached for the zemi and held it in her hands. "The only reason I know about these," she continued, "is because I overheard my mother giving Isaura the items." Juana paused. "I saw them walking toward the shed in the back and I followed, listening in on their conversation from the door." Juana paused. "I was angry. Ay Dios mío, I was the oldest daughter, so I didn't understand why she skipped me and went to Isaura." She handed the zemi to Ty and rose to look out the window. "I felt like my mother had chosen a favorite," Juana continued. "And I was upset, so I tried to take the items from Isaura."

Ty immediately stood up and began gathering the objects, but Juana turned away from the window and shook her head. "Please don't worry," she said. "I would never try to take them again. I learned a long time ago that's not how it works."

Ty continued to pack everything but asked, "What do you mean you learned that's not how it works? How do they work?"

"Hmm," Juana said, pushing her glasses closer to her face. "I don't know much, but when I asked Mami why Isaura and not me, she told me it's not about favorites or rank in a family, but about a feeling. A feeling that the woman who is chosen will take the responsibility seriously." Juana paused. "Isaura was the right person. I know that now. The fact that I tried to steal them was proof that I didn't understand." Before Ty put the amulet away, Juana reached for it. "You know who this is?" she asked, lightly touching the carving on the front of the amulet. Ty shook her head.

"She is Atabey, a Taíno goddess. The supreme goddess," she said, kissing the amulet.

"That's it!" Ty exclaimed, memories tumbling quickly to the forefront of her mind. "I knew it looked familiar. There's an Atabey Market across the street, and, I don't know, but I think José or Hilda drew this same picture on the chalkboard in their store."

"Atabey Market?" Juana chuckled. "Ay, qué cosa," she said. "They must be Taíno."

"Yeah, I guess both Hilda and José," Ty said in awe. *Why didn't I know this?* she wondered.

Everything was put away, back in the shoebox under her bed, but Ty was curious about something. "So did Abuela forgive you for trying to steal her stuff?"

Juana shook her head. "No, m'ija, she didn't, even though we talked to each other afterward and it all seemed good." Juana paused, playing with the crucifix hanging from her neck. "I believe she carried them everywhere she went until she married your grandfather. When she moved out, she took them with her, and I never saw them again."

It now makes sense why Abuela wasn't as close with Juana, Ty thought. *Abuela probably never forgave her for trying to do that.*

"Tía Juana," Ty said. "You said you knew she would pass them on to me. Why did you say that?"

"You are confident and wise," Juana said. Ty gave her a look. "You are," she insisted. "You are not afraid. She must have seen that and decided you were the right choice." Juana looked back out the window and added, "And our ancestors leave signs."

"Hold up, what?" Ty interjected.

"I can sometimes see them, and I had a vision in a dream once that all of our ancestors were standing in a circle around you. I woke understanding that you would be the next to receive the items."

Before Ty could make sense of what Tía Juana was saying, the door to her room opened again, but this time Esmeralda entered. "I thought I saw you come in here," Esmeralda said, eyeing them. "What's up?"

"Nothing," Juana and Ty said in unison, making Esmeralda give them even more of a questioning look.

"Ay, Benny and Milagros want to say goodbye before they leave," she said. Juana kissed Ty on the forehead and left the room. Esmeralda closed the door. "What the hell was that about?" she asked.

"Nothing, really," Ty said, backing away from her mother and plopping herself on her bed. "She wanted to know what was up with me."

Esmeralda made her way to the little chair by the window and sat in it. "Did she tell you about some vision she had?" she asked, rubbing her eyes, and Ty felt her insides do a flip.

"What do you mean?" Ty asked, immediately sitting up.

"Relax," Esmeralda said. "If she said anything like that to you, pay her no mind. She's nuts." Her mother sighed. "Man," she said, moving past talk of visions. "I am so tired and tomorrow Benny and Milagros will be back. I don't know if I'm going to be able to take it."

Ty wasn't sure how to respond. Her own mind was still spinning around Tía Juana. *Could she actually see their ancestors in a dream?*

"And if that Milagros makes another stupid comment, I'm going to pick up Abuela's old stereo and throw it at her." Esmeralda shook her head.

"Wow, Ma," Ty said, hoping her mother was kidding. "What's she saying now?"

"She's pissed, I think," Esmeralda continued, "that Juana doesn't want to stay with her. She's taking it all personal, like it's about her. She thinks I had something to do with Juana wanting to stay here, like I'm talking about her behind her back. Ty, pah-leez, one," she counted out on her fingers, "I don't even want Juana here. And two, I am not thinking about her at all. Besides, if Milagros cared about Juana at all, she wouldn't have sent those ugly-ass Crocs."

Esmeralda glanced toward Ty's bedroom door then said, "They must be gone by now, right?"

"Do you want me to check?" Ty asked.

Esmeralda frowned. "Nuh," she said, making her way to the door herself and listening intently. "I don't hear anything out there, so I'll take a chance."

"Ma," Ty called to her before she left.

"What?" Esmeralda asked, ear still against the door.

Ty wanted to tell her about the items, about what she and Juana really talked about, about how much pressure she was feeling to keep the family together, how much she wanted Alex home for good, how much she wanted Dad home for good, and last—but not least—how much she wanted her grandmother back. But she didn't say any of that.

"Good night," she said, as her mother slowly opened the door and quickly left the room.

Chapter 23

"**C**UATRO, I gotta talk to you," Alex said, barging into Ty's room without knocking.

"Ay." Ty jumped. It was only about 9:00 A.M., but, luckily, she had finished getting dressed and was pulling her hair back away from her face. "Why are you tryna scare me like that?"

"I'm sorry." Alex turned and quietly closed the door. He was already dressed in jeans and T-shirt, the bruise on his cheek almost invisible.

"I talked to Eddie late last night or early this morning, however you want to look at it, and he told me I'm not safe here."

Ty watched Alex as he started to pace. "What?" she asked. "Why? Jayden?"

Alex nodded. "Eddie told me they all been talking about getting back at me for what I did. Ty, I feel like a walking target now."

"No," Ty said, a little too loudly, then lowered her voice. "We gotta do something. How about we call the police, or you go back to Dad's?" She hated that she had to make that suggestion but *what else is there?* she wondered.

"What are the police gonna do? Nuh, I already called Dad and told him to get me after he gets off work. Tomorrow, we will go straight to the funeral, then I will go back with him."

"I hate this," Ty said. "You can't hide the rest of your life. Besides," Ty started to choke up, "you supposed to be here with me." She turned away so he couldn't see her cry, but he did.

"I want to be here, Ty," he whispered, "but . . ." He stopped and took a deep breath. "We'll get through this okay. Let's get through the funeral first, then we can figure out something."

Alex always tried to be positive, but Ty couldn't understand how he could be now.

"What are you going to do today?" Ty asked, composing herself.

Alex shrugged. "Lay low. Stay inside until Dad gets here, then bounce as fast as I can."

"Did Eddie say anything else?" Ty couldn't help but ask. "Did he give you any advice or tell you what to avoid?"

"Nuh, because I went off on him," Alex shared. "This is all his fault, you know?"

Ty nodded. It was all she could do now, even though her mind was racing. Alex was right. This was Eddie's fault, but Ty couldn't be mad at him. It felt like they were all forced into some kind of crazy game like *Survivor*. There had to be more they could do. There had to be.

The Perez family was a somber sight. Esmeralda and her children sat quietly in the living room, all engrossed in their own thoughts. Even Luis was uncharacteristically still next to Ty, letting her stroke his hair. The doorbell rang and they all jumped to get it, but Luis was the fastest. When Luis opened the door, there stood Uncle Benny and Milagros.

"Hey there," Benny said. He had brought coffee and donuts for everyone, which Esmeralda allowed to be set down on her living room table.

Juana, who hadn't made an appearance yet that day, came out of Abuela's bedroom and kissed everyone hello. Today she wore a similar outfit to yesterday, but instead of a white, flowy shirt, she had on a dark one with dark pants and sneakers along with her signature jewelry.

Izzy, who had lagged behind the others, walked over to Ty and whispered, "Hey girl, I have a message for you."

"A message?" Ty questioned. "From who?"

Izzy glanced around her to be sure no one was listening

before continuing. "Eddie." Ty felt her stomach hit the floor as Izzy continued. "He's outside and told me to tell you that he was sorry." Izzy furrowed her brow. "What's he sorry for?" she asked.

Ty grabbed Izzy's hand and walked with her toward the front door. "Where is he?" Ty asked.

"He was at the corner a minute ago," Izzy offered.

Ty peeked toward her family as they made small talk in the center of the room. *How can I get away?* she wondered. As if reading her mind, Izzy said, "I got you, girl," then turned to the rest of the group. "Dad," she said. "Can I have the car keys? I left my bag in the car." Benny passed the keys over. "Come out with me for a minute, Ty?"

"Thanks, Izzy," she said as they walked outside.

"You know," Izzy said, "I really did leave my bag, so I didn't lie." Ty had stopped listening to her as she searched for Eddie. She walked a few paces and noticed how eerily serene it felt in the Dent. No music, no laughter, no kids screaming. It was as if the whole neighborhood had decided to be still along with the Perez family.

Ty thought she saw something move near a tree on the corner of her street. "I'll be right back," Ty said to Izzy, finding Eddie leaning against the tree, arms folded.

"Hey, Ty," he said as she approached.

"Hi," she replied, noticing the deep circles under Eddie's eyes. He looked disheveled, like he had been sleeping in the same clothes for days.

"Um look, I just wanted to tell you that I'm sorry about

your grandmother," he said. "You know you were there when my brother died and I wanted to try to be here for you, but . . . I should go. You shouldn't be seen with me right now."

"I know I shouldn't," Ty confirmed then quickly added, "but I'm here and I need to know what happened to you. How did you become a Crawler? And why didn't you ever talk to us about it?!"

"I messed up, okay?" Eddie shook his head. "I messed up. I hate thinking you think that I'm a bad guy or something."

It was Ty's turn to shake her head. "I don't think that, but I am worried about Alex. How are we going to get out of it, Eddie?" she pleaded.

A new voice entered the conversation. "Eddie, my man," it said, coming up from behind them. Ty swiveled to face a young man who Ty recognized from the Dent. It was Ernie Santos—one of the two Crawlers that Alex said he had fought with.

"Who is this?" he asked, eyeing Ty. As he neared her, Ty could see bruises on his face that were old and fading. *Alex got him good*, Ty thought.

"No one," Eddie said, moving away.

Ty knew she needed to get out of there, but as she turned to walk away, she heard a familiar voice say, "That's Alex's sister, man."

It was Jayden Feliciano.

Jayden stood next to Ty, moving his eyes from the top of her head to the bottom of her feet in a slow, deliberate motion. "What's up, Ty," he said, smiling, although there was nothing friendly about the greeting. "You grown up now," he said, lingering on her hips and breasts.

"Jayden," Ty said, crossing her arms against her chest. "You grown too," she said. "That big, baggy black sweatshirt can't hide that stomach."

Eddie and the other kid with them chuckled, but Jayden gave them a dark look, causing them to stop laughing immediately. It was then that Ty noticed that Jayden also had faded black and blue blots on his face.

"You, always the queen of the comeback," Jayden said, inching closer to Ty and practically touching her with his protruding stomach. "But there's gonna come a day when you ain't gonna be able to comeback, you know what I'm saying?"

Chapter 24

"C'MON, TY, we gotta go!" Izzy screamed, inching her way toward the group. Jayden took a step back, which allowed Izzy to grab Ty's arm and pull her back toward the apartment. Once inside, Izzy put her arm through Ty's and marched her toward her bedroom.

"What was that about?" Izzy asked. "Eddie is cute and all that, but those other two, no, just no. They were trouble."

"I know, Izzy, I know," Ty said as she disengaged herself from Izzy's grip. She didn't want to talk about what had just happened. The truth was, she was furious. No matter what Alex said about Jayden, he would always be that awkward kid who annoyed the girls with cruel practical jokes. Yet he seemed to make Eddie and Ernie Santos tremble with fear. *What in the actual hell are they afraid of?* Ty wondered.

"Let's go back in the living room," Ty said.

"Are you sure you're good?" Izzy asked.

Ty nodded. "I'm good, but, honestly, I really want a donut, girl."

Izzy smiled. "Me too! I hope no one took the chocolate cream-filled one. That one was mine."

Alex had Ty cornered in the kitchen. They hadn't had a moment alone all day because, after Ty had come back inside to claim her donut, the family had engaged in reminiscing about Abuela and planning for the inevitable funeral tomorrow. Now the family was distracted. They were in the living room anticipating the dinner coming from Atabey Market.

Alejandro had arranged it. He had let Esmeralda know he'd taken care of everything before he left to work an extra shift. In a rare moment of gratitude, Esmeralda thanked him and made a point of telling everyone what he had done. Now they waited. Ty offered to set the table and Alex followed with questions.

"I know something happened when you were outside this morning," Alex probed. "Did you see Eddie?"

Ty reached for the plain white plates in one of the kitchen cabinets. She wasn't sure if she should mention Jayden and

Ernie, because Alex was already looking tense. Besides, there was nothing he could do about it.

"He wanted to tell me he was sorry for Abuela and for everything."

"You gotta be careful with him, Ty," Alex said. "Just stay away from him from now on. That's the best thing, okay?"

Ty didn't respond, even though she knew that Eddie wasn't the problem. Those other two were a different story though. They went looking for trouble.

Finally, the doorbell rang. "I'll get it," Ty said.

Ty was excited to see Hilda and José from Atabey Market standing at the door with a large container filled with food. Ty took the container from Hilda's hands. "Please tell me there are alcapurrias in there," she said, showing them into the house.

"Claro que sí," Hilda affirmed.

Alex snuck up behind Ty, grabbed the container from her, and then took off jogging toward the kitchen. Hilda and José chuckled and made their way into the living room.

"We just wanted to share our condolences," José said.

"Yes, we won't stay, but we are sorry for your loss," Hilda shared.

"Please stay," Esmeralda said, to everyone's surprise. "You are welcome too."

Hilda and José smiled and took off their jackets, introducing themselves to the family they did not know. Ty followed her mother into the kitchen, where Alex had already made a plate for himself.

"I'm surprised you invited them in, Ma," Ty said under her breath while grabbing an alcapurria.

"You know Hilda and José love to talk," she whispered. "Well, they can entertain Juana and Milagros for a bit while I go into my bedroom." Esmeralda put a few savory items on a white plate and moved swiftly into her bedroom. Ty and Alex exchanged knowing looks, then went back into the living room.

"I'm so sorry for your loss," José said specifically to Ty when she returned, and Ty gave a half smile in acknowledgement. José looked different today than usual and Ty realized that he had on actual clothes versus an apron and a baseball cap. And she finally saw his hair, which was dark brown with a little white at the corners near his ears. He was chubby, *probably from eating good food all the time*, she thought. His chocolate brown button-down shirt was bursting across the chest, revealing a white T-shirt underneath.

"I'm glad you're here, because I wanted to ask you a question about Atabey," Ty said.

"My store?" José asked, placing his hands on his hips, which made his shirt stretch even more across his chest.

"Well," she thought for a second, "yes and no, I guess. Why did you name your store Atabey? I mean, I know who that is now, but why did you choose it?"

José shrugged. "It was my idea. I'm very proud of being Borinqueño, so I knew if I ever had the chance to open a store, I would name it something Taíno."

"Borikén is Taíno too, right? That's what the Taíno called

the island of Puerto Rico?" José nodded and Ty continued, "How did you learn of Atabey and how do you know that you are Taíno?"

"I guess I've always known." He paused. "Since I was a child, my family talked about being Taíno. It was part of what made us great," he said. "When I got older, I asked around and did a little reading and learned about Atabey and other gods. Why are you asking?"

"Yeah, why are you asking?" Alex asked, apparently overhearing the conversation. "Abuela used to talk about us being Taíno too"—Alex turned to José—"I just figured that was part of our background."

"Exactly," José said. "I never questioned it."

Ty didn't want to be misunderstood, "No, I don't want y'all to think I'm questioning it!" she pleaded. "I am just wondering how you know for sure and I was wondering about Atabey. Is she a goddess everyone knows?"

"Atabey, as in Atabey Market?" Alex asked, furrowing his brow.

"Yes," José said. "I named my store after the Taíno goddess Atabey. She may not be famous, but she is well known among many Puerto Ricans."

"Why didn't I know about her?" Ty wondered. It was a question she had meant to ask herself, but she voiced it. José nodded.

"There isn't a lot written about the Taíno," José said, crossing his arms across his chest and resting his chin in his hand. "We were led to believe that they were extinct.

That they were an ancient people from a faraway time, but that wasn't true at all." José shook his head. "The Taíno survived and they live in all of us, especially those of us from Caribbean islands like Haiti, Dominican Republic, Cuba and, of course, Puerto Rico. You know that Puerto Ricans have the most Taíno DNA? I was reading an article about that and it made everything my mother, grandmother, and great-grandmother told me about my ancestors all true. That we are still here."

"What are you all talking about?" Hilda asked as she and Tía Juana joined them. Ty looked into the kitchen, where Milagros, Benny, and Izzy were sitting at the table eating.

"Atabey," Ty said. "I was curious about how you came up with the name of the market."

"We love being Borinqueños, you know," Hilda said. "We wanted to show that love in the store and in everything we do."

"Qué maravilloso," Tia Juana said in praise of Hilda's statement. "I'll have to come visit your store before I go back to Puerto Rico. Every time I pass it in the car, I see that beautiful mural on the side. Did you paint it?"

Hilda shook her head. "Ay, no, Señora," she said. "A young man from the neighborhood, John Williams, painted it. His brother Eric was shot and killed in that park across the street." Hilda pointed in the direction of the park. "And they didn't find who did it yet. It's sad because he was so young. You know his mother visits the mural every day? She is heartbroken."

"I would be too," Tia Juana said, then asked, "what are the police doing about it?"

"Not much from what I can see," José responded. "But a few residents are getting together to see what we can do. We met once already."

"That's dope," Ty said. "Is it a big group?"

José shrugged. "It's us," José pointed to Hilda then back at himself, "Mary from the library, a teacher from City Main High School, and Mrs. Williams right now, but we hope it will grow."

"Let me guess," Alex interjected. "Ms. Neil is one of the teachers from City Main."

Ty shook her head and said, "Yeah right!"

Not getting the inside joke, José said, "No, but we can ask her. Does she live in the Dent?"

"Doubtful," Alex said.

"It's Ms. Carruthers," Hilda offered. "Do you know her?"

"Yes, she's amazing," Ty said.

"Vamos a comer," Tía Juana interrupted, and Ty realized that Aunt Juana hadn't gotten any food yet. Hilda and José followed her into the kitchen.

As they stepped away, Alex asked, "What was with all those questions about the Taíno?"

Ty wanted to talk to Alex about what Abuela had told her, but she didn't feel like it was the right time. "I just learned that Atabey is a goddess and wanted to know why José named his store after her, that's all."

Alex gave her the *Do you think I'm stupid?* version of the

look and Ty exhaled, puffing her cheeks. "Okay, fine," she said, giving up. "Abuela gave me a story about the Taíno when she came to visit me the night she passed. I'm trying to learn all I can."

"What did she say?" Alex asked.

"You guys talking about Abuela?" came a little voice to their right. Ty had thought Luis was in his room, but there he stood. She quickly put her hand on his shoulder.

"No, Luis, not really," she said. "Hey, everyone is in the kitchen eating. You should go get an alcapurria if you want one."

"Ugh," Luis yelled. "Why is everyone trying to feed me when I want to talk about Abuela?" he asked, then stamped off toward the kitchen.

Chapter 25

ON WEDNESDAY MORNING, a small group of family and close friends buried Isaura Ramos. It was an unseasonably warm, bright October day and the sun reflected off the top of the shiny pearl casket as it was lowered into the ground. Ty was grateful to see people from her community and her life there to pay their respects. Besides her family, Hilda and José, Mary from the library, and Vin and his parents were there. Ty caught Vin's eye and tried to smile, but it probably looked more like a grimace, given how she was feeling.

Around the small crowd, the air was mostly still. There was the occasional sniffle or subdued cry coming from the mourners, but otherwise it was a respectful and quiet tribute. Ty held onto Luis's hand as they said their final goodbyes. He buried his petite, dimpled face into her waist, not wanting to look at the casket. Although they all loved Isaura, Ty felt the loss most. There hadn't been enough time to ask her questions and absorb more history. She vowed to remember her sense of humor, her directness, and her courage. Before they'd left that morning, Ty had held the items Abuela had given her close to her chest. As she stood over her grandmother's resting place, she closed her eyes, remembering the night Abuela had given her the objects and how they felt in her hands. She made a silent promise to keep the heirlooms safe so they would be passed on to future generations.

After the service, people were milling about on the sidewalk outside the cemetery offering condolences. Ty's stomach was in knots. She felt a weird disassociation from her surroundings, like she had forgotten the mundane reality of being human and become this creature that only felt the emotion around her, and the grief was overwhelming. Déjà vu washed over her. She remembered that she had felt similarly twice before—when her grandfather passed away and when her father left for prison. It felt as though the sadness clung to the air, limiting the oxygen, making it hard to breathe.

"Ty."

Ty turned to face Izzy. Her eyes were swollen and her nose red.

"This was hard," she said. "I can't imagine how you feel. You were really close to her."

Ty gave her a hug then wiped her own tender eyes. "I feel lost without her."

Izzy was pensive for a moment, as if she were looking for the appropriate response, *but, really*, Ty thought, *what could anyone say?* Ty was surprised.

"I wish I had spent more time with her," Izzy finally said. "I also wish I'd helped you more. I know you took on a lot. I should have done more."

The two locked eyes for a moment and Ty slowly nodded. "Thanks, Izzy, for saying that," she said. The two hugged again and, over Izzy's shoulder, Ty noticed her mother gesturing toward her to get into Alejandro's car. Juana was already in Benny's car with Milagros. Everyone was eager to leave.

"We should go," Ty said. As Ty made her way toward her father's car, she took one last look toward the cemetery, silently saying goodbye to her abuela Isaura.

At home, before Alex and Alejandro left, Alex had given Ty a hug and kissed her on the forehead, and Alejandro had given her and Luis a hug each, telling them he loved them. He'd also offered Esmeralda a hug. At first, she'd hesitated, but then she'd collapsed into his arms. Then, overcome with emotion, she'd flown out of the room. Alejandro had started after her but then stopped, immobilized, then quietly turned and left. Ty and Luis also went to their rooms alone.

Ty felt numb. She was tired of crying, tired of observing, and tired of problem solving. She faced her bedroom window and fixated her gaze upon a nearby tree. It had only been a few days since her grandmother had given her the items and told her the family tale.

She closed her eyes and imagined a warm Puerto Rican sun on her face—something to comfort her. When she opened her eyes, something moved outside the window. *Did the owl come back?* she wondered. Instead of an owl, it was a small bat hanging upside down in a tree. *What the . . .* It sat there, comfortably—as if it had a message. She tapped on the window and the bat flew off the branch in her direction before disappearing.

Ty couldn't remember anyone ever mentioning bats in the Dent. *Juana,* she thought. *Everyone says weird things happen when she's around. Hmm.* Ty reached for her journal. *Juana said our ancestors leave signs. What if the bat is trying to tell me something?*

She wrote a few things she remembered about bats, how they came out at night and had some sort of special meaning for the Taíno, something related to death. Ty realized that the bat made himself visible to her on the day of her grandmother's funeral. *It has to mean something, right?* she wondered.

Then Ty felt inspired. She sat down and wrote this short fable:

> Bat approached the Moon Goddess and asked if there was anything he could do to be out in the open during the day. The Moon Goddess told him she could make it so he could fly in the bright sun, but she warned that she did not know what might happen to his flying at night. Bat agreed and the next day he was happy to fly in the bright sun. But, after about ten minutes, Bat grew tired. The sun was too hot and bright for him to continue, so he found a cave to dwell in during the day.
>
> That evening, when Bat came out, it was now too dark for him to see. He was miserable, so he approached the Moon Goddess once again and asked her to reverse her work.
>
> The Moon Goddess hesitated, saying that this time, he would have to do something for her in exchange. Bat said he would do anything. The Moon Goddess then explained that she was the protector of souls and that from that day forward, when she elevated a soul, he was to appear to the mourners and honor them.
>
> Bat agreed and from then on, the Moon Goddess and Bat and his descendants worked together.

The little fable helped relieve her from her stress for the first time that day, and she hoped the calm feeling meant she could sleep. She pulled out the zemi from under her bed and held it close to her heart. She no longer thought it was ugly, but instead thought it to be one of the most beautiful things she'd ever seen. She put it next to her on her pillow, allowing its presence to be a comfort to her. She pushed all thoughts out of her mind and fell into a deep, solid sleep.

Chapter 26

Luis was sulking at the kitchen table. "Why can't we just have the whole week off?" he asked.

"I know, right?" Ty said, pouring milk over her breakfast cereal. She'd asked her mother the same question early that morning and had been told the district wouldn't allow it. "It's mean as hell," Ty said, unable to hide her annoyance.

Luis flew from the table and stomped toward his room.

Ty yelled after him, "At least we only have to get through today and tomorrow!" She hoped that would help but was doubtful.

When they were both dressed and ready, they grabbed their backpacks and headed out the door. She took Luis to school more often since Alex left—the duty split between Ty and her mother and it was her turn. The two siblings plodded slowly down Denton Street to the park entrance. The elementary school Luis attended was across the park, and there was usually a bunch of people ambling through it in the mornings to get to the school, so she felt safe enough to do the same.

"Is Abuela really not coming back?" Luis asked as they marched along.

"She's really not, Luis," she replied, letting a wayward breeze wash over her face.

"But she could be a ghost, right?" Luis asked.

Ty thought about that. How could she explain her grandmother's visit the night she passed, or the strange things that had appeared since her death? "Maybe," was all she could think to say. They walked the rest of the way in silence, the rustling of fallen leaves under their feet providing a consistent soundtrack.

"Look," she said as they neared his school, "there's Savion." Ty pointed to another boy who was waving in their direction. The two boys were in the same class, and Savion was the only friend from school Luis ever mentioned. Luis ran excitedly toward him and hugged him, before they skipped and jogged their way toward the entrance of the building. A teacher stopped them. "No running," she said, then added, "you boys need to learn to follow the rules."

Luis and Savion immediately stopped and, heads hanging, followed the rest of the students into the school. Ty instantly became agitated. "They were just excited to see each other," she said, approaching the teacher. "It's not like they were going to run screaming into the building."

The teacher glared at Ty. "Of course not," she said, "but you can't be too sure," then moved on to scold another student. Ty wanted to follow her, tell her to chill, but then thought better of it. It was not the way she wanted to start the day. As she made her way back through Denton Park to get to her own school, she scolded herself. *Why didn't I fight harder to have more days off?* she wondered. *What harm would two more days cause?*

Ty took a quick look at her phone to check the time, and breathed a sigh of relief that she was still early. Suddenly, she felt as though she were being watched. She scanned her surroundings, checking the park to see if there were still lots of people hanging about. There weren't. Only two male figures in the distance. She quickly looked away and picked up speed, but they were faster and made their way toward her.

"Hello again, Ty," Jayden said, now standing next to her. "Why you rushin?" Within seconds, Ernie Santos was by Jayden's side.

"What do you want?" she asked, boldly staring Jayden in the eyes. There was something about Jayden that wouldn't let her be afraid of him, but she trusted Alex. As she studied Jayden's and Ernie's faces, it was clear this was a no-win situation. She tried to walk away, but they blocked her path.

"Look," she said, ignoring the frantic beating of her heart, "I have to get to school, so you need to back up." The words rang loudly in the morning air, but neither of them flinched or obeyed.

Instead, Jayden smiled. "School, huh? You should stay with us. We could teach you things," he said, getting closer, his lips practically on her face. "You used to be so little," Jayden continued. "And now you are all grown up."

"Ugh," Ty replied. "You are so nasty."

The clear disgust on Ty's face must have triggered Jayden, because he grabbed her arm. "I'll show you nasty."

"Don't. Touch. Me!" she screamed.

"Hey," she heard another voice yell. "Leave her alone!"

Eddie quickly wedged himself between Ty and Jayden, forcing Jayden to release her.

"We good now, Taína," Jayden said, pushing Eddie to the side. "But you tell Alex that he needs to man up and find me or I will find *you* again and, next time, no one will be able to help you."

Ty backed slowly away, keeping her eyes on all three of them, all dressed in black, each scrutinizing her every movement. It was only when she was out of the park and back on Denton Street that she began to sprint. When she reached the hot yoga studio on Main Street, she slowed down to glance back. No one had followed her. Overcome with relief, fear, and sadness, Ty began to shake. *I gotta get Alex out of this!* she thought. This wasn't Jayden putting gum in her hair again, a problem she could handle. This felt like life or death. One wrong move and she or someone she loved would be damaged, or worse, gone forever.

A hand touched her shoulder and she screamed.

"I didn't mean to scare you," Eddie said, holding onto her shoulder. "I'm sorry. I just wanted to see if you were okay. Did they hurt you?" he asked.

Ty wanted to give into her sadness and crumple right there on the sidewalk, but her grandmother's words rang in her ears, *there is no time for tears,* and she regained her courage.

"Eddie," Ty said, "what are they gonna do to Alex? And what are they gonna do to me?"

"Nothing," Eddie said. "They aren't going to do anything to you, I promise." Eddie glanced behind him, then began ushering Ty toward school. "Look, Alex was trying to help me, you know what I'm saying, but now they got it in for him."

Ty sneezed, and Eddie reached into his pocket and pulled out a packet of tissues with a Dora the Explorer design.

"Dora the Explorer?" she asked.

He shrugged. "They're my sister's."

Ty used a tissue, but looking at the little cartoon face of Dora made the situation feel ridiculous. "How did this happen?" she asked. "You know what happened to your brother. Is that what you want for yourself?"

"No," Eddie said, "that's not what I want, but what else am I gonna do?" Before she could answer, Eddie continued, "You know my mom doesn't get enough money from disability." He paused. "Jayden gave me some money to help pay rent. I took it, then did a couple of small jobs to pay him back. Then we couldn't pay the light bill, and Jayden was there. It's like I'm always going to end up owing. I just keep going in deeper and deeper."

"You gotta stop, Eddie," Ty said. "Tell your mom what's going on, because you know she wouldn't want you doing that for her. Come back to school and get a legit teenager's job."

Eddie smirked. "A job? Where?" he asked. "At that coffee shop back there that only hires White kids or that yoga studio over there? What am I gonna do there? Mop sweat? They prolly want you to have a college degree to do that."

"That doesn't mean that the only other thing you can do is to join the Night Crawlers and sell drugs or whatever. You can go back to school, Eddie."

Eddie shook his head. "Like school is gonna help. I don't care how many new principals they get, you feel me? They still don't really want us there." Before Ty could interject, Eddie continued. "I have nowhere to go to get out of this mess. The Dogs and the Crawlers just go on killing each other and it's like no one tries to stop it. No one cares, okay?"

"I care," Ty said.

They were now at the entrance of City Main High School facing each other. "I'm really sorry, you know?" Eddie said. "I know you believe in me and, well, the other reason they trying to get you is to get me scared too. To keep me in line. But you know I'm not gonna let nothing happen to you, right?"

At that moment, Ty believed him. Eddie was about

to turn and leave when she dropped her backpack on the ground, hugged him, and said, "I do believe in you and I'm going to do everything I can to help." He hugged her back, then left without saying a word or even looking back in her direction.

"Ty," came a voice from behind her. She turned, thankful to see Vin, but he looked stressed. "What is that about?" he said, pointing to Eddie's back as he walked away. "Hold up. Are you crying?"

Ty grabbed her bag and as she walked said, "Vin, I can't right now. Can we just go into the school please?" Ty pushed open the main entrance and paused at security, where she showed her school ID, then walked through the metal detectors. There were several students in the halls, so Ty bobbed and weaved her way through to get to their first-period class, which was English with Ms. Neil. Vincent was hot on her heels though.

"Seriously though, Ty," he said. "Did Eddie make you cry? Are you guys together?"

"No," Ty answered. "I like him, but he's, I don't know." She couldn't finish her thought because she didn't know how to finish.

"Yeah," Vincent said. "Be careful. I heard some things about him."

"I will," Ty said as Ernie and Jayden flashed in her mind's eye. She wanted to push their faces out of her head, so she changed the subject. "By the way, thank you again for coming to my grandmother's funeral. I really appreciated it."

"Of course," Vin said. "I'm so sorry again about her passing. She was a dope lady."

You can say that again, Ty thought. "Yeah, this week was so hard," she said. "But I hope my grandmother is somewhere, happy."

Vincent grinned. "I hope so too," he said. "When my grandmother died, we had a party to celebrate her life because she had such a big personality."

"I wish we had thought of that," Ty said. "But on another topic, I started that history project Ms. Carruthers assigned and it's kinda dope." Today, their topic choices and a brief description were due.

"You had time to start on that with everything going on?" Vincent asked.

"Yup, I actually had more time than I wanted, so I tried to keep busy," Ty said, then whispered, "I wish we had her now instead of Ms. Neil. I don't want to have to deal with her today."

As they entered their English classroom and took their usual spots next to each other, none of the other students were sitting at their desks. They were mostly in small groups talking about sports or TV or friends. There were two boys standing by the door who were speaking in Spanish. Usually, Beatriz hung out with them, but today they were on their own.

Ty leaned toward Vincent. "Has Beatriz been to school?" Ty hadn't heard from Beatriz since last Friday, the last time Ty had been in school.

"She been out since Friday, Vincent said. "I think she's skipping."

Her phone vibrated in her pocket. She pulled it out to see a text from Alex that read:

CALL ME.

Ty quickly texted back:

I can't right now. U okay?

Suddenly the phone was pulled from her hand. She looked up to see that it was Ms. Neil. "No texting in class," she said, placing the phone facedown on Ty's desk.

Ty gave Vincent a knowing glance. Class hadn't officially started yet, but Ms. Neil was already targeting her. Not only that, Ms. Neil hadn't even acknowledged Ty's absence or the death of her grandmother. Ty wasn't going to let Ms. Neil get to her. Ty put her phone away, but when she did, she saw Alex's reply:

Call me as soon as u can.

Chapter 27

Ms. Neil started class by asking students to pull out their copies of H. G. Wells's *The Time Machine*. Half the class had it and half the class did not. Ms. Neil warned the class that she was going to begin deducting points for students who didn't bring their books. A student raised his hand and said, "I haven't got the book yet because there ain't no more in the library."

Ms. Neil looked skeptical. "I ordered plenty," she said, as if it were the student's fault, or worse, as if he were lying. The student sucked his teeth and shrugged.

Ms. Neil began her lecture anyway, even though the half

of the class without books met her with blank stares. Ty's mind drifted. Her thoughts and attention were on Eddie. How sorry he looked. How deep he had gotten in with the Night Crawlers. The situation with his mother and sister, and, of course, the fact that he had said that the Crawlers knew Ty was his weak spot. *Eddie made some bad decisions, but did he really have a choice?* Ty wondered.

"Ty-na?" Ms. Neil yelled. "Did you hear what I just asked?"

Ty looked alert, thinking on her feet. "Yes, but I don't have a book."

"I assigned it on Monday," Ms. Neil said. "Let me guess, you also didn't find any in the library."

Ty was trying to figure out how to respond in a way that wouldn't get her kicked out of class when Vincent came to her rescue.

"Ty-ee-na's grandmother just died," Vincent countered on her behalf. "She's been out since Monday."

It looked as though Ms. Neil had a retort on the tip of her tongue and thought better of it. Instead, she said, "Make sure you have your book tomorrow."

After class, Ty and Vincent headed toward their history class. "Thanks for having my back in there."

"She was looking to start something," Vin said.

"Like, all the time. Hold up, I gotta call Alex." Ty dialed, but Alex didn't answer. She quickly texted him:

I just tried u. I will try again in 45.

"Did you get him?" Vincent asked as they walked into their history class.

"No," Ty said, noticing a faint scent of citrus. She turned to see Ms. Carruthers had joined them, rubbing her hands, blending in hand lotion. "Hi Taína, Vincent," she said. "I'm so sorry for your loss," she offered. "I know your grandmother was important to you. Do let me know if I can do anything."

Ty felt an unexpected lump swell in her throat at her kind words. Because she didn't want to cry again or sound shaky, she only grunted in response.

Ms. Carruthers walked confidently to the head of the class. Even though she looked like she could be a high school student herself, Ms. Carruthers had to be well into her twenties—her braided hair, big red glasses, and sneakers added to her youthful look. She got the class to order by clapping her hands. "So," Ms. Carruthers began. "I asked you to pick a topic that you learned a little about in middle school and be prepared to share about that subject with the class. Once you select an area, you are going to go more in depth on that topic, do research, then a create a presentation later this year. So, you'd better pick a topic you like!" Ms. Carruthers examined the class. "Who wants to share first?"

A few students raised their hands, but Ms. Carruthers called on Vincent. He stood and presented that his topic would be the Civil Rights Movement.

He let the class know that his mother's uncle had been a Black Panther, and he was really curious about who they were and the work they did in communities. He also discussed freedom riders and how he hoped to focus on what happened with lunch counter sit-ins and other protests. When he was done, everyone snapped their fingers as Ms. Carruthers clapped.

Instead of asking for another volunteer, Ms. Carruthers said, "Why don't we go on to the next person and then move around the room until everyone has gone?" She nodded at Ty, but then caught herself. "Taína," she said, "are you ready to share or do you need more time?"

Ty stood. "I'm ready," she said. She was not someone who was afraid to speak in class, but for some reason, her hands were shaking, and her voice began to quiver. "*Ahem*," she cleared her throat. "I want to do a project on colonization and the Taíno. Um, they are the first people of Puerto Rico, where my family is from."

Two other Puerto Rican students said "wepa" in unison.

Ty smiled. "Um, I learned a little about colonization in the seventh grade, but I wasn't into it, to be honest." The class laughed.

Ty continued, "The Taíno created some amazing things. They invented hammocks, and we still use words from their language today, like *hurricane*, *canoe*, and *barbeque*." Ty paused to see if she still had the class's attention. She did. "You know, the Taíno were nice to the Spanish, but being nice didn't help them at . . . all." Ty used her hands for emphasis. "Most of them died. The ones that didn't die had to blend in with the colonizers, or they would be killed or become slaves. A lot of people said that most of them died because of diseases and stuff, right? But that wasn't the whole truth. Spaniards treated them like shh—, I mean, horribly. They beat them, raped women, took their land, and tried to make them slaves. I guess blaming only the diseases is an easy way out, you know what I'm saying?"

Ty paused to read her notes. "I learned about a cacique named Anacaona. A cacique is like a head person, like a boss, and people loved her. She was assassinated. She had a daughter named Higüamota, who got away. I have a book about Anacaona that I'm reading now, so I will let you know what happened to them." Ty glanced toward Ms. Carruthers. "Okay," she said. "I think I'm done."

Ms. Carruthers grinned, then started clapping. Other students joined in and Ty felt good. By the time all the other students presented their topics, there was a buzz of excitement in the room, with students asking questions and, in some cases, considering new topics. The school bell rang, and Vincent said to Ty, "Dope topic."

"Yours too," Ty said. Vincent's phone buzzed and then got quiet.

"You okay?" she asked.

"Yeah, um, it's Imani."

"What?" Ty said. "I thought you were done with her."

"I am, but she wants to talk to me." Vincent packed up his things quickly. "I'll see you later. I'm gonna see if I can catch her before my next class." He grabbed his bag and took off.

"Good luck," she said, grabbing her bag and gathering her things. *I hope Imani lets him down easy.*

As she closed her bag, Ms. Carruthers joined her at her desk. "I'm really excited to learn more about the Taíno along with you," she said. "My fiancé, Pierre, is from Haiti. Leogane to be exact, and there's a statue of Anacaona in the town square. I visited last year, and I remember thinking I need to learn more, because I hadn't heard of her."

"Really?" Ty said. She knew she had a limited window to call Alex, but this new information stopped her cold. "What was it like?" Ty wondered, thinking about the carved portrait of Anacaona on the box. *I wonder if the face of the statue looks like the one on the box.*

Ms. Carruthers smiled. "You know what, I'll bring in the pictures I took. It was a real learning experience for me. I knew very little at the time about the Taíno."

"I would love to see the pictures," Ty said as her phone started to vibrate. "I'm sorry, Ms. Carruthers, but I have to take this call."

Ms. Carruthers waved her away as Ty walked out of her classroom.

"Hallo," Ty said.

"*Cuatro*," Alex said.

"Ay," she exclaimed leaning against a locker. "You got me nervous as hell. What's going on?"

"Eddie texted me and said that Ernie and Jayden were messing with you. What happened?" Alex asked.

Ty quickly filled him in and then reassured him. "Look, Imma just avoid them as much as I can. I don't need to go through the park to drop Luis off, and I can ask Vincent or someone else to walk with me in the afternoons." Ty paused then added, "I'm not worried."

"I am, though," Alex said. "I made them look bad, you know? They're not gonna let it go. I need to come back home and deal with this."

Out of the corner of her eye, Ty could see Mr. Callahan roaming the halls. He gave Ty a get-to-class look.

"I gotta go," she said to Alex before he could respond, and then added, "you *stay* where you are, you hear me! Do not come home."

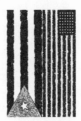

Mayagüez, 1919

"Mami," Clara called out to her mother, Ides. "Are you coming out?"

"Momentito," Ides said from her bedroom window. The window overlooked the back of the house, where there was an expanse of lush greenery and the beginnings of farmland. Clara, her eldest daughter, was sitting on the ground playing "teacher" to her four siblings, who sat lovingly attentive in a circle around her. She was making sweeping gestures with her arms, drawing pictures in the air. Ides was unclear what Clara was describing, but she could tell that her daughter was perfectly content with what she was doing by the elegant use of her slim hands.

The fabric of Ides's long, flowy dress touched her ankles as she turned gracefully from the window and made her way to a chest at the foot of her bed in the center of the room. She lifted the top of the chest and knelt to reach inside it. Years ago, she'd discovered a hidden compartment on the side of the chest that looked like a little shelf. Ides had always thought it odd that there was this extra piece of wood in the chest and jostled it loose one day to discover an empty space. She had been using the spot ever since to hide her treasure—historical items given to her by her mother.

Her mother, Anna, had passed the sacred objects onto her when Ides herself had been twelve years old. Anna had told Ides that she was becoming a woman and it was time for her to learn more about who she was to help her grow into who she was becoming.

"You are strong, smart, and honest," Anna told Ides. "You have a great capacity to love and care for others. These are traits you received from your ancestors." As Anna handed the objects to Ides, she'd said, "We have had to keep secrets about who we are and assimilate, but I know you will always respect our history and legacy. When you have a daughter who is just as warm and wise, pass these along to her to help keep our story alive."

Ides stood and glanced back out the window. Clara was teaching her siblings a dance. Love emanated from Clara. It looked as if she was born to be a leader by the way she stood tall and the way she interacted with her family. Not only did her siblings gravitate toward her as the eldest, but others in the community also commented to Ides about how smart and capable Clara was. The elders, in particular, often commented how the gods had smiled upon Clara and she was destined for great things. Ides had always known Clara would be the one to receive the inheritance.

She returned her attention to the box and, from it, Ides removed the list that contained the names of her ancestors and made her way to her bed. She loved to spread open the fabric and read the list of names. It reminded her that there was more to her life than the current space and time she occupied. Instead, she was part of a long lineage that stemmed from the greatness of Anacaona, who, after so many generations, seemed almost like a mythical, god-like creature.

Her hands moved along the names of the generations of women who had lived on the very farm she now worked. Her family had come to Mayagüez before it was even named Mayagüez in 1760. Much had happened since then—so very much.

A squeal of delight broke Ides from her thoughts. She returned to the window to see her children were no longer alone. Her husband, Hector, and her brother Gonzalo had arrived. They'd joined the children in their dancing, causing the little ones to jump and holler with excitement. Gonzalo was in uniform, proudly displaying the ornaments of the American army. The war of 1898 had finally given Puerto Rico freedom from Spain, which had been a long time coming. But, now they had new landlords in the Americans and Ides was wary. Before native islanders could assert their governance of the island, Americans settled in and around Puerto Rico, planting their flags where Spanish ones once flew. Replacing one flag with another suggested life would go on as normal, but things had never been normal, and they would never be. There was always someone looking for what they could take.

Ides quickly put away the wooden box and walked out of the house to greet her brother. Her husband, Hector, had gone inside the house with the children and Ides and Gonzalo were alone under the afternoon sun.

"Ides." Gonzalo smiled. "You look well."

Ides smiled despite her misgivings about what the uniform represented. "You look well too," she said. Then, because she couldn't help herself, added, "Even with that uniform on."

Gonzalo chuckled. "Ides, you will never change," he said, gesturing toward a shaded area under a large Flamboyán tree. The fiery leaves created a canopy.

"I know," Ides said. "There are very few opportunities to make a living in Puerto Rico and being part of their army helps you take care of your family." She understood why Gonzalo had joined the American army, but it didn't make it easier for her to accept. Ides never ceased to worry about his life, especially when he had fought alongside Americans in World War I.

"Don't you ever wonder," Ides continued, "what life would have been like for us had we stayed Borikén? What it would be like to be on our own as a nation?"

Gonzalo shook his head. "After the war, I just wanted

to live a simple life here with my family." He paused. "You know, we have American citizenship now. That could give Puerto Ricans a lot more opportunities."

Opportunities for what? Ides wondered. *To get farther and farther away from who we could have been?*

"Ides." She heard her husband, Hector, call for her and it was a good thing. She didn't want to argue or debate the island's past or present. She had to look toward the future and pray that Clara and her potential daughter and daughter's daughter would continue to do their part to preserve who Boriqueños were, regardless of the struggles and strife that would come with these new "opportunities," and make their history known.

Chapter 28

*H*E BETTER NOT COME BACK to the Dent, Ty fretted as she walked toward the library after school. How quickly things had changed from her wanting Alex to come home to wanting him to stay away. She still missed him and of course wanted him home, but she wanted things to be normal first. Normal would be a life that did not include the threat of guns, drive-by shootings, unnecessary suspensions, boys making threats, and murals of dead children. That would be basic normal—a foundational level of safety and support that should be expected in a country like America. She also wanted her family back together and, as a young Puerto Rican girl, wanted to feel welcome and safe in her own neighborhood. Her bilingualism seen as an asset, her knowledge of history encouraged and championed.

Ty pushed the library door open to find Mary sitting at the front desk.

"Taína," Mary said. "How are you and the family doing?"

"Fine, I guess," she said, surveying the library. "Do you know if that computer in the kids' section is taken?" she asked.

"It is," Mary responded. "Everyone is out of school now, so they get signed out quickly."

"Do you want to use my computer?" Sofia asked, appearing with laptop in hand.

Ty waved hello and grunted, "Thanks."

Sofia motioned with her head for Ty to follow her as she moved swiftly through tables, chairs, and bookcases. The buzz in the library was a soft hum. Kids were trying to keep their voices down but would often forget and need to be reminded. Adults were shuffling papers, books, and their own laptops as they acquired and processed information. Sofia found a free table in the back of the library and sat.

"How's your research going?" Sofia asked, opening her computer.

"I've been reading the book I checked out," Ty said, "but I'm wondering what might have happened to Anacaona's daughter, Higüamota. Do you think there's a way she could have made it to Puerto Rico?"

Sofia shrugged. "I know Anacaona was murdered in what is now Haiti. Let's see what we can find," Sofia said, navigating to Google and typing into the search box. "Look," she said, pointing to the screen. "She did have a daughter named Higüamota, but no one seems to know what happened to her. I would guess she probably died in Haiti too."

Ty wasn't sure where Higüamota had died, but she knew one of her ancestors had made it to Puerto Rico at some point. She had hoped there would be more information. "Where can we find more information?" Ty asked.

"Good question. You know," Sofia said, "there's not a lot about the Taíno recorded anywhere. They didn't write stuff down and, when the Spanish came, the Spanish documented what they saw, but it was from their perspective. The Spanish saw the Taíno as uncivilized."

"Really?" Ty asked, not necessarily looking for a response. It was more of a statement because Ty saw the Taíno as incredible. It would have taken unbelievable strength and courage for them to have survived all they had endured.

"Here," Sofia said, handing her a couple of books. "I found these books after you left last time. One will give you a little more backstory on the Taíno. The other is on Puerto Rico and will give you information about the history of the island after it became a territory of the US."

"Thanks," Ty said, taking the books. "How *did* the US get Puerto Rico? And how did we become citizens?" Ty asked, realizing in the moment that she'd always taken her US citizenship for granted, never really thinking about the history.

"The Spanish-American War," Sofia said simply. "The US won Puerto Rico, sort of, I don't know how else to describe it, and Puerto Rico has been a territory of the US ever since." Sofia turned toward the front entrance and noticed Mary gesturing toward her. "Hold on. I'll be right back," she said.

Ty sat at a table and opened the book about the history of the Taíno first. The first thing she saw was a map of the Caribbean and the names the Taíno had given the islands before others had changed them. Haiti was once Ayiti, but since the Dominican Republic and Haiti shared the same island, their former name had been Ayiti/Quisqueya. Cuba was always Cuba, it seemed, or Cubanascnan, and Puerto Rico used to be Borikén. Ty turned the page to the introduction. It was written by a professor from the University of Mayagüez in Puerto Rico. Ty read a little of it, but two paragraphs stood out:

The US National Science Foundation funded a study of Puerto Rican DNA and found that 61 percent of all Puerto Ricans have Amerindian mitochondrial DNA, 27 percent have African, and 12 percent Caucasian. Mitochondrial DNA is only inherited from your mother and unlike the DNA inherited from your father (nuclear DNA) it does not change or blend with other DNA over time. What does this mean? It means that the majority of Puerto Ricans have Native blood.

The idea that the Taíno were extinct had been a popular and dominant narrative for many years, but we now know that to be untrue. This new research shows that there was assimilation and Puerto Ricans became a mix of Taíno, African, and Spanish ancestry.

"You look like you've seen a ghost."

Ty jumped as if Anacaona had appeared by her side.

"I'm so sorry." Sofia chuckled. "I didn't mean to scare you, but your face was like white, girl. What were you reading?"

Words floated through Ty's mind. *DNA*, *assimilation*, *Native blood*, *extinct*, *untrue!* Ty voiced none of this. "I feel like every time I pick up a book or look at a website about the Taíno, I learn something new."

Ty's phone vibrated in her pocket—a set reminder to get Luis. "Damn," Ty said absentmindedly. "I thought I had more time, but I gotta get my brother from school," she said.

"Sure. I'll keep seeing what I can find for you about Higüamota. And before you go," Sofia said, "I wonder if you'd let me interview you for a story I'm writing on amazing young women."

"Me?" Ty asked, startled. "Amazing? Why?"

Sofia giggled. "I have yet to meet someone so young who was as interested in their ancestry as you are, to the point where you are in the library researching and learning. And that conversation we had about oppression was dope." Sofia grinned. "Besides," she continued, "it would give me the chance to write about Anacaona and her daughter in some way."

Ty liked the idea and said, "Yeah, sure."

"Yass," Sofia said, snapping her fingers. "Would you mind asking your mom to sign this permission slip?" Sofia went into her bag again, pulled out a folder, and handed it to her. Even though Ty politely took it, she knew her mother would probably not sign it. She packed her things, silently vowing to give it a try.

After saying goodbye to Sofia and Mary, Ty made her way to Luis's school. She wasn't going to chance running into Ernie or Jayden, so she took the long way around the park, where there were more people in plain sight. Not that it was much better, because she had to go through the Denton Street Dogs' territory. The Crawlers and the Dogs had a longstanding history of conflict, which, in Ty's opinion, was so stupid. But after that morning, she thought she'd take a chance on the side of the Dent that the Dogs ruled.

This side of Denton Street was different than the side Ty lived on. She was close to Main Street, Atabey Market, and the park, but once you passed the park, the homes looked more dilapidated and unkempt. There were abandoned cars and trash in the streets, some of which Ty kicked with her feet as she walked. She saw a couple of young, familiar-looking men standing in front of a boarded-up house near Luis's school. Her heart raced, but then she saw they were wearing jeans and white sneakers—not Night Crawlers' black.

Denton Elementary School gave Ty an inexplicable sense of dread. Nothing about it gave anyone the impression that it was a place of learning for children until you read the sign that said Denton Elementary School. There wasn't a visible playground, no colorful, decorative elements, nor any sense that there was joy in the confines of its three stories of brick walls. The windows on the first floor were dark and covered with bars, so you couldn't see inside the classrooms. It made her feel as if she were in trouble for something or going to visit someone who was in trouble—a mini prison, lifeless and cold.

Ty rang the building's doorbell and waited. When she felt the door click, she opened it and entered the abyss. A police officer sat at a desk by the door.

"I'm here to get Luis Perez," she said, eyeing the posters on the walls that said things like "stay in line" or "no running in the hallways" or "no talking in the hallways." She desperately looked for signs that said anything about hope or aspiration but there weren't any.

"I have a note here," the officer said, holding a piece of paper in his large hands, "that Luis is in Principal Moriarty's office. You should go that way." The officer pointed down the corridor to his right.

Ty trudged to the office. The dread she'd felt outside mounted as she entered the formal office space. A woman sat at a desk working on a computer.

After a minute of waiting to be acknowledged, Ty said, "Excuse me."

Without looking up, the woman lifted a single finger by way of response.

Ty tried to be patient but all she wanted was to find her brother and bounce. A man walked into the office past Ty and asked the woman, "Where's the key for the staff lounge?"

The woman grabbed a set of keys from a hook and handed them to the man without saying a word. The man was not fazed. He took the keys and left.

"Excuse me," Ty said, head tilted to the side and eyebrows raised. "I'm just here to get my brother."

The woman finally focused on Ty. "What's his name?" she asked.

"Luis Perez," Ty said.

"Oh yeah, right," she said. "He's with Mr. Moriarty. Hold on, I'll let him know."

After a minute, Mr. Moriarty came out from the back with Luis.

"Hi, I'm Mr. Moriarty," the man said, holding out his hand. Ty shook his hand, pretending this was the first time she'd met him. It wasn't. She had met him on Luis's first day of school six weeks ago.

"I'm Taína, Luis's sister," she said.

"I was hoping his mother would be here, because Luis was a little out of control in class today and in the after-school program," Mr. Moriarty said sternly. "I called your mother and left a message, so she knows what happened, but I haven't heard back from her yet."

Ty glanced at Luis, who buried his head in her stomach. "What did he do?" Ty asked.

"He wasn't listening to the teachers," Mr. Moriarty said. "And he said he didn't want to do any of the assignments. Three of his teachers called me about it at different times and one time the school resource officer had to go and talk to him. Finally, I just brought him to my office."

Ty tried to imagine a scene where a police officer would come into a first-grade classroom to get a student. She couldn't, so instead she shared, "He's been sad. Our grand-mother died this past weekend."

Mr. Moriarty crossed his arms against his chest. "Of course. That's why I brought him to my office, but I hope tomorrow he is ready to be back in school."

"Ready?" Ty questioned. "It might take him a while. She was important to all of us." Ty realized her voice was getting louder, so she took a deep breath, hoping to calm herself.

"I understand," Mr. Moriarty said slowly, "but I can't have him acting out in class."

"Okay, fine," she said, knowing she needed to get them out of there before she continued to debate him on this topic. "I'll talk to my mom tonight." Before Mr. Moriarty could respond or continue his overview of Luis's bad behavior, Ty took Luis's hand and marched him firmly out of the building.

Outside, Ty turned to Luis and asked, "What's up, Luis? Why were you acting out like that?"

Luis kicked a small rock across the sidewalk. "I hate school," he said finally. "Why can't I just be home with you or be with Dad and Alex?" he asked.

"We all gotta go to school, Luis," Ty said.

"Alex doesn't," he said, stamping his foot.

"Yeah, but Alex got in trouble in school. You don't want to get into trouble in school." Ty said the words, but they felt hollow. Weren't they the same words her mother had said to her about the way she'd acted in school last Friday? *Maybe it wasn't the same situation*, she thought as she reached for Luis's hand and headed toward Denton Street.

"Why aren't we cutting through the park?" Luis asked, pulling his hand away from hers.

"Because," Ty said, "I want to go this way now." She wasn't about to tell Luis that she was avoiding the park because gang members were threatening her.

"Aww man," Luis said, stamping his foot. "I don't want to go the long way."

Ty gave Luis a long stare. "C'mon. Will you trust me? We need to go this way, okay?"

Luis sulked the whole way home. Her mother wasn't home yet, so Ty made something to eat and let Luis watch his iPad. When Esmeralda arrived, Ty was sitting on the couch skimming the book on Puerto Rico.

"Where's Luis?" Esmeralda asked, dropping her bags onto the floor. "There was a message from his principal that he was acting out in class."

"In his room, Ma," Ty said, closing her book. "I know what happened, though. Mr. Moriarty told me when I picked him up."

"What is it with my kids?" Esmeralda asked, placing her hands on her hips and leaning forward to be more at eye level with Ty. "Why are all of you acting so bad in school?"

Ty couldn't help but roll her eyes. "Ma, c'mon. Can't you see that Luis is sad and upset, and this is how he's trying to get someone's attention? And Alex and my situations are completely different."

"Abuela, right?" Esmeralda asked, sitting down and rubbing her eyes repeatedly.

"Yes, Abuela," Ty said. Her mother was so lifeless, showing no reaction, almost like she didn't care. Ty felt frustrated. She needed to see her mother acknowledge what was going on, react to something. "But that's not it," Ty said, hoping to get through to her. "He also is hurting because of Dad and Alex."

Esmeralda squinted as if she were trying to comprehend the words Ty had just uttered. "What are you trying to say?" she asked. "Your father and I split years ago and Alex is still around. It's not like he's dead."

"But things have changed a lot in the last three years, Ma," Ty pleaded. "Alex and Dad are not home anymore and Luis misses them."

Esmeralda stared blankly at her daughter, and then got up and escaped into the kitchen. Ty followed, insistent, hoping to get more. Instead, Esmeralda grabbed a sponge from the top of the kitchen sink and began to wipe the counter of non-existent dust and grime.

"Ma," Ty pushed. "Did you hear me?"

Esmeralda continued to wipe. "I heard you," she said, "but I don't agree with you."

"Ma—"

"Luis was fine before Abuela passed away, okay? I don't think anything else is bothering him."

Esmeralda wiped the counter a few more times, put the sponge back, and straightened the dish towels hanging on the handle of the stove.

"Really?" Ty asked. "Because anytime I talk about Alex or Dad, Luis gets real quiet. He comes into my room every night, now, because he doesn't want to be alone. And he told me today that he didn't want to go to school anymore, because he wants to be with Alex. Maybe you don't think anything else is bothering him, but I'm here *way* more than you, and there are a lot of things bothering him!"

"Are you throwing the fact that I have to work in my face?" Esmeralda responded. "I have to work or else we won't be able to stay here. Do you think I want to be away from my children?"

"Sometimes," Ty responded quickly. "Sometimes I do think you want to be away."

Esmeralda pulled the dish towels off their perch and began folding them again, but this time with intense energy. "If I don't work then we're screwed, Ty, so I'm doing the best I can," she said.

For about ten seconds, all Ty could hear was the ticking of the kitchen clock. She waited awkwardly, wondering if her mother was going to say something other than that she was doing the best she could. *How about acknowledging the fact that I'm doing the best I can?* Ty wondered. *Maybe even saying something like, "Hey, Ty, I think you are a great kid. You help me so much and I love you."* Ty was slowly accepting that her mother was never going to say words like that to her, which made her even more aware of the loss of her grandmother.

Ty couldn't take the silence anymore, so she asked, "Can we keep Luis home from school tomorrow at least?"

"I can't take another day off work," she said. "And you need to be in school too, so you can't stay home with him."

"Seriously? Abuela just died. Don't we get time to grieve?" Ty held back tears, but her mother was unmoved.

"You went to school today. What's one more day?"

"What about Benny?" Ty pleaded. "I heard him say he took a couple weeks off." *Like normal human beings*, Ty thought bitterly.

"No way," Esmeralda snapped. "There's no way in hell I want him here gloating like I need his or Milagros's help. No way."

"You know that Benny is not like that, Ma." Ty stamped her foot. "He has always been there for us."

Esmeralda shook her head. "Not always. When your father was arrested, he said really nasty things about him that hurt a lot. Like your father was good for nothing, and I had bad judgment and all that." Esmeralda continued to shake her head. "That's why I don't give him any information that he can use against me."

Ty didn't respond because she'd never heard Benny say anything like that. "Ma," Ty said slowly, "maybe he was just reacting to the situation, you know? Sometimes people say stupid things when they get upset." Ty knew that better than anyone.

"Well, he never apologized or anything, and I haven't forgotten his words." She paused. "It's best that Luis go to school. You'll see. He'll get back into a routine and be fine."

Yeah, Ty thought, *because that's how it works, right? People just keep going and ignore their feelings, like you.*

"You're still working a short day tomorrow, right?" Ty asked, giving up the fight.

"Yep," Esmeralda said, trying to sound unaffected. "I'll take Luis to school before work, then pick him up after."

"Okay," Ty said. "Um, Ma," she continued, figuring now was as good a time as any to ask, "could you sign a permission slip for something?"

"For what?" Esmeralda asked suspiciously.

"Someone wants to interview me for a college news-paper. She's doing a feature on young women. I met her at the library, and she asked to interview me. I would like to do it, but she needs your permission." Ty stopped.

"Who is this person and why are you talking to strange people at the library?" Esmeralda asked.

"She's not a strange person, Ma!" Ty exclaimed. "Her name is Sofia and she's a student from Canvas College who is a library volunteer. I met her there because I was researching something for school, and she helped me. She used to live around here and she's Dominican."

Esmeralda used her hand to visually dismiss the idea. "No. Why does she want to know our business?"

"She doesn't want to know our business!" Ty snapped. "We're not that important."

"No," Esmeralda said. "Let her interview someone else, if we're not that important."

Mayagüez, 1972

"¡VEN, CUCA!" Isaura called out to her favorite pig. She stood inside the pen holding a peeled banana in her hand. Cuca snorted rapidly and loudly as she approached the rich fruit, then grabbed it whole. Isaura laughed. She would miss Cuca la Puerca Rica—the name Isaura had given her when they first met—because Isaura liked the way Cuca walked around the pen as though she were royalty.

A rustling of hay and the scratching of a rake filled her ears while the scent of freshly turned soil pervaded her nostrils. She wanted to remember all of it because today she was leaving for the United States, and she didn't know if she would ever be back. She glanced toward the main house and there stood her husband, Otilio Ramos, speaking to her father. *I'm married*, she thought. *I can't believe I am married and moving to a strange country today.* Isaura's feelings moved from fear to excitement to worry back to fear again as she gripped her bony arms. "Flaca" they nicknamed her because of her thin frame. She wondered if she would make any friends in America and if they would affectionately call her Flaca like her family did. Feeling she was not alone, Isaura turned to see her sister, Juana.

"In the pigpen again," Juana said. "You will miss your pigs when you are in the United States." There was no emotion in her voice, and Isaura wondered if she cared one way or the other.

"Yes, I'm sure you'll be happy when I'm gone," Isaura countered, peeling another banana while Cuca snorted and grunted in anticipation. She and Juana had been avoiding each other for almost a year since Juana had tried to take the amulet and zemi from her.

"No, I won't be happy," Juana said, playing with the gold crucifix around her neck. "I feel like you haven't accepted my apology and still think I'm a thief."

Isaura feigned shock. "When did you apologize?" she asked. "I don't remember."

"¡Ay, Dios mío!" Juana spat. "I apologized a hundred times!" For a moment, it looked as though she were about to join Isaura in the pen, but Juana avoided anything dirty, so she remained planted outside the simple wire gate. "One day you are going to realize that we are family and yes, I made a mistake. I was envious that you were chosen over me, the oldest. I didn't understand, but now I do. It's about legacy and love. It's about making sure we never forget our ancestors and how powerful they are. I don't need items to know all that, because it's not about them. It's about knowledge. We were given the gift of knowledge and now we must preserve and share it."

Isaura watched Juana closely before giving her a big, gaptoothed smile. "That's the most sense you've ever made!" Isaura laughed.

"Wait a minute," Juana said. "I make a lot of sense. What are you talking about?"

"Sometimes," Isaura stated. "But most of the time you are talking about omens and visions." Juana was known in the area as the neighborhood soothsayer. If you wanted your future told or help with a problem, you'd go to Juana.

"I know you never really believed that I had connections to things you can't see or understand," Juana said. "But I did have a vision about you." She paused and Isaura looked intrigued.

"Okay," Isaura said. "Tell me. One last vision for the road."

Juana smiled. "You are going to live a good, long life, Isaura. You will have your ups and downs, struggle with America and Americans. But you will have children who love you and a daughter and granddaughter who will keep the legacy going."

Isaura became serious. "Will I be happy? Will my children be happy?" Isaura asked.

"That's up to you and them," Juana said. "You all will have more power than you will think."

Otilio called to Isaura from a distance, and it was time to say goodbye.

"I hope you can forgive me one day and we can be friends as well as sisters," Juana said.

Isaura patted Cuca on the head, exited the pen, and gave Juana a hug. "Goodbye," was all Isaura said. It was time for Isaura to go. Her destiny awaited her on the mainland, USA.

Chapter 29

VISIONS FROM THE DAY invaded Ty's thoughts as soon as she closed her eyes. Jayden's grabbing her arm and Ty feeling his hot breath on her cheek as he threatened her, Eddie's crumbling face as he handed her a tissue to wipe her tears, Ms. Neil's judgmental and hateful staring, Luis's begging to stay home, and her mother's head shaking at every request Ty made. But not all of the images were bad. A memory of Abuela smiling also appeared and, even though Ty grieved her loss, remembering that she had always been happy to see Ty made Ty feel loved and appreciated.

Picking up her phone, Ty noticed it was almost midnight.

She imagined everyone would be asleep by now, so she crept out of her room. She used the flashlight feature on her phone to illuminate the still, dark living area then paused at Abuela's bedroom door. She had avoided the room all week, but Ty needed comfort and didn't know where else to go for it.

As she opened and entered the quiet room, everything was as Abuela had kept it. Tidy, sparse, yet full of her personality. Ty walked toward Abuela's dresser, where there were three framed photos. One was of her and her husband, Ty's grandfather Otilio, leaving Puerto Rico in 1972. *She looked so young and happy*, Ty thought. Another one was of her grandmother's mother, Clara, taken in 1980. Ty had heard Abuela talk about that visit and seeing her mother. *It must have been hard for Abuela to be away from her family to build a new life here.* Ty thought. *And here we are in this mess! What would Abuela do?* Ty wondered as her phone vibrated in her hand. It was Alex.

"Alex?" Ty answered.

"Hey, sis," Alex said. "I'm glad you're still up. I couldn't sleep and wanted to see how you were doing. Did you see Ernie or Jayden again?"

"No," Ty said, "and Mom is dropping Luis off at school tomorrow, so I am just gonna pretend like that never happened." Ty hoped Alex wouldn't probe, because she was actually finding it difficult to forget what happened. It was Jayden's negative energy and that breath on her cheek!

"I'm so amped," Alex said as if he hadn't heard her. "It's me they want, and I don't want you to be in the middle of it. This has nothing to do with you."

"I know, but it's not your fault," Ty insisted. It was too risky. Ty couldn't fathom losing her brother too. She'd just lost Abuela.

"No, like I said before, it's Eddie's fault."

"Alex, Eddie's kinda stuck. He got in deep, but you know he has to take care of his mom and younger sister," Ty said, remembering the Dora the Explorer tissue pack he'd had.

"I know that," Alex snapped. "Still. I'm coming home tomorrow."

"No!" she pleaded. "Alex, please listen to me. It's too hot here."

"I know, Ty, I know, but Eddie texted and said if I came back—" Alex started.

"What? You and Eddie are friends again?" Ty asked.

"Yeah, he's been texting me. You know I'm not mad at him even if this is all his fault." Alex sighed loudly. "He needs to get away from those guys, but first I gotta take care of me and you."

"Right," Ty said picking up the photo of Abuela from 1972. "You can take care of us better if you stay where you are. Besides," she tried, "you gotta watch out for Dad too."

Alex chuckled. "Yeah right," he said. "You know, Dad needs Mom and she needs him, but they both act like they don't need each other. All he does is ask about Mom. How she's doing. If she's seeing anyone."

Ty gasped, "Mom seeing someone else? Who would she see?"

"Right. She don't like to talk to people."

Ty grimaced at the thought of her mother in a relationship with someone other than her dad. "What do you think it will take for them to get back together? I mean, Dad is trying. He's got a job now and he's not seeing anyone, right?"

"No," Alex said, "but there's this woman next door who keeps coming over to see if we need anything. She's always gassing up Dad, but there's no way. Besides, I said I'd tell Mom if I see him even look at someone else."

"See," Ty said, "that's why you need to stay right where you are."

"Nice try, sis," Alex said, then changed the subject. "How are you doing? I mean Abuela's death was rough for you— well, for all of us, but you, I don't know, you always had a special thing going."

"Yeah, I miss her, you know?" Ty said. "I didn't realize how much she taught me."

"Are you ever gonna tell me what she said to you that night she visited you?" Alex asked.

"Let me tell you in person," Ty said then backpedaled. "I mean . . . I'll come out and visit you at Dad's and tell you."

"Nice try, again, sis," Alex said. "I'm gonna ask Dad to drop me off tomorrow, so I can stay the weekend. Then I will deal with the Crawlers."

"Alex . . . ," Ty warned. "No seas tan estupdio."

"I'm not being stupid. I'm being responsible. This is my fight, Cuatro. I gotta fight it."

"But—"

"I gotta go. That lady from next door is knocking on the door. Imma go tell her to leave before Dad gets weak."

"Wait—"

But Ty was too late. Alex had made up his mind.

Chapter 30

THANKFULLY, TY was having a basic Friday at school—no arguments, no drama, and some learning. Right when she was thinking the rest of the day would be just as basic, she saw a missed a call from her mother. A few seconds later, there was a voicemail notification. Ty quickly listened to it before her teacher was able to notice. The message was simple, but desperate. "Come to Luis's school now," her mother had recorded. Ty looked at the time. Class ended in five minutes. She'd have to wait to call back.

When class ended, Ty immediately called her back with no luck. A student could not leave the school without a parent's permission, so Ty frantically tried her mother a few more times, but still no answer. All she wanted to do was skip her last class—English with Ms. Neil—and run to her mom and Luis. She didn't want to have to interact with Ms. Neil while worrying about her mother and Luis. Maybe her mom would call back and she could get a pass to leave. She plodded into Ms. Neil's classroom, never taking her eyes off her phone, willing it to ring. It didn't. Ms. Neil, however, did stop her as she sat.

"Make sure that phone is put away before class starts," Ms. Neil said, standing over her desk. Ty nodded absent-mindedly.

"Did you hear me?" Ms. Neil added, standing by the desk waiting for a response.

"Did you not see me nod?" Ty asked before she could stop herself. *How was she supposed to continue to pretend that she was this obedient person who had no emotion?*

"Watch the attitude, please," Ms. Neil warned.

Ty opened her mouth to respond when Vincent, who had entered the class and sat next to her, stopped her. "Ty," he said under his breath. "Let it go."

Ms. Neil backed away to talk to another student. Ty leaned toward Vincent and whispered, "I'm just worried about my mom. She left me this crazy message and now I can't get her. I don't know what to do. Ms. Neil is not going to let me come back to the class if I leave to make a phone call."

"If you're worried about your mom, you should go see Mr. Callahan. Maybe he'll help."

That seemed like a good idea to Ty and exactly what Mr. Callahan had said to do, so Ty raised her hand. Ms. Neil didn't acknowledge her even though she was looking in Ty's direction.

"She's pretending she can't see me," Ty said, turning to Vin.

"Just call out to her," he suggested. "Maybe she can't see you."

"She can see me, Vin," Ty said, reaching her tipping point. She stood and gathered her things. As she placed her backpack on her back and turned to leave the class, Ms. Neil approached.

"Where are you going?" Ms. Neil asked, walking toward her.

"I need to see Mr. Callahan. There's an emergency at home," Ty said over her shoulder then purposefully walked toward the door.

"Wait a minute," Ms. Neil said. "You can't leave without my permission, and I haven't given it yet."

The classroom went still and quiet. Ty faced Ms. Neil, aware that all eyes were on them.

"Ms. Neil, I raised my hand to ask for permission," she said, calmly at first, then she gave into her panic. "Look, I've got a real emergency happening at home, so I don't have time for this."

"I warned you about your attitude, didn't I?" Ms. Neil placed her hands on her hips, challenging Ty. Ty felt a lump in her throat form from frustration and worry.

"Are you for real?" Ty couldn't help but yell. "I told you I had an emergency situation at home and you're going on about some attitude I may or may not have." Ty sucked her teeth and waved her hand. "I need to go!" Ty was out of the room in seconds.

Ms. Neil hadn't said anything more, but that didn't surprise Ty. Ms. Neil was probably thrilled that Ty was giving her a reason to kick her out of class. Ty clenched her teeth and dialed her mother again. This time she answered.

"Ty, come to Luis's school now," Esmeralda pleaded.

"Ma, I'll be right there, but I need per—" Ty tried to get the words out before her mother disconnected but didn't make it. *How am I going to get out of school without Mom's permission?* Ty remembered the back door near the cafeteria where Alex and Jayden had fought and wondered if the door's alarm was still off. She surveyed her surroundings, then walked quickly to the cafeteria.

No one was around. When she found the door, she opened it and stepped out onto the street without a sound. She moved quickly and stealthily the long way around, so as not to be noticed, and still arrived at Denton Elementary in less than ten minutes.

Inside Luis's school, a different school resource officer was at the desk. She told him who she was and he sent her to the principal's office. A sense of dread quickened her pace and her heartbeat as she entered the office door. Ty found her mother and Luis sitting in chairs across from the principal. They were in deep discussion as another school resource officer stood in the room nearby. As soon as Luis saw her, he began wailing.

"What happened?" Ty asked. Luis didn't answer, but got up and ran to her, grabbing her and holding her tight as if she'd disappear if he didn't.

"He has to learn," the principal said to Esmeralda as if Ty wasn't there, "to not yell out in class. He was disruptive, which is when Officer Jones was called into the class."

"But why did you handcuff him?" Esmeralda asked. "Why would you do that?"

"What?" Ty asked, but no one looked at her or responded. She tried again. "What?" she said much more loudly. She looked at the resource officer. "What did you do to him?"

"Taína—" Esmeralda snapped.

"What the hell happened?" she interrupted, kneeling to Luis's level. "Luis," she said softly. "What did they do to you?"

Luis continued to clutch his sister. "I was talking in class," he said, trying to catch his breath. "The teacher told me to stop talking. I said I had a question and she said to be quiet. I yelled at her. I asked her why no one was listening to me." Luis started crying anew and Ty hugged him tighter.

"What happened after that?" she asked. Ty had to lean in close to understand his words.

"The teacher called the principal, who sent the police to get me. He tried to get me to leave, but I didn't want to. I only wanted the teacher to listen to me."

"What did the policeman do?" Ty insisted.

"He held me down and handcuffed me. It hurt my arm so much that I was screaming." He showed his wrists and arms, where there were scratches. "They pulled me here," Luis said through labored, gut-wrenching cries.

"Cálmate," Ty said, hoping the word would have the same relaxing effects it did when her grandmother had said it to her. "It's okay, Mom and I are here." She stood, making her body erect even though she was shaking.

Everything was in Technicolor and in stereo—like Ty was seeing things clearly for the first time ever.

"Are you hurt?" came a question from somewhere. Ty snapped her head toward the voice and saw the woman who had ignored her yesterday watching them, waiting for a response.

"Is he hurt?" Ty repeated. "What do you think? Have you ever been handcuffed?" Ty asked, getting closer to the woman. "It prolly hurts. It prolly hurts a lot!"

"There's no need to yell," the principal said, folding his arms. "We can all be civilized here."

Hearing the word *civilized* made something in Ty snap. For a quick second an image of her ancestors flashed before her. They had been labeled *uncivilized* for simply existing, and that description somehow made it okay for others to oppress them. A seven-year-old child had been handcuffed by these savages and somehow she was acting in an uncivilized way by telling them that was wrong. She added "Are you for real? Are you kidding me?!" as punctuation. Esmeralda got up and joined her, lifting Luis and holding him.

"Look," the principal said, "let's talk about this calmly. If you want to do an incident report then Officer Jones will take one."

"No. I don't want to talk to him," Esmeralda said, silencing everyone in the room with the tone of her voice. "I am going to go to a police station right now and file a complaint against you, Officer Jones," she pointed toward the officer, "and this school."

"Mrs. Perez," Officer Jones said. "There's no need. I didn't act in an inappropriate way. I did what I needed to do to protect other students." The robotic tone of his voice made it sound like he'd said these words many times before, and that thought scared Ty.

Ty turned toward Officer Jones. "You didn't act in an inappropriate way?" she said. "Are you like crazy or something? You handcuffed a seven-year-old."

The principal pursed his lips in naked judgment of Ty's behavior. "Hey, watch your tone. We did the best we could under the circumstances."

Ty marched over to the principal's desk, leaning over it and facing him undeterred. She said, "You tell me, Mr. Moriarty, what tone should I be using? What tone would you use if you found out your seven-year-old brother or seven-year-old son had been handcuffed and dragged through his elementary school, leaving marks on his wrist? I'd really like to know, so please go ahead and tell me how I should act. I want to know what's acceptable to you."

"I know this is upsetting," Mr. Moriarty said, not

responding to Ty's specific request, "but we only had the safety of the other students in mind when we intervened."

"You mean to tell me you don't know how to calm a seven-year-old down without handcuffing him?" Ty asked, realization dawning. "Wow. You don't see anything wrong with this, do you? Why are you a principal? Do you even like children?" Mr. Moriarty tried to respond, but Ty only talked louder to indicate she was not finished yet. "Have you ever even talked to Luis?" she asked. "If you had ever talked to him, you would know that he's loving, kind, and funny as hell! You wouldn't ever think of handcuffing him if you'd spent five minutes getting to know him. Maybe you just don't see kids that go to this school as actual people. Is that it? Or is it only the children that don't look like you that get treated this way?" she asked.

"Now wait just a minute," Mr. Moriarty said, swiftly interrupting to counter. "Don't try to make this about race. This is about behavior."

Ty gave Mr. Moriarty the *Do you think I'm stupid* look and then turned toward her mother saying, "Let's go, Ma." Ty walked past Esmeralda and waited. Esmeralda didn't follow. Instead she faced the cast of school personnel assembled in the office. Ty noticed that even with the weight of Luis in her arms, she stood tall. "This boy that you handcuffed is my son, Luis Perez," Esmeralda finally said, breaking into sobs. "Maybe you think you can do this to us because we're poor or you think you can get away with it because—like you said, Mr. Moriarty—this is about behavior, right? But it isn't about that. It's about keeping us in line by making us feel worthless for being who we are and you feeling like you can treat us any way you want. That you can treat a seven-year-old who is crying out for help like a criminal. You should all be ashamed of yourselves."

With Luis still in her arms, Esmeralda walked past Ty, who dutifully and swiftly followed her out of the main entrance of the school. No one pursued them. No one apologized. No one made any effort to find out if Luis was okay.

Outside, Ty allowed the deep, painful feelings she'd been harboring to rise to the surface of her skin. She hoped the afternoon breeze would carry some of her anger away. Lifting her eyes, she watched her mother and Luis engage in a deep embrace on the dingy sidewalk, and she jogged to catch up to them.

"Ty," Esmeralda said. "You know how I always tell you to keep your mouth shut?"

Ty nodded, thinking *Not now, Ma. Not today of all days!*

"Well," Esmeralda continued, wiping her eyes. "Today was not that day. Thank you for fighting for . . ." A cry escaped her mother's throat and she stopped to collect herself. "Why would they do that?" Esmeralda said, shaking. "What made them think they had the right? He's only a little boy." She pulled Luis closer to her. "I'm so sorry, m'ijo. You didn't deserve that."

"But I talked out in class, Mommy, and didn't do what they told me to do," Luis said.

Esmeralda blinked and shook her head. "M'ijo," she said fiercely, "nothing you could do would make you deserve that." Esmeralda paused. "I am so sorry. I am so sorry," Esmeralda repeated as she continued to hold onto Luis. Ty was sure she would be in trouble herself at school, but there was no place she would rather have been than there with her mother and Luis.

Chapter 31

"**I** WISH I'D LISTENED when you said to keep him home," Esmeralda said, sitting on the couch with Luis as Ty paced. It was growing dark outside, the days getting shorter. Soon it would be time for dinner, but right then, the three of them weren't ready to move on with the day. They were still in shock. They hadn't even called the rest of the family. "Luis," she said, squeezing his hand, "this is my fault. I know now you weren't ready to go back to school. I knew it, but I didn't do anything! I'm so sorry."

Luis remained silent. His listlessness caused Ty to want to do something more extreme than ignoring the relentless calls Principal Moriarty was making to Esmeralda's cell.

"Ma, we can't just send him back to that stupid school."

"What can we do, Ty?" Esmeralda asked. "I mean, we're kind of stuck. We filled out a report at the police station, and I left a message at the superintendent's office, but what else can we do?"

Ty had an idea. "Give me a minute, Ma," she said, running into the kitchen. She looked through a small, neat pile of papers on the counter and found the permission slip Sofia had given her. It had her cell number on it, so Ty slid her phone out of her pocket.

"Hallo," Sofia answered cheerfully.

"Sofia, this is Taína, Ty," she said. "Listen, I need your help." Ty proceeded to tell Sofia what had happened that day at Luis's school and asked if it would be possible to gain some publicity about it.

"Oh my God, I'm so sorry," Sofia said. "They shouldn't do stuff like that, but they do—and he's only seven years old!"

"I know," Ty said. "I need them to get into trouble for this, because it's like they think it's okay to treat us some kind of way."

"Hmm," Sofia said. "I'm going to write a piece for our school newspaper right now. Can I come over to interview you and your mom?" she asked.

Ty glanced guiltily toward her mom, but said, "Yes." She gave Sofia the address and told her they would be there all evening.

"Okay, I'm coming over." Sofia paused. "I'm also going to call my professor to see if we can get other news outlets to cover it. She used to be a news reporter. Are you okay with that?"

Once again, Ty felt a pang of guilt, but still said, "Yes."

"Okay, I'll see you soon then!" Sofia said, disconnecting.

"Who's coming here?" Esmeralda asked.

"Ma," she said, returning to the living room and sitting next to her. "We can't just let this be. Mira Luis," Ty said, pointing toward Luis. "He should know that it's not okay for people to treat him like this. This is some control shh—, I mean trash, and we can't let them oppress us. We have to fight."

Esmeralda was silent for moment, then threw her head back. "Ay Dios, m'ija," she finally said. "You sound like your abuela. She was always talking about how our people were held back, and we should fight for what's right."

"Exactly. But to do that we have to ask for help." Ty paused. "Ma. I know that you don't want Sofia in our business, but it's the only way to get the story out. It's wrong and people need to know."

They all sat quietly together. Luis lay in Esmeralda's arms as she lovingly rubbed his hair. "You know," she said, "I have learned to accept that this is my lot in life because that's just the way it is." Esmeralda choked up.

"I know, Ma," Ty said, comforting her.

Esmeralda took a deep breath. "I don't want that for you or Alex or Luis. Alex is so much smarter than me or your father. I don't understand what he's doing. He can be whatever he wants to be, but he's caught up in stupid things."

"Alex is trying really hard," she said. "He got into a fight because he was defending a friend, Ma. That may have been a bad choice, but he's not doing bad things. Don't give up on him. He needs us too, just like Luis."

Esmeralda nodded, tears flowing down her cheeks.

"Ma, let's call Alex and Dad. They should be here with us, and we can figure out this fight as a family."

Esmeralda wiped her eyes and said quietly, "Call Benny too."

Ty dialed the first number, before her mother could change her mind.

Chapter 32

"**A**LL THESE PEOPLE came for me?" Luis asked. A good many people had assembled in his living room. Sofia had come with Professor Martinez to interview the family. Benny, Juana, and Izzy had come right away, followed later by Milagros. Alex and Alejandro were there as well, but Alex looked pre-occupied. At one point, he tried to get Ty's attention about something, but there wasn't a good time to talk under the circumstances.

"Yes," Ty replied. "Like we said earlier, what happened to you today was wrong. Now, we are going to make sure more people know about it."

Luis scanned the room as if imprinting the images of everyone there into his brain.

Professor Martinez had been adamant that she come along with Sofia. Before deciding to teach full time in the journalism program at Canvas College, she'd been a newscaster. She still had connections in print and broadcast journalism and was going to pitch the story everywhere she could. When she arrived, Ty could tell she was serious. She firmly shook everyone's hands after learning their names. She told the family that these types of incidents were happening more frequently in schools, and she was absolutely disgusted that it had happened to Luis.

Sofia made her way over to Ty and Luis.

"Is it okay if my friend asks you some questions?" Ty asked.

Luis nodded.

"I'll sit with them in the kitchen," Juana said as Luis, the professor, and Sofia walked toward the kitchen. Juana was particularly horrified by what had happened to Luis. Ty had never seen her so upset. She kept repeating, "We have to do something. We have to do something." Now, she clung to Luis, acting as his protector.

Ty surveyed their small apartment, feeling a sense of pride that her family had come together like this. They were all angry, and as Professor Martinez said, there is nothing like a group of angry people to make real change happen.

"Could I play a game on my iPad?" Luis asked as he returned from his interview.

"Sure, m'ijo," Esmeralda said, and for the first time all afternoon, Luis seemed happy about something.

"He's such a great little boy," Sofia said. "I can't believe anyone would feel the need to do that to him."

"It's like they're afraid of us," Ty said. "Mr. Moriarty said it was a safety issue. That's such trash."

With that statement, everyone in the room began talking at once, agreeing and conferring. Professor Martinez moved closer to where Ty was standing. "We've interviewed everyone, and now I'd like to talk to you before we leave," she said.

"Sure," Ty said. "Do you want to go into the kitchen or my bedroom?" she asked.

"Bedroom is fine," the professor said as she and Sofia followed Ty down the hall.

"You must be so angry," Sofia said as they settled into Ty's room.

"I am," Ty said, "but I didn't want to get too amped because my dad and brother are mad as hell. We had to stop them from going to the school and raising hell." Ty noticed that Professor Martinez had pulled out a notebook. "Don't put that in there," Ty said, pointing to the notebook.

The professor grinned. She had perfect white teeth and her brown eyes crinkled on the sides when she smiled. Her thick, curly dark hair did not seem to have one bit of frizz. It hung healthily, hitting her shoulders. On her wrists were thick silver bangles that Ty could tell did not come from the places she shopped, where you could get three silver bangles for $1.99.

"I won't put that in there. I promise," she said. "Do you mind if I record?" she asked, pulling out a small recorder with a mini-cassette.

"Wow," Ty said. "Look at that. It's like old-school."

Professor Martinez chuckled.

"And sure, I don't mind," Ty said.

"We know what happened at the school based on what your mother and Luis told us. We also plan to call the super-intendent and principal for comments, but we want to know about how this made you feel. We think readers will want to know how this has affected you as his big sister who is also still in school."

Ty didn't answer right away. A jumbled mess of thoughts ran through her head. *How did this make me feel?* "Yo," she started. "How doesn't this make me feel? I mean, it feels like if you're different, if you're Black, Brown, or speak with an accent, or are poor, you have to be perfect all of the time. There's no room for anything else. We can't be mad, we can't grieve, we can't be emotional, we can't share frustration, because if we do, we are told we are not being respectful or acting out. Like Luis's principal. He told us we couldn't be upset when we found out what happened. That we had to be *civilized*." Ty looked down at her blue nails and took a breath.

"You know," she continued, "a week or so ago, one of my teachers insulted another student in class, and I defended them. Later she told me that I could no longer speak in class, because I talked too much, or I talked in a way she didn't like. I mean, I know I need to clean up how I say things, like using less curse words when I'm upset, but that doesn't mean that everything I say is bad or offensive—and it shouldn't get me kicked out of class.

"I don't understand these rules that seem to be only for me or for Alex or for Luis. My brother ended up in a fight recently. He never gets into fights. He was trying to keep a kid from getting bullied. But *he* was suspended. There wasn't one person who asked him why he was fighting. No one tried to help him figure out the situation he got into. After that, it's been like double punishment. The person he stuck up for got the gangs' attention in the Dent. Now, we have to deal with crazy gang members."

Ty hoped she wasn't rambling, but she was trying to make sense of everything in her head. Professor Martinez and Sofia remained silent.

"And now Luis. You know, my grandmother died not even a week ago. Not even a week!" Ty finally broke, allowing the tears to fall. "But it's like we didn't have time to grieve or even a pass. No one even thought that maybe he's just sad about our grandmother. Aren't they supposed to be professionals and help kids, calm them when they're hurting? The principal at Luis's school was all like, 'He has to learn to respect' and all that, which I guess he thinks handcuffing him and dragging him to the office is supposed to teach him? No. That will only teach him to hate and to be afraid. He would learn respect if he'd been shown respect!" Ty paused, composing herself.

"They didn't want to know if there were other reasons for him to be tired or sad or cranky or impatient—*like any other person.* They just were like, you need to respect us and be quiet, no matter what, because, what, he's Puerto Rican? Are we supposed to not have feelings? Are we supposed to be okay with whatever treatment we get?" Ty wiped her eyes. "I'm sorry," she said. "I don't think I'm answering your question, but you asked me how all of this is making me feel, and it's like I don't know if I have the words to describe how I feel. It's like I am holding the anger and pain of many, many people who came before me. I don't know how Luis is gonna get over this, because he's like traumatized now. How do we get past this?"

"I wish I had an answer to that question, Taína," the professor said, wiping her eyes as well. "I'm sorry I'm emotional, but I feel everything you're saying." Professor Martinez sat up straighter, full of conviction. "We have to break this cycle, but the oppression lives in us too. We carry it with us, and we need to grieve our losses, heal, and then continue to fight to be treated fairly and with kindness."

Sofia handed the professor a packet of tissues from her pocket.

Professor Martinez took out a tissue and directed her gaze firmly on Ty. "But remember, the pain can connect us. By telling our stories, listening, and seeing how alike we all really are, we can find ways to help each other, to be there for each other during times of need." Professor Martinez then turned to Sofia, who was listening intently. "That's why I went into journalism, and I know that's why you want to be a journalist too, Sofia."

Sofia nodded.

"I wanted to find the truth of things and I wanted to elevate stories of the oppressed. I believed, I still believe, that the less silent we are about our pain, the more we will collectively heal and overcome."

Ty's thoughts of her friends and family swirled around in her mind. She instantly thought of her mother. She had been silent about everything and maybe that was her way of protecting herself. While protecting herself, though, she'd also cut herself off from the people in her life who cared about her and could help make her feel better. Ty thought about her father, who held his feelings close, as though they would drown him if he let them go, and Eddie, who never talked about his brother's death. She especially thought of the objects that were sitting in an average shoebox under her bed, passed down for over five hundred years. They were shrouded in secrecy and, because of that, an entire lineage of women had been silent. It was a lot to take in.

"Ty," Professor Martinez said gently, "I think I have enough. To be honest, I'm eager to get home and write this. I plan to get it out to circuits tonight if possible. Sofia, I'm hoping you will come with me, and we can work on this together," she said.

"I would love to!" Sofia said, beaming.

"Thank you so much, Ty," Professor Martinez said as Sofia nodded. "Sofia told me you are a brilliant young woman, and I couldn't agree more."

Ty watched them leave her room but didn't follow. She

gently closed her bedroom door and allowed herself to cry a little more. No one, besides her grandmother, had ever said she was smart or brilliant, and here were two incredible Latinas telling her just that.

She knelt down by her bed and brought out the objects that her grandmother had given her. Touching the zemi and amulet, she hoped it would guide her understanding—help her figure out what she should do next. Suddenly loud voices were coming from the living room. Ty quickly placed the items back and headed toward her family.

Chapter 33

"**W**HAT HAPPENED?" Ty asked, finding Alex standing just outside the living room in the hallway.

"Milagros said that maybe Luis will learn a lesson now," he said.

"What?" Ty asked.

"It's about to get lit." Alex stood with his arms folded across his chest as if assuming a battle stance, ready to join the adults at any second.

"Mira," Milagros said, "I didn't say it was good that happened to Luis. I said he may learn something from it. That's all." She ran her fingers through her hair; the gesture was like a challenge.

Esmeralda accepted the challenge. "You know what he just learned—" Uncle Benny stood between them, lifting his hand to silence Esmeralda while shooting a warning glare at Milagros.

"Milagros," he said firmly, "getting handcuffed at seven years old is never a good thing, never-ever for any reason."

Milagros threw her decorated talons in the air and exhaled. "You all are living in la la land, for real. This one," she said pointing to Alejandro, "was in jail. That one," she said, pointing to Alex, "is on his way to jail." She looked at Ty and said, "And this one has no respect for adults. It's good for Luis to learn now that he can't get away with acting like this. You can't go around being ghetto all the time."

You would have thought she'd physically slapped everyone in the room. Yelling ensued. Juana wanted to know what Milagros thought about her too. Others were shaking their heads or rolling their eyes. It became louder and louder until Esmeralda said, "¡Ya! That's enough!"

Esmeralda stood almost toe-to-toe with Milagros and said in a measured voice, "I don't know why you are like this, Milagros. I really don't, but it seems like, from the first moment you met me, that you didn't like me, and I don't know what I did to you."

Benny was about to interrupt, but it was Esmeralda's turn to lift her palm and do the silencing. "Sorry we are not perfect like you. But we are trying our best to make it. Yes, we've all made mistakes, but if you think for one minute that my seven-year-old *baby* deserves to get treated like a criminal, handcuffed, and dragged through the halls of a school so that he can learn a lesson, then I would rather be *ghetto* than be like you."

Alejandro stood next to his estranged wife and held her hand. She did not push him away, so Alex and Ty joined them, all waiting for Milagros to respond.

"Fine," Milagros said. "Maybe we just need to go." She grabbed her coat and bag, then turned back. "By the way, you have it all wrong. At the beginning I tried hard to be your friend, but you never let me. Once Isaura came to live with you, you shut me out. It's like all of you were against me and I didn't need that." She put on her coat and headed to the door. "And why can't you just be grateful? We do a lot to help you. Benny gives Ty money all of the time, so she can do things since you can't afford it, but you still don't appreciate us."

"What did you say?" Esmeralda asked, blocking Milagros's path. "My daughter would never ask you for money."

All eyes in the room turned toward Ty.

"Ma, I would never ask Milagros for money, I only—"

Benny interjected. "Look, I am your brother and Ty is my niece. I love you both." He paused, choking up. Ty reached out and touched his arm.

"She doesn't ask me for things," he continued, "but sometimes I give her a few dollars, because I know she likes to do things at school that sometimes she doesn't have money to do. It's not a bad thing, okay?" He turned to Milagros. "You didn't have to go there," he pled as she looked away.

"You know," Esmeralda said as her face hardened. "It's

just like Abuela used to say. Friends are like money in your pocket unless there's a hole in it. Family can be worse."

Everyone groaned. "What does that even mean, Ma?" Ty said. "I mean, Benny was just trying to help, you know? That saying is like they are sucking something from us."

"What are you talking about, Ty?" Izzy chimed in. "I thought that meant people are untrustworthy or something."

"Who gives a hell?" Benny screamed, throwing his hands up in the air. "The saying never made any sense."

Everyone started yelling at once while Luis put his fingers in his ears and chanted, "La la la la la."

Juana, who had been observing from the couch, stood and put her arms around Luis's shoulder. "Ya!" came a voice that didn't even sound like Juana's. It was a loud, confident boom of a voice that stopped everyone. "This is not worth arguing. We need to be here for each other now more than ever." Juana turned her gaze toward Ty. "Did Benny help you when you needed it?" she asked.

Ty nodded, looking guiltily away from her mother.

"Bueno, then stop this stupidese," Juana said. "Let it go." She looked lovingly toward Luis and guided him to the sofa, where he leaned against her, resuming his game.

"Vámanos," Milagros said, heading out the front door without looking back.

"I'm not leaving," Benny said to Izzy and Juana, "but let me go out and tell Milagros I'll be home later."

"I'll go home when you do, Dad," Izzy said.

Juana wasn't getting up to leave. Benny and Izzy stood

by the door looking at Juana and waiting for her to make a decision. Finally, Juana said, "¿Y qué?" Which was the equivalent to her saying, *don't even think about asking me whether I'm leaving. I'm staying put!*

Benny ran out to give Milagros the update. It was a quick conversation because he was back within seconds. When he returned, he said, "Esmeralda, I'm sorry. I know she can say the wrong thing sometimes."

"Sometimes? *Hmpf.* That's who she is all the time—with me anyway."

"She's not a bad person," he said quietly, then added, "she did try with you, but you never seemed to give her a chance."

"Benny," Ty interrupted. Now was her chance. The family seemed ready to work their issues out and Ty was done with the fighting between her mother and Benny. "Did you ever say anything really negative about my mom or dad when Dad was arrested?"

"Taína," Esmeralda warned.

Benny looked flushed. "I don't know," he said. "I might have, but I don't know," he repeated. It was then as if realization struck him in the face. "Wait a minute," he said, turning to Esmeralda. "I said something the day it happened. I was pretty mad because you are my sister and I only wanted what was best for you, and," he turned toward Alejandro, "sorry, bruh, but you were not best for my sister at that time."

Alejandro exhaled. "You're not wrong. At the time, I wasn't good for your sister or my kids, but I want to be a good husband and father." Alejandro paused, catching Esmeralda's eye, and added, "Believe me, I'm working hard on that."

"I know you are," Benny agreed, "which is why I don't feel that way anymore."

Benny moved closer to Esmeralda. "You've been holding that against me, haven't you? And Milagros too? She had nothing to do with that. She was trying to get to know you, but now she feels like you all hate her." Benny placed his hands on his sister's shoulders. "I'm sorry," he said. "I never meant to hurt you."

Esmeralda made eye contact with Benny and gave a small nod of acknowledgment.

Ty couldn't help herself. She clapped and said, "Oh my God, this is so dope!"

Esmeralda gave her daughter a look that told her to leave well enough alone.

Alex then tapped her on the shoulder and whispered, "I need to tell you something." Ty nodded and they headed to her room.

Ty was smiling from ear to ear. "Alex," Ty said when they were alone. "I wasn't sure if I should say something, but, then I thought, damn, that prolly needs to happen!"

Alex didn't acknowledge what she'd said. He walked over to her bedroom window and gazed out of it toward the park. "Ty," he said nervously. "When I got out of Dad's car, I saw Ernie standing on the corner. He must be casing our place or something, but he was for real waiting for me, because when he saw me, he bounced."

"What do you think that means?"

"I don't know, but I don't think it's good," Alex said. He then sat down on the bed and confessed, "Ty, there's something that I haven't told you."

Ty's heart raced, a familiar sense of dread overtaking her body. "What? What didn't you tell me?"

"I heard from Eddie that Jayden was the one who shot Eric Williams," Alex said.

"Are you serious?" Ty asked. Realization was dawning on Ty. "What do we . . . I mean . . . what does that . . ." Ty wasn't sure she wanted to know more. It was like all these fragmented pieces were coming together in her mind to create a picture that put her family at risk in a way she hadn't imagined. She thought of Eric Williams's mother standing in front of his mural, Jayden's threats, Alex fighting. Suddenly, she knew why Eddie was trapped, why everyone feared Jayden. He had killed and could do it again. This was a whole other level of bad.

"You need to get out of here!" she yelled. Gone were the feelings of joy she'd felt about her mother and Benny. Those were replaced with straight-up terror.

"They saw me," he said. "They know I'm in here, so they're probably waiting for me to come out."

"Do you think they would try to come inside our apartment?" Ty asked, nervously glancing out the window. "Should we call the police?"

Alex gave her a sideway glance. "What can the police do? Jayden or Ernie haven't done anything yet, and I don't know for sure if Jayden killed Eric. It's just what Eddie told me. I got nothing."

"What about Eddie?" Ty asked. "Should we text him and see what's up? Maybe he can do something." Ty picked up her phone, desperate.

Alex shook his head. "Nah, he's one of them, Ty. It's sad but, the more information we give him, the more trouble he gets into. We need to leave him alone."

The sound of a huge crash and glass breaking rang out from across the apartment. Ty and Alex ran from her bedroom into the living room. Someone had thrown something through the front door window, shattering the glass into many pieces.

"What is it?" Ty and Alex asked at the same time.

Benny knelt on the floor with Izzy to see what came through the window. Juana made the cross over her chest. Luis began to sob. "They are coming for me!" he screamed.

"No," Esmeralda said, grabbing Luis and holding him in her arms. "This has nothing to do with you! What is it, Benny? What came through the window?"

Benny lifted a rock and turned it around in his hands. Written on it were the words, *Time's up.*

Chapter 34

"THIS IS MY FAULT," Alex said. "It's my time that is up."

"Alex," Alejandro said, "tell us what is going on now!"

Frantically, Alex shared everything from Eddie's involvement with the Night Crawlers to the rumors about Jayden to the fight he'd had with Jayden and Ernie, which had led to his suspension from school and their harassment of Ty to get to him.

Alejandro reached for Ty. "What?" he said, hugging her. "If they had done anything to you, I don't know what . . ."

"Llama a la policía," Juana said, cutting Alejandro off, and Benny agreed. Benny unlocked his cell to dial 911, leaving Alex and his father to give each other a knowing look.

"I don't know if that's a good idea," Alejandro said. "It may make things worse for Alex. Maybe we should go talk to them."

"What?" Esmeralda yelled. "No way. There's no way you or he is doing that." She grabbed Alejandro's arm as if holding him back.

"Hear me out," Alejandro continued. "If Benny, Alex, and I go and find these kids, we can tell them to call a truce and leave us alone."

Alex shook his head. "No. That's too dangerous. They might kill us all." Alex regretted his choice of words because Luis started to cry again. "I'm sorry, little man," he said to Luis. "Look, we can call the police, but we can't tell them anything. We can't snitch on the Crawlers. They are too strong in this neighborhood."

The blue-and-red rotating lights of a police car shone from outside their shattered window. "Someone must have already called the police," Izzy said, opening the front door. Mrs. Lopez from upstairs was on the sidewalk. "Over here, officers," she said, waving her arms as if she weren't already noticeable in her curlers and housecoat.

A White police officer exited the passenger seat and a Black police officer exited the driver's side. They both walked purposefully toward the apartment. The White officer went directly to inspect the window while the Black officer acknowledged the family standing in the living room. "I'm Officer Washington and that's Officer Greeley," he introduced himself and his partner. "What happened here?" he asked, looking at the shattered glass on the floor.

Benny had a phone in one hand and the rock in another. He showed them the phone and guiltily said, "I was just getting ready to call you," as if not calling the police were a crime. "Someone threw this rock through the window. We were trying to figure out what it was and why anyone would do that." Benny handed the rock to Officer Washington while the other officer continued to examine the hole in the window.

"It says *Time's up* on it," Officer Washington noted, lifting the rock for all to see. "Does that mean anything to any of you?" No one said a word.

Officer Washington homed right in on Alex, held his eyes, then looked away. "Has anything happened recently that might have caused someone to do this?" Officer Washington glanced back at Alex. "Or maybe this was a mistake and was meant for someone else?"

"Um . . . ," Alex said, feeling the pressure of being singled out. "Like a week ago, I did get into a fight with a couple of guys," he said slowly. "Then I noticed that some guys have been following me around the neighborhood. I don't know who they are. I wonder if the rock might be for me."

Officer Washington was still. "You don't know who these guys are?" he reiterated. "Then why did you get into a fight?"

Alex was always good on his feet. "They jumped me. I didn't see it coming."

"They jumped you? For no reason?" Officer Washington asked. Officer Greeley finished his inspection of the window and came to join his partner. They both removed their caps and revealed shaved, shiny heads. Alex didn't respond because he wasn't sure if he was actually being asked a question or not. Officer Washington watched the rest of the family in the living room. "Can anyone else think of anything?"

Luis raised his hand. "Luis," Esmeralda warned, "this has nothing to do with you, remember?" But Luis still wasn't sure.

"What is it, son?" Officer Washington asked.

"I got in trouble in school today," Luis said solemnly. "Maybe the principal and the police are coming for me?"

Officer Washington knelt to Luis's level. "This wasn't meant for you, young man. No one is coming for you because you got in trouble in school."

"They handcuffed me, so I thought I was arrested," Luis said.

"Sorry, Officer," Esmeralda interjected. "They treated Luis really bad at school today. Now he thinks this is all for him, but this has nothing to do with him. I keep trying to tell him that."

Officer Washington stood and asked, "What school does he go to? Have you filed a complaint?" He made a notation in his notepad for the first time since he'd entered the unit.

"Denton Elementary School, and yes, I filed a complaint, but nothing's gonna happen." She sat on the couch, hunching her shoulders in defeat.

"Well, let me look into it, anyway," he said, then turned to Alex. "If you think of any reason why anyone would throw a rock through your window with the words *Time's up* on it, please call us," he said, handing Alex a card. Officer

Washington took the rock with him as he and Officer Greeley exited the apartment.

Juana appeared with a broom and began sweeping up the glass. Alejandro found some cardboard to temporarily cover the hole in the window. Alex paced back and forth in the living room.

"Alex," Izzy said. "You've got to calm down." She stopped him from pacing by blocking his path. "It's gonna be alright, okay? They are not going to come back here tonight."

"Right," Alex said, "but they will be back tomorrow. What if something happens to Mom or Ty or anyone? I couldn't forgive myself."

Chapter 35

BEFORE ANYONE could say anything in response, Alejandro walked over and said, "You were trying to do the right thing, but it didn't work out. I get it. It's like you wanna do right, but the only way to do right is to do wrong." He paused, then continued, "Alex, we can make this better. How about we talk to Eddie or talk to his mother and see if she can help?"

Alex thought about it for a minute, then said, "I don't know. I don't know." Alex scanned the apartment, walking slowly toward his bedroom. "I gotta think for a minute. I'll be right back."

Ty was worried. Her father seemed to be at a loss for how to help Alex, and she could feel Alex's hopelessness mounting. "I'm going to go to my room for a minute," she said, needing to get away, but Izzy followed her.

"Girl, this is a mess," Izzy said, plopping on Ty's bed. "And, wow, it's like how much more can happen this week? This day?"

Ty ignored her and said, "I'm gonna text Eddie and see how bad this thing really is. I don't know, Izzy. I gotta believe Eddie is still good and will help us."

"Yeah, you keep thinking that," she said, waving her hand dismissively.

Ty blocked Izzy out of her thoughts and texted Eddie, "Where r u? Is Alex safe?" Within one minute she got this response: Keep him home.

Ty tossed the phone on the bed, almost hitting Izzy, who protested, "Hey, watch it." Then Izzy grabbed the phone and read Eddie's response. "Girl," she said.

Ty took off her glasses and stared at the image in the mirror. *What am I going to do?* she wondered. She turned and leaned against her dresser when she saw half of the box jutting out from under her bed. "Izzy," she said. "Can you get Alex for me?"

Izzy nodded and left the room as Ty put her glasses back on, reached for the box, and put it on the bed. She pulled out the carved wooden chest and lifted the lid. Immersed in her thoughts, she didn't hear Izzy return.

"Cuatro. Alex is not in his room," Izzy said quickly. "I

went after him and his bedroom window was wide open. I think he left."

"Oh no," Ty said. "Did you tell my mom or dad?"

"No," she said. "I came here to tell you."

"Ty." Luis entered the room. "Alex left. Is he going to die?"

"Oh my God, no!" Ty shouted. "Luis, it's gonna be okay. I promise."

He ogled the wooden box. "I heard what Abuela said that night she was a ghost," he said, lowering his voice. "She gave you special powers, like a superhero. The powers are in the box, aren't they?"

"What's he talking about, Cuatro?" Izzy asked.

"What?" Ty ignored Izzy for the moment. "Did you overhear everything Abuela told me that night she came to my room?"

"Yeah," Luis said. "She gave you that stuff," he said, pointing to the box. "And now you gotta use them or the principal is gonna come for me and those gang people are gonna get Alex."

"No, baby," Ty said. "No one is coming for you, but . . ." *they might be coming for Alex*, Ty finished the thought in her head. She had to think fast. Maybe the objects could help her. Ty gently removed all the items and placed them on the bed. "It may be time to try to open this amulet thing," Ty said.

"Okay, you need to tell me what's up, because things just got weird," Izzy said, pointing to the box and the objects.

Ty gave Izzy the short version of her discussion with

Abuela and stopped her from asking questions. "I'll explain more when I can, Izzy," Ty said. "But Abuela told me when it was time to open it that I would know." Ty reached for the amulet, wondering what to do. There wasn't an instruction manual, so she started to run her fingers over the metal clasp that held the two halves together. She placed the necklace in the palm of her hand and felt the weight of it. It was warm and she thought she felt it vibrating. Whether it was time or not, Ty knew they had to try, so she picked at the medallion's locket mechanism to pry it open.

It didn't budge. Ty tried and tried. "C'mon," she yelled desperately pulling at the clasp, willing it to open. As tears formed, Ty felt another presence in the room.

"Taína!" Aunt Juana called. "Que haces?" Juana's face was illuminated by light. Ty swiveled to see the moon through her window. It was full, low, and glowing with more intensity than she ever remembered seeing it at any time in her life. Ty felt sure—it was time.

"Tía Juana," she said. "Abuela said to me that this was the year that I would come into my power. I thought she meant that I would have a good year of school, but I don't think it's what she was talking about. I think she meant that I would understand: my heritage, my ancestors, my family, even this neighborhood. Why we are all here. It *is* time. It is our time to heal and fight, and opening this may help."

Juana nodded, filling her with confidence to do what she needed. Once again, she reached for the clasp and gently caressed it until it unlocked. They all waited for something to happen, for the house to shake, for the moon to explode, but nothing happened. Ty and Juana peeked inside the medallion and Ty touched what looked to be a dusty, ashy residue. It felt a little bit like mesh but was not as thick or solid.

Ty placed the amulet around her neck, grabbed the zemi off the bed, and put it into her pocket.

While Ty didn't notice anything out of the ordinary, she felt different. Stronger than a moment ago, like she could take on anything. Images of women danced before her like holograms filling the room. Some of the images felt familiar, as if she had seen them somewhere before, but they were hazy. She imagined Anacaona—who had been groomed to be a leader, a ruler, a boss—and a feeling of calm washed over her. Action was now as clear as the full moon. She picked up her cell phone and started making phone calls.

Chapter 36

"**W**HAT DO YOU MEAN Alex is not here?" Esmeralda asked, running into the back of the apartment then frantically returning. "He is gone! Call the police now!"

Alejandro touched Esmeralda's hand and squeezed it. "You do that," he said. "But I'm going to find him." He turned away quickly to leave, but Ty stood in his way. Almost twenty minutes had passed since Luis told her Alex was missing. Ty had formulated a plan of action, then come out to tell her parents Alex was gone.

"Wait!" Ty yelled. "I know where he is and he needs us now." Ty moved past her father and toward the front door.

"How do you know where he is?" Alejandro asked as he followed her.

"I got a text from Eddie," Ty said, showing her phone, "telling me—"

"Where is he, Ty?" Alejandro interrupted, grabbing her by the shoulders.

"Follow me," she said, pulling away from him and running out the door before anyone else could stop her.

"Taína," Esmeralda yelled as Ty, her mother, and her father stood on the sidewalk in front of their unit. "Don't get involved in this!"

"No, Ma," Ty said calmly, and she glanced toward Mrs. Lopez, who was in her window watching them with interest. "We are all involved now whether we like it or not."

Out on the sidewalk now stood Izzy, Benny, Juana, and Luis. There were a few people walking toward them as Ty tried to get a good look at Denton Street Park. As the figures came into view, Ty said, "Yes!"

Ty ran to greet them. "Vin," she said. "It's so dope you came." Vincent and his mother came forward. "You know it," he said.

Behind them were a few others. First, Ty saw Sofia and Professor Martinez. "Thank you for coming back!" Ty yelled. "We gotta go, though, because Alex is in trouble." Ty was about to walk off when Esmeralda grabbed her arm. "What is this?" she asked as more people continued to join them.

"Ma," Ty said. "You were right. No one is coming to save us. We are the only ones that can make this right, but we can't do it alone. We need other people, Ma. All these people are our family and belong to our community. They are tired of hoping things will get better. They are here to make things better. We can all help each other because as a group we're even stronger and more powerful," she explained, moving quickly to the front of the crowd.

"Hilda, José," Ty said as the store owners came forward. "You came!"

"Claro que si," Hilda said.

"Ms. Carruthers," Ty said as her teacher came toward her. "How did you hear about this?"

"We called our neighborhood group and we are ready," Hilda interjected.

"Yes, we are. This is my fiancé, Pierre," Ms. Carruthers said, pointing to a tall, handsome, dark-skinned man wearing a red flannel jacket. Ty remembered that he was from the same town in Haiti that Anacaona was from and felt an instant connection with him as she shook his hand.

Behind them, Ty saw a small figure walking softly toward her. It was her classmate Beatriz Machado. Ty ran and hugged her.

"Gracias por venir," Ty said, thanking her for coming. Beatriz beamed and in confident Spanish said, "Of course. I wouldn't miss the chance to help."

Out of the corner of her eye, Ty saw Benny move into the street and hug someone. When they parted, Ty watched as he and Milagros came toward the sidewalk.

"Okay, everyone," Ty said. "We need to go." The group

followed her across the street to Denton Street Park. At the entrance, the group stopped as Eric Williams's mother came into the light of the streetlamp.

"My son Eric was killed right here at this spot," she said quietly as Ty faced her. "No more," she added, as Ty touched her arm. Ty noticed her other son, Johnny, was there too. He was the one who had painted the mural of Eric on the side of Atabey Market.

"Taína!" someone called, and she turned. Mary the librarian made her way toward her. "I came to help. What can I do?" Ty faced the entire collective that had formed. She was not able to process that all these people had come because she'd called. Instead, she simply said, "Everyone, follow me."

The moon seemed to be as close to them as the trees blowing in the October wind. Ty felt a strange sense of connection, like she was part of something bigger than Denton Street. She was part of a history and a legacy—part of a strong lineage with the moon as its guide and power.

In the distance, by the monkey bars where Luis had just been playing only a week or so ago, was a group of young men in black. They were standing in a circle surrounding what looked like two figures who were on the ground. Ty instinctively knew the two figures were Alex and Eddie.

"Hey," Ty screamed, causing them to turn. "Leave them alone!" The young men parted and she could see that Alex lay unconscious at their feet. Eddie was on the ground next to Alex, beaten but alert.

Jayden stepped forward, gaping at the group in confusion.

"Look," he said, puffing out his chest. "I don't know who y'all are, but you need to go."

"Where's Alex?" Alejandro asked, coming forward, but Ty held him back with her hand.

"I see him, Dad," she said. "He's on the ground behind them."

This time she could not hold her father back. He ran for Alex, but Jayden pulled out a gun and pointed toward Alejandro's chest. He immediately backed away with his hands in the air.

"Y'all better back up!" Jayden yelled, and the group obeyed.

"No," Ty said, facing Jayden. "We are not going anywhere. Alex is my brother and I need him." She pointed to the people behind her. "They all need him." Jayden continued to hold the gun toward Alejandro.

"What happened to you, Jayden?" Ty screamed. "What happened to all of you?" she asked, pointing to all the men who were blocking the group's path to Alex and Eddie. "We shouldn't be doing this to each other. Our ancestors, our people fought for survival and for freedom. What are you fighting for, Jayden? Who are you fighting?"

"Our ances . . . ?" Jayden started with a confused look on his face, but Ty didn't have time to get Jayden up to speed on everything, so she tried to move past him. He turned the gun toward her. Ty moved her gaze toward the moon, feeling a sense of oddly timed peace. Out of the corner of her eye, Ty saw something move. She looked to her right and noticed a white owl with yellow eyes sitting majestically and curiously on a tree branch. The owl felt normal to Ty, as if it made more sense for it to be there than the gun still pointed toward her chest.

Fixing her gaze back on the gun, Ty grabbed her father's hand, who silently turned to hold Esmeralda's hand, who reached out and held Luis's hand, who held Izzy's hand, who held Juana's hand, who held Benny's hand, who held Milagros's hand, who held Hilda's hand, who held José's hand, who held Vincent's hand, who held his mother's hand, who held Ms. Carruthers's hand, who held her fiancé's hand, who held Mary's hand, who held Mrs. Lopez's hand— she'd joined them at some point, still wearing her curlers and a housecoat—who held Beatriz's hand, who held Sofia's hand, who held Professor Martinez's hand, who held Eric's mother's hand, who held Johnny's hand, who reached around to hold Ty's hand. Without realizing it, Jayden, the other young men, Alex, and Eddie were now encircled by the group.

"We're here to make sure you don't hurt anyone else," Ty said, feeling something pass through her, making her feel ten feet tall. "We are the children of rulers, kings, queens, and warriors," she said. "We are not gonna fight you. We can't!"

Ty closed her eyes to allow the power coursing through her body to completely take over. When she opened them, Abuela was standing face-to-face with her. Ty almost broke the circle to reach for her, but Abuela mouthed "no" then turned to face Jayden and the rest of the boys in the center of the circle. She held out her hands and Ty saw that an inner circle was forming of women who she instinctively knew as the long line of women listed on that faded, browning paper and cloth hidden away in an old box. They were strong and beautiful, and looked very much like Ty, her mother, Izzy, and many of the other women in the outer circle. Ty faced forward and in her direct line of vision stood the proudest of the women. She had long black hair and dark eyes, and Ty knew it was Anacaona. Ty let the mounting frustration escape her mind and body as she saw the vision of Anacaona lift her arms, causing all the other women in the inner circle to lift their arms along with her.

Anacaona began speaking softly, and Jayden stood his ground with his gun pointed at Ty. The other young men stared in awe at the circle of people that had formed around them. Ty couldn't tell if everyone could see Anacaona and her daughters, or if only she were able. The group seemed so transfixed that it was difficult to tell what anyone was seeing or thinking. All Ty understood was that all of the young men were now in the center of the group, and they seemed unsure about what they were doing. Ernie kept turning from person to person in the group, not sure where to pause.

Jayden's hand began to shake. He could have shot his way through the crowd, but he seemed only to be able to stand with the gun in his wobbly hand.

Ty turned her attention back to Anacaona, who was moving her lips as if in silent prayer. Ty closed her eyes to listen and found that she could hear what Anacaona was saying and found herself repeating the words loudly for everyone else to hear.

"This is our moment," Ty repeated. "And we need to be ready for what's next. We can only do that if we mourn our past, accept our power, and help each other realize our future.

"These young men are not the problem, but a symptom of a problem that has been with us for hundreds of years. There is only one in this group who has killed, and he should be punished for his crimes."

Ernie backed away from Jayden and joined the circle. Jayden suddenly fell to his knees, dropping the gun in the process. Eddie, still in the center of the circle, kicked the gun away from him, toward where Eric's mother was standing. She glanced at it as if it were the most repulsive thing she had ever seen.

All eyes were on Jayden, who seemed inconsolable. "I'm sorry," was, at first, all he managed to get out of his mouth through sobs. Then he said, "I didn't want to shoot Eric."

Eric's mother finally broke the circle by kneeling and lifting the gun. "Don't touch that," José yelled out, but Eric's mother held it up and away from her as if it were infected.

"Is this the thing that killed my son?" she asked in tears as her other son, Johnny, Eric's brother, held her free hand.

"Drop the gun," a voice from behind said, startling the group. Everyone turned to see Officer Washington and Officer Greeley running toward what was left of the circle.

"Drop the gun," Officer Washington yelled again. Eric's

mother let it go and it hit the ground with a thump. Both Hilda and José ran to her side to comfort her and Johnny with an embrace.

Ty scanned her surroundings. The inner circle had disappeared and there was no sign of her grandmother or any of the other women who had materialized. In the distance, something moved then flew away.

"Was that an owl?" Izzy asked, standing next to Ty.

Ty nodded. "You didn't notice it when we walked into the park?" Izzy shook her head.

Esmeralda and Alejandro ran toward Alex, who was now conscious and trying to sit.

"Oh my God," Ty heard her mother say. "Are you okay?"

"What's going on?" Alex asked, but no one answered. It might have been that no one knew exactly what was going on or it might have been that there was simply too much going on.

"Whose gun is this?" Officer Washington asked, but no one immediately spoke.

Eric's mother pointed to Jayden. "It's his," she said quietly. The officers walked over to Jayden, who was still kneeling on the ground but, instead of sobbing, he was vigorously shaking his head as if waking from a nightmare.

"What happened?" Jayden asked, examining all the people around him as if noticing them for the first time.

Alejandro spoke first. "You tried to kill Alex, then you tried to kill me and Ty."

"You also confessed to killing Eric Williams," Mary

the librarian said, stepping forward. Backing her up with vigorous head nodding were Sofia and Professor Martinez.

Jayden stood. "I did?" he asked, clearly perplexed about what had gone down over the last ten minutes. He peered over at Alex then toward Eric's mother, as the reality of the situation began to take shape. "It wasn't just me, yo," he said, holding his hands in the air and speaking quickly. "It was all of us."

"You were the only one with a gun, though," Alejandro said.

"And the only one to say you didn't mean to shoot Eric," Hilda said.

"C'mon," said Officer Washington to Jayden. "Let's talk at the station." He looked around at everyone standing in the park. "I'm not sure what happened here tonight," Officer Washington said, "but we will need to get all of your statements." Everyone stared at the officer then slowly started talking to each other. Ty heard Ms. Carruthers say to her fiancé, "Wasn't it wild that we all went into a circle?" And Vin say to Beatriz, "Can you believe Jayden killed Eric?"

Ty realized that no one had seen what she had seen. *What did I really see?* Ty asked herself. *Maybe I wanted something to happen, and my mind made it up.* She had almost convinced herself that her visions were hallucinations when she caught Aunt Juana in what looked like a standing prayer. When she was done, Juana took the crucifix she wore around her neck, kissed it, and held it toward the moon.

"Ty." Eddie joined her. "That was crazy," he said, shaking his head. Ty noticed that he was bleeding.

"I know, right?" Ty said. "I'm not sure what even happened." She reached out to touch his bloody lip. "Are you okay?" she asked, but he quickly pulled her to him, giving her the biggest hug she had ever gotten in her life.

"Hey," someone said, and they quickly pulled apart. Alejandro walked over to them. "What are you doing?" he asked, coming into Eddie's personal space.

"Sorry, sir," Eddie said. "I, um, just, well, it's been a, well." Eddie just stopped since he wasn't making any sense.

"Dad, it's okay," Ty said. "Can you hear that?" she asked, happily changing the subject. "I think an ambulance is coming for Alex." Not only was an ambulance arriving, but so were more police cars. Officers Washington and Greeley must have called for backup.

"Eddie," Ty said as her father returned to Alex. "Promise me you won't go back to the Crawlers. Promise me!"

"I never wanted to join in the first place," Eddie said. "Ty. You have to believe me."

"You can get out now, right?" Ty asked.

"Yeah, I mean Jayden was the one holding things over me, and it's not like he's working for someone, at least from what I've seen," Eddie said, watching Jayden being taken by Officer Washington into custody. "That's not me at all. I want to be someone you respect," he said earnestly.

"You are, Eddie," Ty stated. "I know you did what you had to do." Eddie nodded and Ty scanned the crowd again, trying to make sense of everything. One of the police officers pulled Eddie aside and began to ask him questions as Vin joined Ty.

"Yo," he said. "That was intense."

Ty grabbed his sleeve and moved him away from the police officer taking Eddie's statement.

"What did you see tonight, Vin?" Ty asked.

"Not much," he said. "After we all held hands, I heard like someone whispering, but I didn't hear what they said. Then Jayden just kinda fell to his knees and said sorry. It all happened really fast."

Ty wasn't sure whether to feel disappointed that people didn't see what she saw or relieved.

Vin's mother called to him. "I better go," Vin said. "Let me know how Alex is. He looks pretty beat up."

Ty rushed to where her family was just as Alex was being placed onto a stretcher.

"Alex," Ty said. "How you doing?"

Alex tried to smile, but he looked slightly crazy. "Wow, Ty," he said. "Did you do all of this?"

She scanned the scene and said, "I think I did."

Chapter 37

THE NEXT DAY Ty woke to find a foot in her face. It took her a moment to remember that Izzy had stayed over and was sleeping in her bed. Because the bed was small, they'd slept in opposite directions, hence the foot sitting right under her nose. She quickly moved her face away and got out of bed.

It was a miracle Ty had finally fallen to sleep. Everyone had waited up until two in the morning, which is when Alex came home from the hospital with her mom and dad. He was fine, a little bruised and sore from being punched multiple times, but fine.

Even though she had tried to doze, Ty's mind had raced most of the night, and when she did finally fall asleep, her dreams were a collage of all the things that happened that week—her grandmother dancing, white owls, women praying, the moon shining, and Eddie smiling.

Ty yawned and headed to the living room to check on the family. Benny was still asleep on the couch and Juana was asleep in Abuela's room. She assumed Luis, Alex, and her mom were also still asleep in their rooms.

Returning to her room, Ty disengaged her phone away from its charger and powered it on to find quite a few messages. Perplexed, she peeked at the text messages first. The first was from Sofia:

Hey, last night was crazy, but so dope. Professor Martinez and I went back and finished the article about Luis and posted a link to it on Twitter. Here's the link.

Ty clicked on the link, which took her to Professor Martinez's tweet about the article, and the tweet had been liked one thousand times. *Wow!* Ty thought. *That's a lot.* She then viewed how many times it had been re-tweeted and it said more than two hundred times. She quickly clicked on the link to the article in the local newspaper. It was a pretty scathing review of the school system and the way school resource officers were used versus counselors. Ty noticed she had been quoted as saying:

> If you're Black, Brown, or speak with an accent, or are
> poor, you have to be perfect all of the time. There's
> no room for anything else. We can't be mad, we can't
> grieve, we can't be emotional, we can't share frustration,
> because if we do, we are told we are not being respectful
> or we're acting out.

Ty felt oddly disconnected from the words because so much had happened since she'd uttered them, but they were all still true.

She then saw that she had direct messages. The first few were old messages that she deleted right away. But she also had about twenty new messages, some from friends and some from newspapers asking for interviews. Ty didn't know what to do with those requests, so she left Twitter and went back to her text messages. There was a second from Sofia saying:

> Check out this thread on Twitter. People want to help
> your family get Luis out of that school.

Ty clicked on the link and saw that there was a Twitter thread started by a few angry people who were upset at the way a seven-year-old baby, according to them, had been treated.

> If he were White, you know that would never have
> happened.

Because they don't have money doesn't mean Luis should have to go back to that school.

Somebody should do something.

There were even tweets tagging the principal of the school and the superintendent of the district, admonishing them for having school resource officers in an elementary school in the first place. But the most amazing tweet was from Professor Martinez, who wrote in response to the post that said *somebody should do something*:

I just started a GoFundMe page for Luis to get him into another school. Here's the link.

Ty followed the GoFundMe link and more than $2,000 had already been raised for what was described as the "Free Luis from his elementary school prison" project.

Ty was flushed with excitement. She returned to the rest of her text messages. The next was from Vin.

Alex good? Beatriz and I will be at Denton Park around 2. Meet up with us if you can!

Ty smiled. *That was how it used to be,* she thought. They would meet up and hang out at the park before things got hot there. She hoped things were getting back to that basic normal she wanted.

The next text was from Eddie. At around two-thirty in the morning, he'd written:

Sleep tight, my princess.

Ty could no longer contain her nervous energy. She jumped up and started dancing to the music in her head. Time to wake the family. She headed first toward her mother's room, gently knocked on the door, waited a few seconds, and then entered.

"Ma?" she said, but didn't get a response. Something on her mother's nightstand reflected the light from the door. It was a huge ring of keys laid comfortably next to a lamp.

"Dad?" she yelped as both her mother and father sat upright. "Oh my God! Mom and Dad. Are you back together?"

Chapter 38

"TY," HER MOTHER YELLED. "Get out of here!"

Ty ran back into the hall and unceremoniously opened the door to Alex and Luis's room. Luis was watching his iPad and Alex was still asleep. "Alex," Ty said quietly at first then yelled, "Alex!" making him jump into a seated position.

"What? What's going on?" Alex said groggily. For a moment, Ty felt bad for waking him. His face looked like a big black-and-blue bruise, but her guilt lasted only for a moment.

"Alex, oh my God, Mom and Dad are back together!"

Alex smiled then winced in pain.

"Yay," Luis said, putting his iPad down, standing and

jumping. Ty joined him and the two of them were holding hands jumping around the room trying to avoid the little plastic figures strewn on the floor.

"I wish I could join you," Alex said. "But my head feels like a truck ran over it."

"It looks like it too," Luis said matter-of-factly, making Ty giggle.

"Damn, two against one here. That's messed up."

Luis ignored the remark and turned to Ty. "I'm hungry," he said.

"Oh yeah," Ty said. "It's late. C'mon." Luis followed Ty as she happily made her way into the kitchen.

A little while later, everyone else was awake and in the kitchen. Benny helped Ty pull together some breakfast and brew coffee. No one flinched when they saw Esmeralda and Alejandro walk into the kitchen together.

"Now that everyone's together," Ty announced over the din, "Ma, Dad, you are not going to believe this, but the article about what happened to Luis came out today, and it's getting mad attention."

"Really?" Esmeralda said, trying to get to the coffee. "I saw that I had a bunch of messages on my phone, but I haven't listened to them yet."

"I'll get your phone," Alejandro said. "Let's see what's happening."

Ty glimpsed at her own phone. There were a few more texts. She read another one from Vincent: Did that really happen to Luis??? You still meeting us at the park?

Another message was from Sofia: Channel 5 wants to interview you all!

Ty set the device on the table, but didn't share the texts with anyone. She didn't know what to do with all this information yet, and she didn't know how her mom would react.

Alejandro returned to the kitchen and handed Esmeralda her phone. As she drank her coffee and read the article, she mumbled under her breath.

When she was done and looked up from her phone, Ty blurted, "Sofia says that Channel 5 wants to interview us!"

"Wow," Esmeralda said.

"Check your messages," Izzy said. "What do they say?"

Esmeralda listened. "There are like ten messages here. One is from Professor Martinez. Hold up. There is one from Mr. Moriarty and the superintendent."

"You know why?" Ty asked while sucking her teeth. "Because people on Twitter, Facebook, and Instagram are going crazy about the story and they are tagging the superintendent and Mr. Moriarty, asking for answers."

"*Hmpf*," Esmeralda said. "Now he is apologizing." She tapped the phone angrily. "Delete, delete, and delete," she said bitterly. "Wait," she said. "Listen. There's one from Officer Washington." She put the message on speakerphone.

"Hello, Mrs. Perez. This is Officer Washington. I wanted to let you know that I visited Mr. Moriarty, Luis's school principal, at his home and asked about the practice of handcuffing seven-year-old boys. He didn't seem to have

an answer other than he was following the school resource
officer's lead. I plan to speak to the school resource officer.
I will keep you posted."

"Yes!" Alex screamed, startling everyone. "What? I hope he gets into serious trouble."

"Play the message from the principal," Alejandro said. "Let's see what that guy has to say."

Esmeralda rolled her eyes. "Okay, fine," she said, then played it.

"Mrs. Perez. On behalf of the school, I want to apologize
for what happened to Luis. It will never happen again.
Please accept my apology."

"Yeah right," Alejandro said. They then listened to the message from the superintendent, who also apologized and offered Luis a seat at any elementary school in the district.

Esmeralda dropped her phone on the table. "Good," she said. "If I can help it, Luis will not be going anywhere near Mr. Moriarty and that school again."

"Mom," Luis said almost in a whisper. He had been sitting quietly at the table eating his cereal up until that point. "I don't want to go back there. Can I just go to work with you?"

"No, m'ijo," Esmeralda said gently. "You have to go to school, but maybe we can look at different schools in the area since the superintendent said we could move you to another school."

"Wait," Ty said. "I should have mentioned this before, but Professor Martinez started a GoFundMe for Luis. Let me see . . ." Taína said, scrolling through her messages. "Oh my God. It's at like five thousand dollars now."

"No way," Izzy said, scrolling through her own phone.

"Let me see that." Esmeralda snatched Ty's phone out of her hands. "People are actually donating money to send Luis to private school. Who are these people?"

"They are on Twitter and Facebook," Izzy said, showing them the article link and the fact that it now had over ten thousand likes.

"But," Esmeralda said, "we can't take strange people's money. That's weird."

"Maybe," Benny said, cleaning out the now empty coffee pot to make another batch of brew. "But people are trying to help, I think, trying to take responsibility for each other," he said.

"Is that right?" she asked, then there was silence. After a time, Esmeralda asked, "What made you call all those people last night?" All eyes turned toward Ty.

Alejandro spoke first. "We all came together for Alex and it was amazing," he said. "I felt connected to everyone there, and I was so grateful. I don't know what we would have done if anything had happened to Alex."

Esmeralda remained still, never taking her gaze off Ty.

"Yeah," Ty said. "That all happened and maybe a little more." Ty smiled, thinking about how she'd opened the amulet.

"Taína, cuídate," Esmeralda said, looking over at Alejandro and glaring at Ty.

Ty realized her mother thought she was talking about how Ty found them that morning. "No, what I meant was—" Ty started.

Alex interrupted, "Let it go, Cuatro."

"Oh, yes," Ty said. "Not touching that, besides we need to get ready if we are going to talk to reporters!"

By the afternoon, the "Free Luis from his elementary school prison" GoFundMe project had raised more than fifteen thousand dollars. They had all talked to reporters throughout the morning and the article had gone viral.

Ty sat on one of the swings at Denton Park while Luis and Izzy sat on the other two, each trying to go higher than the other. It was two o'clock and Ty was looking forward to seeing her friends. As if on cue, Vin and Beatriz walked toward them.

"Hey!" Ty waved.

"Hey back," Vin said as he neared. "Little man," Vin said, running behind Luis and pushing him higher. Luis squealed with delight as Vin ran behind Izzy, pushing her too.

"Nooooo!" Izzy screamed playfully.

Beatriz smiled. "Taína, ¿Como te sientes?"

"I feel great," Ty replied. "After everything that happened in the last two weeks, damn, you'd think I'd feel like trash, but I feel like everything's gonna be alright, you know?"

"Last night was off the chain," Vincent said, joining them and shaking his head in disbelief.

"That's a good way to put it," Beatriz said, then added, "I told Vincent I'm going back to school tomorrow." She shrugged. "I don't know about that school though. They need to change how they treat us."

"I think we should go into Principal Callahan's office on Monday," Vin said. "And tell him that we want a student advisory group to help address issues at the school. What do you think?"

Beatriz and Ty nodded and snapped. "We should also do something outside the school to help, maybe at the middle school or elementary school," Vin continued.

"Mr. Moriarty will do whatever you ask him to do now that he's got news people in his face." Beatriz laughed. "Seriously, we should do something at that elementary school too," she said, waving her hand toward Denton Elementary School on the other side of the park.

"Maybe we could volunteer for a peer mentoring program. If there isn't one, we can propose they create one."

"That's a dope idea!" Izzy exclaimed, joining them. Luis had run off to the monkey bars, where a couple other children were playing. Izzy let her eyes wander toward him, then turned to the group. "But Luis is probably going to go to a different school. He won't be there anymore."

"¿Y que?" Beatriz shrugged. "There are a lot of other kids in that school that have to deal with all that, you know what I mean? Just because Luis isn't there don't mean that we shouldn't do something there."

"Hell yeah," Vincent said.

"I know I don't go to school with y'all, but I'll help too!" Izzy said to new snaps.

"I think we should teach about the history of the Taíno people," Ty said, jumping off the swing. "Maybe Ms. Carruthers will help."

"Maybe we can take over Ms. Neil's class?" Vincent joked.

The mention of Ms. Neil made Ty recall that she was probably in trouble again because she'd walked out of class Friday. *Will they hold that against me?* she wondered. At least taking action made her feel better about going back to school on Monday and dealing with the consequences.

"Oh hey," Izzy said, pointing to the entrance of the park. "There's Alex with Eddie."

Ty felt heat rise to her cheeks.

Alex and Eddie strolled up to them. "What's up?" Eddie asked, eyes only on Ty. She noticed that his lip looked a little swollen and he had a nasty bruise forming on the side of his mouth. She wanted to reach out and touch him, but she knew she couldn't.

"Have you figured out how to change the world?" Alex asked. It was amazing that he could even smile given that his beat, swollen, and bruised face made it look like he had some kind of skin condition.

"We're getting there," said Ty. "You know, we got jobs for you both."

"Do you?" Alex said. "I guess we gotta get back to school first." He pointed toward himself then Eddie.

"What's up with that?" Vincent asked. "When *are* you both coming back?"

Alex placed his hands in the front pockets of his jeans. "I was just talking to my mom and dad, and we are going to see Principal Callahan on Monday and explain everything. I think he'll let me back in or else we will have to send a bunch of news reporters his way." Alex chuckled then groaned through the pain.

"Yeah," Eddie said. "My mom and I are also gonna head in too. They gotta let me back, right?"

"They better!" Ty said. "I can't wait to have you back in school."

Alex rolled his eyes. "Okay, I'm going to catch up with little man," Alex said. Izzy followed him, waving at the group.

Vincent looked at his phone. "I gotta bounce," he said. Ty would have asked him if he was off to see Imani, but Vincent had already told her they were officially, *officially* over. He seemed to be taking it well, but Ty noticed that he smiled a lot with Beatriz. "Are you ready to leave?" he asked Beatriz. "I can walk you home."

"Yes." Beatriz grinned as the two of them made their way out of the park.

Ty was alone with Eddie. "Yeesh," she said, pointing to the bruise she'd noticed earlier. "That looks painful."

"Nah," he said, "it's good." He grinned. "How are you doing?"

"I'm good. Tired, but good." Ty noticed that he was no longer wearing black. He had on baggy blue jeans, a white T-shirt, and a blue hoodie. "No black?" she asked.

"Nope," Eddie said quickly. "Not for me anymore."

Ty caught his eyes lingering on her face and she immediately looked away. "Um, any word on Jayden or Ernie or any of those guys?"

"You didn't hear?" Eddie asked as Ty shook her head. "Jayden admitted to killing Eric at the police station last night," Eddie said, causing Ty to gasp. "You know I believed the rumors I heard about that, but I didn't know for sure. And I don't know what made him tell the truth, you know? It was like he wanted to get it out, like, be free." Eddie paused and shifted a little on his feet.

"Ernie," he continued, "threw away his Crawlers clothes and gave his money and stuff to me. I told him I didn't want any of it and we gave all our stuff to another brother in the group. He took it and went away. I don't know what's gonna happen to the Crawlers, but I hope they just go away for good. There aren't that many of them left."

"Me too," Ty said. The Night Crawlers seemed to have taken a hit, but Ty wasn't sure it was the end of them yet, especially with the Denton Street Dogs still hanging around.

"Um," Eddie continued, "I talked to José about a job at Atabey Market."

"That's great," Ty said excitedly. "Atabey is dope. I go in there a lot after school."

Eddie was pensive for a minute. "Did I miss out on

anything at school while I was gone? I mean, Vincent? I saw him leave here and just wondered, you know, if you guys are still just friends."

"Friends," Ty confirmed. "He's always been a friend."

"Good." He smiled. "That's what I wanted to know." Eddie stared boldly at Ty, taking in every inch of her features. "I wish I could kiss you right now," he whispered, causing Ty to guiltily look toward Alex, Izzy, and Luis while she composed herself.

She had fantasized so many times about kissing Eddie that her mind was going in all kinds of directions. All she could do was be honest and whisper back, "I wish you could too."

Eddie smiled. "Yeah, I'm not gonna try that because I already got a lecture from Alex."

"What?" Ty said, embarrassed and annoyed.

"Nah, it's all good," Eddie said. "I would do the same with my sister." He paused, distracted by a shriek from Luis who was being chased by Alex. "Well, I better get back home," he said. "My mom has been really worried about me not being home a lot the last few months. So I'm going to stay at home with her tonight and have dinner and watch telenovelas or some program she used to make me watch when I was little."

Ty couldn't help but chuckle.

"Don't laugh," he said, teasingly. "Hey, maybe tomorrow you could meet me somewhere—just the two of us."

"Yes, I'd like that," Ty said, probably too quickly, but Eddie didn't seem to mind.

Chapter 39

LATER THAT NIGHT, when Ty was finally alone in her room writing, trying to capture everything she had seen the night before, she heard a knock on her door. "Come in," she said. Her mother walked in with a brown paper bag and paper plates.

"Oh my God," Ty said, dropping her notepad on the bed. "Is that what I think it is?"

Esmeralda smirked. "Yup," she said, giving Ty a plate and pulling the alcapurrias out of the grease-stained bag. "José just came by real quick to drop them off."

"Yay," Ty said, taking a bite out of the dark brown piece

of heaven. "*Mmm*," she said. Esmeralda sat, picked up Ty's notepad, and started reading.

"What is this?" Esmeralda asked, looking over the notes.

"I was writing a story," Ty said, licking her fingers. "I'm imagining that Abuela was with us last night, helping us." Ty paused. She was unsure whether she had actually seen Abuela and her great-grandmother and great-great-grandmother and on and on, but it felt like she had.

"Ma, there's something you should know," Ty said, finishing the last of her food and reaching for her worn shoebox. She boldly extracted the precious objects and explained the whole story: how Abuela had given her the items, what she'd said about what they were, and the story about how Ty would know when it was time to use them.

Esmeralda listened, then reached for the list of names. "Wow," Esmeralda said. "She gave this to you the night she died and told you that story?"

Ty nodded, worried that her mother was going to shoot it all down with a negative response, but Esmeralda remained pensive. She took a big bite of the alcapurria and chewed slowly. It was as though the chewing was buying her time to collect her thoughts.

When she was done with her alcapurria, she said, "I'm thinking about what Abuela told you about why she gave these to you and not to me, but I knew why right when you said it. You've always been fearless. Even when you were a little girl. You never second-guessed yourself like I did. And it's like you and Abuela understood each other. I don't know.

I was different from her." Esmeralda wiped her hands on a napkin. "The last two weeks have been crazy. Hell, the last few years! I've learned a lot.

"And you know what? I can't be afraid anymore," Esmeralda said, choking up. She composed herself. "I'm sorry," she said, as a tear fell down her cheek. "I just can't believe everything that has happened to my children these past two weeks."

"It's okay, Ma," Ty said.

"It's not okay," she replied. "I know that, so I will try to do better. I promise. And before you and Alex go off talking about us to Benny, your father and I are getting back together."

Ty smiled.

"I know you, Alex, and Luis are all going to be happy about that. It took me a while to accept some things," she said. "I was so hurt when he got arrested, you know, that I couldn't function. That's why it hurt me so much when I thought Benny was judging us. It was too much to take for me, you know, and I admit I wasn't nice to Milagros or him."

Esmeralda paused, then shrugged. "You know what, though?" she said. "Your father did his time and he's trying really hard, and, well, the truth is that I love him. I will always love him, and I don't feel ashamed of that anymore. I don't love a criminal. I love Alejandro. And I know that, regardless of his bad decision, he's a good man."

Ty hugged her mother and said, "I'm so happy you and Dad are back together."

"Oh, check this out." Esmeralda pulled out her phone

and said, "Look," showing Ty the screen. Esmeralda had been tracking the GoFundMe project, and it had surpassed the goal of twenty-five thousand dollars.

"Are you kidding?" Ty asked.

Esmeralda shook her head. "Nope. I learned you can't think the worst of everyone. I mean, look at that!" she said, pointing to the phone. "There is a private school we could send Luis to that's on the other side of Main Street. It would be close to where we are now. Is it stupid to want to stay here?"

"No," Ty said. "I like it here now. This is my community. And where else would we get dope food like this?" she asked, reaching for another alcapurria.

"Yeah, seriously," Esmeralda said. "We are going to be okay."

Ty lifted the amulet and gently glided her fingers across the figure of Atabey. "You know, Ma," she said. "This is really beautiful." She held the medallion in her hand. "But when I opened it, I expected something more to happen, like a hurricane or a tornado."

Esmeralda took the amulet from Ty and studied it. "It is beautiful," she said, "but you didn't need a hurricane, did you?" she countered. "You are a strong and powerful force and people came to help because of you." Esmeralda smiled warmly and touched her daughter's cheek. "You are amazing, Taína, and I love you."

Taína reached for her mother and, as the two women hugged, the bright light of the Moon Goddess smiled upon them.

Chapter 40

"**Y**ass!" Ty screamed, without realizing that she had done so out loud. Everyone in Ms. Carruthers's class turned toward her and laughed. Ms. Carruthers had a questioning look in her eyes, but then the bell rang and class ended.

"Alex back in school?" Vincent asked and Ty smiled.

"That's wonderful," Ty heard Ms. Carruthers say, as she joined them.

"I'm sorry for yelling out in class," Ty said to Ms. Carruthers.

"Oh, no, please don't worry about that," Ms. Carruthers said. "This is a big deal. I am so happy for you."

Ty smiled in relief. "I don't know where he is now, but I'd better find out before I get to English class."

"Yes, that's right!" Vincent confirmed. "Ms. Neil will snatch the phone out of your hand and make you stare at her for forty-five minutes." He meant it as a joke, but Ms. Carruthers frowned.

"What does that mean?" she asked Vincent.

"Well, I mean, I don't," Vincent became flustered and Ty stepped in.

"Ms. Carruthers," Ty started. "Ms. Neil thinks I got a bad attitude and stuff like that." Ty shrugged. "She's kicked me out of her class like three times already because she said I'm disrespectful. I left on Friday because my mother was dealing with what went down at Luis's school. I know she's gonna give me a hard time about it."

Ms. Carruthers exhaled. "I see," she said. "Do you have English now?"

Ty looked at her watch. "Yes, and I can't be late."

"I'll go with you," Ms. Carruthers said. "Why don't you check in with Alex first, because you won't be able to concentrate in class with him on your mind, then I'll walk you to class."

"I'll head there now," Vincent said and took off to English while Ty called Alex.

"What happened?" Ty asked as soon as Alex answered.

"I'm in. We're in, both me and Eddie."

Ty squealed in delight. "Oh my God, that's so dope. What do you have to do?"

"We both have to go to each of our classes today, talk to each teacher, and see what projects or extra work we need to do to catch up."

"I can help you both," Ty said, resisting the urge to jump up and down. "I don't mind studying with you. Vin too. We can help you all catch up."

"Thanks, Cuatro," Alex said. "Okay, gotta get to math class. See you later."

Ty ended the call and smiled at Ms. Carruthers. "Thank you," she said. "You're right. I wouldna been able to think about anything else but Alex if I didn't get to talk to him."

"I'm glad," Ms. Carruthers smiled knowingly, as they made their way out into the hall. "I was so sorry to hear about your brother Luis," she continued. "I didn't know that had happened when I joined you at Denton Park on Saturday. I read about it and even donated to the GoFundMe."

"Thank you," Ty said. "This past weekend was crazy, but everyone's support, everyone coming out to help Alex, everything that happened, it all brought us closer as a family."

"It was a special night." Ms. Carruthers paused. "I mean, I hate that Ms. Williams lost her son, Eric, but I'm glad Jayden finally admitted it. I'm hoping that the Dent community will continue to support one another."

"Me too," Ty said.

"Where is Luis now? I know the GoFundMe was to send him to a different school?"

"Yeah, it was," Ty confirmed, "but my mom and dad are

thinking about it first. We don't plan to move or nothing, so they're trying to decide where's the best place for him."

"Taína," Ms. Carruthers said gently. "If you ever need someone to go with you guys to talk to administration, let me know. I am happy to help."

"Well," Ty said, smiling, "now that you brought it up. Vincent, Beatriz, and I were talking this weekend and we want to do stuff at the school, you know, to make it better, and we could use help."

"Oh," Ms. Carruthers said. "Tell me more?"

"We want to start a student council, so we can share our ideas, because we can be doing more than we are right now," Ty responded.

"What are some of your ideas?" Ms. Carruthers asked.

Ty smiled. "We're thinking about a program where we could go to the elementary school and read to the kids, or be there for them when they get emotional, like my brother did. We also thought it would be dope if Beatriz could have a Spanish discussion group after school for those who want to learn Spanish or get better."

Ms. Carruthers nodded as Ty continued, "I was also thinking about starting a Caribbean history club where we could talk about our ancestors. I would love to start a group around that."

Ms. Carruthers smiled. "I love it," she said simply, while Ty grinned and jumped. "How can I help?"

"We need at least one teacher who believes in the ideas and can support us with Mr. Callahan or anyone else."

"Done," Ms. Carruthers said, as they arrived at Ms. Neil's classroom. "We can talk about it more later," she said. "Go on in so you are not too late."

"I guess I better get this over with." Ty sighed and tried to turn the doorknob, but the knob did not budge.

Ms. Carruthers tried to open the door herself, shaking her head vigorously in confusion. She then loudly knocked on the door. After a few seconds, Ms. Neil herself opened the door a crack and seeing Taína said, "You are late. Go to Mr. Callahan's office, now." She was about to close the door, but Ms. Carruthers stepped into Ms. Neil's line of vision.

"Ms. Neil," Ms. Carruthers said sternly, "Taína was with me finishing something in my class. I offered to walk her to your classroom, because I knew we would be a few minutes late. You need to let her into the class."

Ms. Neil pursed her lips, stepped outside the classroom, and let the door close behind her. "Ty-na is always late or skips my class. This isn't the first time, so I will not be letting her in class."

"I am never late," Ty said in her defense. "And I left your class *once* on Friday, because I had a family emergency."

"Didn't you hear what happened to her younger brother, Luis?" Ms. Carruthers asked. "It was all over the news."

Ms. Neil looked from Ty to Ms. Carruthers then back to Ty again. Her eyes squinted as if she didn't believe a word they were saying.

"Ms. Neil." Ms. Carruthers moved closer to her. "I'm

not sure what you think you are doing, but you need to let *Ty-ee-na* into class. I have explained that she was with me, and I walked her over here with the express purpose of letting you know the circumstances." Ty stepped back to let Ms. Carruthers fill the space.

She continued, "Now, after you let Taína into class, I plan to walk over to Mr. Callahan's office and tell him that, one," she began counting with her fingers, "you are abusing your authority by not allowing a student in your class who was accompanied by another teacher, and two, that you took it one step further by locking the door to your classroom. It's unwelcoming and unnecessary."

"What's going on here?" a voice interrupted. Ty, Ms. Carruthers, and Ms. Neil turned to see Mr. Callahan walking toward them.

Ms. Neil smiled. "I'm glad you are here, Mr. Callahan," she said. "Ty-na is late to my class and I am not letting her in, regardless of whether Ms. Carruthers says she should be excused. She has been continually disrespectful to me, she skipped class on Friday, and now she's late. I don't want her in my class."

"I walked over here," Ms. Carruthers interjected, "to let Ms. Neil know that Taína was with me finishing something. We got here and the door was locked for the express purpose of keeping Taína from entering the class. You," she continued looking directly at Mr. Callahan, "instructed us that we could not lock students out of the class. It seems to me that she is punishing Taína, because she simply and inexplicably doesn't want her in her classroom, which is an abuse of authority in my opinion."

"Is that true?" Mr. Callahan asked Ms. Neil.

"I did lock the door to teach her a lesson." Ms. Neil stated, "But abuse of power? That's really a stretch, don't you think?" Ms. Neil turned toward Mr. Callahan as if no one else were with them. "Ty-na doesn't respect me and she's disruptive, so, no, I'd rather not have her in my class."

Mr. Callahan blinked a few times as if trying to gather his thoughts. He detached a walkie-talkie from his hip and said into it, "Donna, is Ms. Jones still in the office?"

After a pause Donna answered, "Yes."

"Great," he said. "Can you send her to room 121, Ms. Neil's room?"

After another pause, Donna answered, "Sure."

"What are you doing?" Ms. Neil asked.

"You and I need to talk now in my office," he said. "I'm sending a substitute to your classroom to take over for as long as it takes for us to straighten this out."

Ms. Neil turned and pulled open the door to her classroom. Students who were piled against the door fell over each other trying to get back to their desks. She walked to her desk, unlocked the drawer, grabbed her bag, and marched out of the classroom. As she left the room, she faced Ty.

"You really are a smart girl, but you lack discipline and focus. Someone has to push you."

"Is that what you think you are doing?" Ty couldn't help but ask.

"Taína," Mr. Callahan said. "Get to class. Ms. Jones is on her way." Ty swiveled toward class, but turned to Ms. Carruthers and mouthed, "Thank you."

"Anytime," she mouthed back.

Ty felt like she were floating on air as she made her way to the front entrance of the school to head home. She had seen Alex a few times throughout the day but hadn't gotten to speak to him, and now they were going to walk home together for the first time in weeks. As she neared the doors, she saw Alex in an animated conversation with the security guard.

"What's going on?" Ty asked, a sinking sensation in her stomach.

"Can you believe he's a Yankees fan?" Alex asked, laughing and giving the officer a big handshake. As they made their way out the doors, Ty breathed a sigh of relief.

"I thought you two were arguing about something important," Ty said as they walked out onto Main Street.

"Exactly." Alex laughed. "Baseball is important."

"Since when?" Ty asked, hearing Alex talk about baseball for the first time ever.

"I've been watching with Dad and it's alright," Alex said, smiling. "What a day." He sighed. "I felt like I had to crawl on my hands and knees, beg to make up the work for teachers to believe I was serious."

"Did they make it hard for you?" Ty asked.

"A little," Alex replied, pausing to investigate the windows of a yoga studio. "I wonder what they do in there."

"Never mind that," Ty said, grabbing his arm and pulling him away from the window. "What do you have for make-up work?"

"It's good, Ty, really. I'm just happy to be back, and I'll definitely do the work." He paused. "I'm even going to stop at the library to get started on some things."

"I'll go with you."

"Ty, I know you would help me if I needed it, but it's okay." He paused again. "I think Eddie might need your help more than I do."

"Really?" Ty's heart did a little dance. "Why do you say that?"

Alex didn't respond right away then smiled. "Because he told me. He thinks you are smart and all-knowing."

Ty couldn't help but laugh. "Where is he?" she asked.

"He took off to get to work."

"What?"

"He started today at Atabey Market."

Ty made a mental note to stop there on the way home. "I actually have to go to the library, myself," she said, following him off Main Street and toward the library doors. "I want to talk to Mary. I haven't seen her since Friday, and I wanted to thank her for coming out."

"There were so many people!" Alex held one of the library doors open, so Ty could walk in ahead of him. Mary wasn't at the front desk, so she went to find her while Alex made his way to a table in the back to study. Ty finally found Mary in a small room near the main desk, talking to two women. It took her a few seconds to realize that one of the women was her mother and the other woman was Mrs. Williams, Eric's mother.

"Ma?" Ty asked as she entered the room.

"Hey, Ty," her mother said. "How was school?"

Ty took the scene in and couldn't quite believe what she was seeing. The three women were sitting at a small table, looking at papers as Mary took notes. The flyers for the anti-gentrification league and the anti-violence coalition also sat on the table.

"School?" Esmeralda asked.

"Oh, sorry. Fine," Ty finally responded. "Hi, Mary. Hi, Mrs. Williams. Ma, um . . . are you joining these groups?" Her voice was unable to restrain her shock.

Esmeralda sat up in her chair. "Yes," she said firmly. "I am."

Ty knew better than to push further, so she directed her attention to Mary and Mrs. Williams. "Um . . . I wanted to thank you both for coming out Friday."

"No need to thank us," Mary said. "It was the right thing to do."

"Yes," Mrs. Williams added. "I wish something like that had happened before Eric was murdered," she said. "But we helped Alex, which made me realize how much power we have to be a positive change in our community." She sighed then continued, "That's why we're here."

Esmeralda nodded vigorously as though it were the most natural thing in the world for her to be sitting there fighting for the community. "Where's Luis?" Ty asked, changing the subject.

"He's home with Benny. It was a good day today. Alex is back at school, and we had a good talk with the superintendent," Esmeralda added.

Ty suddenly noticed that her mother had combed her hair and was wearing jeans and a bright sweater. She looked younger. She was present, active, and smiling as if she had something to offer. She was beautiful. *She does have something to offer*, Ty thought proudly.

"Esmeralda, you didn't tell us," Mary said. "Is Luis going back to Denton Elementary or somewhere else? Ty, come on in here and sit with us."

Ty went in and sat down at the table.

"We are still talking about it," Esmeralda said, then quickly added, "Principal Moriarty is stepping down and there's going to be someone stepping in for the rest of the year."

"Are you serious?" Ty asked excitedly. "They are really working fast."

"Yes, and they're replacing the school resource officer with a counselor in the school who will help the kids who need more emotional support."

Ty couldn't contain her joy. She leaned over and hugged her mother, who seemed surprised at first but then hugged her back. "Ma, that's so dope!"

"I know," Mary chimed in. "This will help so many kids.

Esmeralda agreed. "I think so too. I was hoping that we'd see Sofia and maybe her professor here today, because it was all that publicity that did it. I wanted to thank them."

Ty hugged her mother again, then got up to hug Mary and Mrs. Williams. "I actually need to get going. But I'd be happy to help with whatever you're working on sometime."

"We're counting on it!" Mrs. Williams said.

Out on Main Street, gliding toward Atabey Market, Ty reached into her backpack and pulled the amulet out. She carried it with her for good luck and it seemed to work. Everything had shifted for the better. She only wished Abuela were there to see it all. At the thought of her beautiful grandmother, she held the amulet in her hand, saying a silent prayer in honor of all of her ancestors.

May the Moon Goddess illuminate the vines that connect us all.

May the light that makes the night sky bright bring continued peace and love.

Epilogue

THE SONG MADE the women feel free and beautiful as they pranced along the beach. Some of them were wading in the shallow end of the ocean water, others were dawdling by the shore, and some were playfully chasing each other across the sand. Anacaona finished her areíto then peacefully watched her daughters.

"Do you think they'll be okay?" Isaura asked Anacaona, her white afro flowing in the ocean breeze.

"Of course," she said. "Our time has finally come. My power has been used well this time, but we will always be here if they need us."

Isaura looked lovingly at her ancestral mother as Anacaona gently touched her weathered face. "We did our part. Now, it's up to them."

With that, Anacaona dashed gracefully and purposefully toward her daughters, joining them in boisterous laughter and loud singing signifying freedom, liberation, and lightness of being.

Author's Note

As a Puerto Rican woman, I had always been told and always believed that I was Taíno. My mother often said, "nosotros somos Indios, Africanos y Españioles." Loosely translated, she said, "We are made up of Indian, African, and Spanish ancestry." Growing up, I knew a lot about the Spanish and a little less about my African ancestors, but very little to nothing about my Indian—or rather, Taíno—ancestors. What *is* documented comes from early journal writings, letters, and stories shared by Spanish (and other) colonizers—stories that have constituted the dominant narratives we know today, with the most prevalent being that the Taíno did not survive.

I had always been curious about this part of my heritage and did what I could to learn about them. I learned their name was not really Taíno but Arawak, how when they greeted Christopher Columbus, they'd said "taíno" to make their visitors feel welcome, because it meant "good people." Columbus misunderstood it to be their name, and it stuck. I also learned that the Arawak were living on many islands: Puerto Rico (Borikén), Haiti (Ayiti), the Dominican Republic (Quisqueya), Cuba (Cubanascnan), and Jamaica (Xaymaca).

I visited the Taíno petroglyphs in Jayuya, Puerto Rico, and talked to elders where my parents are from in San Sebastian. I learned that beyond petroglyphs, the Taíno did not document their culture and beliefs in contemporary ways (in writing). Instead, they passed on oral histories, which is why many Puerto Ricans have always had a different understanding of Taíno survival, because we've heard stories from our parents, grandparents, and great-grandparents. This understanding went against the grain of historians and anthropologists who needed that written account to legitimize a people.

In my own family, my mother told me stories about her Taíno great-grandmother and how her ways of living and being had passed down to each generation, mother to daughter, eventually reaching her and then me. For example, my mother often spoke of how her grandmother and aunts taught her to live off the land. To this day, she can grow vegetables anywhere, even in the hardest of soils in Boston, MA.

Historical documentation spoke of the Taíno in the past tense, as if they had perished forever, yet Puerto Ricans spoke of the Taíno as if they had never left. I spent years trying to come to terms with what I read against what I was taught and felt deep in my soul: that the Taíno, my ancestors, lived within me.

In 2018, while finishing up a doctoral program in arts and education, I read an article published on Smithsonian.com titled, *Ancient DNA Contradicts Historical Narrative of 'Extinct' Caribbean Taíno Population*. This article chronicled a research project into the DNA of an ancient tooth found in a one-thousand-year-old skeleton. This skeleton was found in the Bahamas and was of a human who predated Columbus. Through the DNA found in this tooth, researchers were able to track the migration of Arawak people from islands in the

Caribbean and discovered that present day Puerto Ricans had the most Taíno DNA.

That was it. That was the "truth" that lived in my blood. See! We are still here! My mother, grandmother, and great-grandmother—as well as many other Caribeños—had shared that truth with the world, but now science backed up what we already knew.

Something reawakened inside me—a need to honor my ancestors by digging deeper and learning more about how they had ensured their survival. I wanted to understand the lengthy history that caused the Taíno to try and blend in with their oppressors—to hide in plain sight. And I felt strongly that my Taíno ancestors had instilled in me, my family, and other people of Taíno descent a deep-seated sense of survival based on love for one's family, land, and culture, and a profound respect for nature.

With renewed vigor, I continued to research and learn. I read all I could on the Taíno. I read work by anthropologists, scientists, fiction writers, and children's book authors (see the list of references at the end of this note) but I wasn't satisfied. I had yet to find a story that presented the Taíno as strategic—a people who understood that genocide was happening and fought back in ways that ensured their survival. I also wondered how historical trauma affects our present-day lives, how the past is connected to the present, and how we articulate the pain and loss of a major part of history through our contemporary lenses. But I couldn't find a work of fiction or nonfiction that shared what I wanted to understand or express.

At a 1981 speech to the Ohio Arts Council, the late amazing literary genius Toni Morrison said, *"If there's a book that you want to read, but it hasn't been written yet, then you must write it."* I took those words seriously, which is what set me on the journey to write *The Moonlit Vine.* A book to name how vital the Taíno were to not only my survival, but also the survival of my family and many, many others. How much their joy, intelligence, and love continue to shape me and others to the present day. They are more than just the people who warmly greeted Christopher Columbus and welcomed him to their islands. They are family. This novel is my way of sharing my deep gratitude and respect for them. And I truly believe they were guiding me through this process, ensuring this work would have an audience.

A first draft of this manuscript serendipitously made its way into the hands of Elise McMullen-Ciotti, an editor at Lee & Low Books. After I had written the first draft, I wasn't sure what I was going to do with it. Writing the novel healed something inside me, and I wondered if that was enough of a purpose for writing it. I shared that feeling with a good friend of mine, Rondi Silva. Rondi asked if she could read the manuscript, which I sent to her. Unbeknownst to me, she knew Jason Low of Lee & Low and talked to him about the work. He asked if he could share a copy with Elise.

At the time, I was embarrassed. I wasn't ready for the work to see the light of day, nor did I think my writing was ready for a professional editor and publishing house to analyze! When Elise reached out to me about the novel, I was floored to learn that she had also been deeply interested in the Taíno. As a member of the Cherokee Nation, Elise works tirelessly to get Native stories out into the world. She acknowledged that there were no young adult novels focused on the Taíno and she had been hoping someone would write one. Out of the sky, *The Moonlit Vine* appeared on her desk. To me, it felt as though our ancestors had had a hand in bringing us together, because the odds of us finding each other in the way we did and at the time we did were slim to none. I humbly acknowledge this truth and thank my ancestors for everything they have done to help me tell this story and make sure it got into the hands of one of the few editors who could understand it. (Thank you, Elise, for all that you have done to champion *The Moonlit Vine*!) I hope the story will resonate not just with Puerto Ricans, but with all of us who feel untold history in our blood and have stories to share because of it.

The Moonlit Vine weaves in historical chapters and content into a contemporary work of fiction. Through this structure, I've shown how historical trauma makes itself known within the lives of present-day descendants of the Taíno and how colonial oppression still exists.

Not all of the characters in the book are works of fiction. Anacaona and Caonabo are very real historical figures— royalty in the Caribbean before Columbus. They ruled in what is now Haiti and are important historical figures in Haiti and the Dominican Republic. I chose Anacaona to begin the matrilineal line to the present-day fictional character of Taína, because Anacaona is Taíno royalty most Caribbean folks have heard of, and Anacaona worked diligently to keep her people safe. I also wanted to show ancestral unity between Caribbean islands that have Taíno ancestors like Haiti, Dominican Republic, and Puerto Rico. Other Caribbean islands have Taíno ancestors, but I focused on the islands where I could have a connective story arc with Anacaona. Since she ruled in present-day Haiti, I imagined that her daughter, Higüamota, made her way across that island to short-term safety on Mona Island.

Higüamota (aka Higuemota) is a real, historical figure. She was the only recorded child of Anacaona and Caonabo. However, there is no written knowledge of what happened to her. She may have died as a child or lived until adulthood. I wondered what she would have had to do to survive. I imagined her receiving important artifacts from her mother and finding her way to Ámona or Mona Island (La Isla de la Mona to Spanish speakers). Mona Island, which lies between the Dominican Republic and Puerto Rico, is currently not a habitable island. Yet there is known Taíno activity there. Archeologists have found Taíno cave drawings on the island, establishing their inhabitance of the island. It was easy to imagine Higüamota hiding there for a time on her travels to nearby Mayagüez, Puerto Rico.

The Taíno have influenced present-day America. Have you ever swung in a hammock? The Taíno invented them. While they didn't have a written language, their words have endured. Words like hamaca (hammock), as well as bar-bacoa (barbecue), canoa (canoe), tabaco (tobacco), yuca, and huracán (hurricane) have been incorporated into both Spanish and English languages.

Finally, the purpose of my doctoral research was to focus on narrative techniques that support liberation and healing of young people who have been marginalized by systemic racism and oppression, and yet this novel took a very personal turn by supporting my own liberation and healing. The healing was unexpected. I had not written creatively for many years and diving into my curiosity and research to support this narrative awakened the creative side of my brain. I began to place my research into a context with real, modern-day people, neighborhoods, and larger societal issues. *The Moonlit Vine* describes how the themes I was encountering in my research play out in schools, communities, and homes. The biggest theme I wanted to convey is that young people have power. They can change their personal life trajectories as well as the quality of life in their communities. This is why Taína, our fourteen-year-old protagonist, discovers and uses her power through the understanding of her history. Her awakening to her ancestral history plays out in the resilience of her present-day life.

I have been humbled and honored to bring Taína to life. Taína is not only me but also many young girls I see in my own community, who are beautiful, powerful, and able to do so much more than society tells them is possible. My niece Tori texted me after reading a draft of the book, "Taína is soooo bold!" Yes, she is, and creating her channeled my own need to be bold. It took me a long time to find my voice again as a writer and as a creative person, and the amazing Taíno, my ancestors, and my fictional character, Taína, both gave me personal power. I hope *The Moonlit Vine* inspires others to reflect, act, and be bold.

Anacaona and Caonabo Ancestry

(based on this fictional story)

Anacaona • Caonabo (1474–1503) Anacaona died in 1503. Before she died, she created zemi and amulet. She gave the items to Higüamota who fled to Isla de la Mona (Amoná).

Higüamota • Guaybana (1482–1540) Higüamota said goodbye to her mother when she was thirteen and never saw her again. She died in 1540 on Isla de la Mona. She had two children: Yayael (boy) and Guanina (girl). She passed on items to Guanina.

Guanina • Cacimar (1507–1580) Guanina died in 1580 in Yagüecax. She had a daughter, Casiguaya, and son, Daguao. She passed on items to Casiguaya.

Casiguaya • Hatuey (1526–1601) Casiguaya died in 1601. She had four children: Augustin (Caonabo), Pedro (Guama), Jimena (Tinima), and Miguel (Hayuya). She passed on the items to Jimena (Tinima).

Tinima/Jimena • Cristobal (1547–1620) Jimena died in 1620. She had three children: (Yuisa) Luisa, (Guaynata) Maria, and (Amanex) Hernan. She passed on the items to Guaynata.

Guaynata/Maria • Gabriel (1567–1634) Guaynata died in 1634. She only had one son, Mateo. She passed the items on to her granddaughter, Antonia.

Mateo • Quiteria (1589–1650) Mateo died in 1650, but he and Quiteria had two children, Antonia and Mateo, Jr. Guaynata passed the items on to Antonia, who was born in 1615.

Antonia • Hernan (1615–1715) Antonia lived 100 years and died in 1715. She had three daughters: Maria, Clara, and Luisa. She passed the items onto Luisa.

Luisa • Lorenzo (1638–1719) Luisa died in 1719. She had five children: Gasper, Alvaro, Anna, Ines, and Julia. She passed on the items to Ines.

Ines • Andres (1665–1750) Ines died in 1750. Had one daughter, Cristina, whom she passed the items to.

Cristina • Juan (1695–1783) Cristina died in 1783 and had three children: Rosa, Magdalena, and Diego. She passed on the items to Rosa.

Rosa • Francisco (1725–1808) Rosa died in 1808 and had four children: Maria; Luisa; Francisco, Jr.; and Antonio. She passed on the items to Luisa.

Luisa • Jorge (1760–1860) Luisa died in 1860 and had three sons: Alonso, Martin, and Miguel. She held onto the items to pass on to one of her granddaughters.

Miguel • Julia (1795–1887) Miguel had three children: Maria, Anna, and Martin. Luisa passed the items on to Anna.

Anna • Gonzalo (1843–1935) Anna died in 1935. She had three children: Beatriz; Gonzalo, Jr.; and Ides. She passed on the items to Ides.

Ides • Hector (1885–1960) Ides died in 1960. She had five children: Clara, Jaime, Enrique, Cesario, and Luisa. She passed on the items to Clara.

Clara • Rodrigo (1909–1986) Clara died in 1986. She had two daughters, Juana and Isaura. She passed on the items to Isaura.

Isaura • Otilio (1950–2018) Isaura died in 2018, but not before passing the items on to her granddaughter, Taína. She had two children: Benito and Esmeralda.

Esmeralda • Alejandro (1978–present) Isaura and Otilio moved to the states in 1972 for a better life. They had their son, Benito, in 1975 and their daughter, Esmeralda, in 1978. Esmeralda has three children: Alex Jr., Taína, and Luis.

Taína (2004–present) Taína receives the items when she is fourteen years old.

Key Moments in
Puerto Rican History

1474   Anacaona is born in Ayiti (present day Leogane, Haiti)

1493   The Arawaks (AKA the Taíno) greet Columbus. It is said Anacaona was one of the first Taíno to greet Columbus and his people.

1496   Caonabo dies

1503   Anacaona is murdered

1508   Spain officially colonizes Puerto Rico

1513   African people are forced into Puerto Rico for the first time (estimated date)

1760   Mayagüez is founded

1873   Slavery is abolished

1898   Spanish American War ends and Spain cedes Puerto Rico to America

1917   The Jones-Shafroth Act is signed, giving Puerto Ricans US citizenship

1950s   With travel to the US becoming easier, the largest migration of Puerto Ricans to the mainland US occurs

Inspiring Boriqueños
(Puerto Ricans)

Hayuya (born c. 1470) was the Taíno cacique who governed the area in Puerto Rico that bears his name (now spelled "Jayuya"). Jayuya is a town and municipality of Puerto Rico located in the mountainous center region of the island.

Mabodamaca (reigned in the 1500s) was a well-respected cacique. He is said to have led his people up the Guajataca River to the central mountain range to escape the Spanish invaders. He fought bravely to maintain their security and way of life.

María Bibiana Benítez (1783–1873?), poet, was born in Aguadilla, Puerto Rico. In 1832, Benítez published her first poem, "La Ninfa de Puerto Rico" ("The Nymph of Puerto Rico"). In 1862, she wrote the first dramatic play by a Puerto Rican person, *La Cruz del Morro* ("The Cross of El Morro"), inspired by the 1625 defense of San Juan against the Dutch.

Mariana Bracetti (1825–1903) was born in Añasco, Puerto Rico, and is believed to have been the woman who crafted the first Puerto Rican flag. Bracetti was an independence movement leader in the 1860s and was involved in organizing the 1868 Grito de Lares, an attempted revolt in the town of Lares. She was arrested and released a few months later, after she was granted amnesty by the Spanish government. The flag she designed, known to many as the Bandera Revolucionaria, is now the official flag of Lares.

Ramón Emeterio Betances (1827–1898), doctor, activist, and writer, was born in Cabo Rojo, Puerto Rico. He got his medical degree from the University of Paris in 1855. He returned to Puerto Rico and worked to save people from a cholera epidemic, which hit particularly hard in the city of Mayagüez. His refusal to give priority treatment to Spanish officers, his creation of an organization that sought to free enslaved people, and his activism for Puerto Rican independence all created tension with the colonial government, and he was repeatedly exiled. His literary works, which included essays and novels, earned him the Legion of Honor award from the French government.

Ana Roqué de Duprey (1853–1933), educator and activist, was born in Aguadilla, Puerto Rico. At 13, she created a school in her home. She went on to direct or establish more schools—including a teacher's academy, a high school for girls, and the College of Mayagüez—and helped found the University of Puerto Rico. She started several publications including *La Mujer*, a newspaper for women, and cofounded Puerto Rico's first organization for women's suffrage.

José Celso Barbosa (1857–1921), physician, sociologist, and politician, was born in Bayamón, Puerto Rico. In 1880, he became the first Puerto Rican to receive a medical degree in the United States. He returned to Bayamón, where he provided medical care. In 1899, he formed a pro-statehood political party. He served in Puerto Rican Governor Charles H. Allen's executive cabinet (1900–1917) and the first Puerto Rican Senate (1917–1921). He established *El Tiempo*, the island's first bilingual newspaper, in 1907.

Pedro Albizu Campos (1891–1965), politician, was born in Ponce, Puerto Rico. After service in an African American unit during World War I, he became a champion of Puerto Rican independence. He joined the Nationalist Party of Puerto Rico in 1924 and in 1930 was elected its president. When conflicts between nationalists and those in power turned violent, he was arrested and imprisoned. After he was released, he continued to agitate for independence, defying new laws that limited speech against the US government, and was imprisoned again. He is remembered for his passionate challenges to the status quo of the commonwealth.

Felisa Rincón de Gautier (1897–1994) was born in Ceiba, Puerto Rico. She was a firm believer in the suffragist movement and was one of the first women on the island to register to vote. She worked in many professions, such as pharmacist, florist, and seamstress, before entering politics and helping to found the Popular Democratic Party. In 1946, she was appointed mayor of San Juan, making her the first woman mayor of any capital city in the Americas; she would be reelected another four times, serving until 1969.

Luis Muñoz Marín (1898–1980) was born in San Juan. Following in the footsteps of his father, who had been Resident Commissioner of Puerto Rico (1910–1916), Muñoz Marín entered politics and was elected to the Puerto Rican Senate in 1932. At first he advocated independence, but changed his views over time. As president of the Senate (1940–1948), he worked with the Roosevelt administration to bring New Deal programs to Puerto Rico. He won the first-ever election for governor of Puerto Rico in 1948, serving a total of four terms. During this time, he successfully changed the island's status from territory to commonwealth.

Rita Moreno (1931–), actress, was born in Humacao, Puerto Rico. Her role as Anita in Robert Wise's 1961 film *West Side Story* brought her fame and an Oscar (the first ever for a Latina woman). She won a Tony in 1975 for her Broadway stage performance in *The Ritz*. Her work in television included a starring role in *The Electric Company* (an accompanying record won her a Grammy) and Emmy-winning guest appearances on *The Muppet Show* and *The Rockford Files*. This made her the first Latina woman ever to win the four biggest awards in American show business, the "EGOT" (Emmy, Grammy, Oscar, and Tony).

Roberto Clemente (1934–1972), baseball player, was born in Carolina, Puerto Rico. He was a baseball player with the Pittsburgh Pirates (1955–1972) and was famed both for his batting and for his prowess as a defensive outfielder. Clemente won four National

League batting titles (1961, 1964, 1965, 1967), was the league's Most Valuable Player in 1966, and won the Gold Glove 12 years in a row (1961–1972). After his untimely death in a plane crash en route to deliver earthquake-relief supplies to Nicaragua, the Baseball Hall of Fame held a special election that waived the usual five-year waiting period and admitted him in 1973.

Sila María Calderón (1942–) was born in San Juan and served in various governmental positions before being elected mayor of San Juan in 1996. She became head of the Popular Democratic Party, and—in a 1998 referendum—she successfully led the campaign to have Puerto Rico remain a commonwealth rather than seeking statehood. Soon afterward, she was elected the first female governor of Puerto Rico (2001–2005).

Richard L. Carrión (1952–), financier, was born in San Juan, Puerto Rico. Following in the footsteps of his grandfather—who cofounded the commercial bank Banco Popular (Popular Bank) in 1923—and his father and uncle—who took over upon his grandfather's retirement—he became chairman and CEO of the bank in 1990. He is now the executive chairman of its parent company, Popular Inc. He chairs the finance committee of the International Olympics Committee. His Banco Popular Foundation has provided scholarships to more than 1,000 students.

Nydia M. Velázquez (1953–), politician, was born in Yabucoa, Puerto Rico. She was the first Latina woman to serve in the New York City Council upon her appointment in 1984. In 1992, she was the first Puerto Rican woman elected to the US Congress, becoming the representative of a district spanning parts of Manhattan, Brooklyn, and Queens in New York City. In 1998, she became the first Latina to serve as ranking member of a full House committee, the House Small Business Committee. In 2006, she became the first Latina to chair a full Congressional committee, the House Small Business Committee.

Sonia Sotomayor (1954–), judge, was born in the Bronx, NY. Sotomayor worked as an assistant district attorney and as a private attorney before being nominated by President George H.W. Bush as a district court judge in 1991. She later served on the US Court of Appeals for the Second Circuit starting in 1998, having been nominated by President Clinton. Finally, she was nominated by President Barack Obama in 2009 as an associate justice of the Supreme Court. She became the first Puerto Rican to be appointed to the role.

Jennifer Lopez (1969–), singer, actress, and dancer, was born in the Bronx, NY. She rose to prominence with her starring role in the 1997 film *Selena*. In 2001, she became the first woman to have a #1 film and album at the same time, with *The Wedding Planner* and *J.Lo*. She has been named one of the most influential or powerful people in the world by *Time* and *Forbes*.

Ivy Queen (1972–), singer, rapper, and songwriter, was born in Añasco, Puerto Rico. Known as the "Queen of Reggaeton," she was among the first female stars in the male-dominated genre. She was inducted into the Latin Songwriters Hall of Fame in 2019.

Bad Bunny (1994–), rapper and singer, was born in Vega Baja, Puerto Rico. In 2018, he was featured on Cardi B's hit song "I Like It." He went on to release several successful solo albums, including *El Último Tour del Mundo*, which in 2020 became the first all-Spanish album to reach #1 on the Billboard 200 chart. In addition to his Latin trap and reggaeton music, he has wrestled in WWE matches.

Laurie Hernandez (2000–), gymnast, was born in Old Bridge Township, NJ. At the 2016 Rio Olympics, she was part of the gold-medaling USA women's gymnastics team and won a silver medal of her own on the balance beam. Later that year, she also became the youngest winner on *Dancing with the Stars*.

References

Alexander, Kerri Lee. "Rita Moreno." National Women's History Museum. 2019. womenshistory.org/education-resources/biographies/rita-moreno.

Atlas Obscura. "Tumbo del Indio—Jayuya, Puerto Rico." Accessed June 21, 2022. atlasobscura.com/places/tumba-del-indio.

"Biography: Nydia M. Velázquez." Congresswoman Nydia Velázquez. Accessed June 22, 2022. velazquez.house.gov/about/full-biography.

Brandman, Mariana. "Ana Roqué de Duprey." National Women's History Museum. 2020. womenshistory.org/education-resources/biographies/ana-roque-de-duprey.

———. "Felisa Rincón de Gautier." National Women's History Museum. 2020. womenshistory.org/education-resources/biographies/felisa-rincon-de-gautier.

Colón, Frances A. "The Untold History of Women in Science and Technology: Ana Roqué de Duprey." White House, March 30, 2016. obamawhitehouse.archives.gov/women-in-stem.

Danticat, Edwidge. *Anacaona: Golden Flower, Haiti, 1490*. New York: Scholastic, 2005.

EnciclopediaPR. "María Bibiana Benítez." September 15, 2014. enciclopediapr.org/content/maria-bibiana-benitez/.

Encyclopaedia Britannica Online. "History of Puerto Rico." Accessed May 2, 2022. britannica.com/place/Puerto-Rico/History.

———. "Luis Muñoz Marín." Accessed June 21, 2022. britannica.com/biography/Luis-Munoz-Marin.

———. "Pedro Albizu Campos." Accessed June 21, 2022. britannica.com/biography/Pedro-Albizu-Campos.

———. "Rita Moreno." Accessed June 21, 2022. britannica.com/biography/Rita-Moreno.

———. "Sila María Calderón." Accessed June 21, 2022. britannica.com/biography/Sila-Maria-Calderon.

"Felisa Rincón de Gautier." Iowa State University Archives of Women's Political Communication. Accessed June 22, 2022. awpc.cattcenter.iastate.edu/directory/felisa-rincon-de-gautier/.

JT. "Biography—Pedro Albizu Campos." Latinopia.com. September 13, 2010. latinopia.com/latino-history/biography-pedro-albizu-campos/.

Keegan, William F. *Taíno Indian Myth and Practice: The Arrival of the Stranger King*. Gainesville, FL: University Press of Florida, 2007.

"Laurie Hernandez." USA Gymnastics. Accessed June 22, 2022. usagym.org/pages/athletes/athleteListDetail.html?id=278528.

Library of Congress. "José Celso Barbosa." The World of 1898: The Spanish-American War. May 14, 2020. loc.gov/rr/hispanic/1898/barbosa.html.

———. "Ramón Emeterio Betances." The World of 1898: The Spanish-American War. June 22, 2011. loc.gov/rr/hispanic/1898/betances.html.

"Luis Muñoz Marín." National Governors Association. Accessed June 22, 2022. nga.org/governor/luis-munoz-marin/.

Olmo, M. C. "Hekití and the Moon: A Taíno Legend." Self-published, Smashwords, 2011.

Picó, Fernando. *History of Puerto Rico: A Panorama of Its People*. Princeton, NJ: Markus Wiener, 2006.

Poole, Robert M. "What became of the Taíno?" *Smithsonian*, Oct. 2011. smithsonianmag.com/travel/what-became-of-the-taino-73824867/.

Porrata, Richard. *Taino Genealogy and Revitalization*. Self-published, 2018.

PuertoRicoTravel.Guide. "Cacique Mabodamaca : A Taino Chieftain of Note." Accessed June 21, 2022. puertoricotravel.guide/blog/cacique-mabodamaca-a-taino-chieftain-of-note/.

———, "Monumento al Indio Mabodomaca—'Cara del Indio.'" Accessed June 21, 2022. puertoricotravelguide.com/cara-del-indio-mabodomaca/.

Reséndez, Andrés. *The Other Slavery: The Uncovered Story of Indian Enslavement in America*. Boston: Mariner Books, 2017.

Rivera, Magaly. "Famous Puerto Ricans." Welcome to Puerto Rico! History, Government, Geography, and Culture. Accessed June 21, 2022. welcome.topuertorico.org/culture/famouspr.shtml.

"Roberto Clemente." National Baseball Hall of Fame. Accessed June 22, 2022. baseballhall.org/hall-of-famers/clemente-roberto.

Rouse, Irving. *The Taínos: Rise and Decline of the People who Greeted Columbus*. New Haven, CT: Yale University Press, 1993.

Solly, Meilan. (2018). "Ancient DNA Contradicts Historical Narrative of 'Extinct' Caribbean Taíno Population," *Smithsonian*, Feb. 22, 2018, smithsonianmag.com/smart-news/ancient-dna-contradicts-historical-narrative-extinctcaribbean-taino-population-180968221/

"Sonia Sotomayor." Oyez. Accessed June 22, 2022. oyez.org/justices/sonia_sotomayor.

Soulet Noemi Figueroa and Raquel Ortiz, dirs. *The Borinqueneers: A Documentary on the All-Puerto Rican 65th Infantry Regiment*. 2007. El Pozo Productions

Wikipedia. "Bad Bunny." Last modified June 19, 2022. en.wikipedia.org/wiki/Bad_Bunny.

———. "Ivy Queen." Last modified June 18, 2022. en.wikipedia.org/wiki/Ivy_Queen.

———. "Jayura, Puerto Rico." Last modified March 17, 2022. en.wikipedia.org/wiki/Jayuya,_Puerto_Rico.

———. "José Celso Barbosa." Last modified February 19, 2022. en.wikipedia.org/wiki/Jos%C3%A9_Celso_Barbosa.

———. "Laurie Hernandez." Last modified June 6, 2022. en.wikipedia.org/wiki/Laurie_Hernandez.

———. "Jennifer Lopez." Last modified June 23, 2022. en.wikipedia.org/wiki/Jennifer_Lopez.

———. "María Bibiana Benítez." Last modified December 19, 2021. en.wikipedia.org/wiki/Mar%C3%ADa_Bibiana_Ben%C3%ADtez.

———. "Mariana Bracetti." Last modified January 21, 2022. en.wikipedia.org/wiki/Mariana_Bracetti.

———. "Ramón Emeterio Betances." Last modified June 15, 2022. en.wikipedia.org/wiki/Ram%C3%B3n_Emeterio_Betances.

———. "Rafael Carrión Sr." Last modified March 5, 2022. en.wikipedia.org/wiki/Rafael_Carri%C3%B3n_Sr.

———. "Richard Carrión." Last modified May 11, 2022. en.wikipedia.org/wiki/Richard_Carri%C3%B3n.

———. "Sila María Calderón." Last modified April 5, 2022. en.wikipedia.org/wiki/Sila_Mar%C3%ADa_Calder%C3%B3n.

Wilson, Samuel M. *The Indigenous People of the Caribbean*. Gainesville, FL: University Press of Florida, 1999.

About the Author

ELIZABETH SANTIAGO grew up in Boston, MA, with parents who migrated from San Sebastián, Puerto Rico, in the 1960s. The youngest of nine, Elizabeth was entranced by the stories around her and became particularly fascinated by those that were not being told in school. These were the stories her mother, father, aunts and uncles, and community elders told her. Today she seeks to capture and honor those narratives and share them with the world.

Elizabeth earned a BFA in creative writing from Emerson College, a master's in education from Harvard University, and a PhD in education studies from Lesley University. Her first loves remain creative writing and teaching, where she creates characters based on her community and supports students in learning to be better overall storytellers.

She still resides in Boston with her husband and son but travels to Puerto Rico as often as she can to feel closer to her ancestors, culture, and heritage.

RESOURCES FOR EDUCATORS

Visit our website, leeandlow.com, for a complete Teacher's Guide for *The Moonlit Vine* as well as discussion questions, author interviews, and more!

Our *Teacher's Guides* are developed by professional educators and offer extensive teaching ideas, curricular connections, and activities that can be adapted to many different educational settings.

How Lee & Low Books Supports Educators:

Lee & Low Books is the largest children's book publisher in the country focused exclusively on diverse books. We publish award-winning books for beginning readers through young adults, along with free, high-quality educational resources to support our titles.

Browse our website to discover Teacher's Guides for 600+ books along with book trailers, interviews, and more.

We are honored to support educators in preparing the next generation of readers, thinkers, and global citizens.

LEE & LOW BOOKS
ABOUT EVERYONE • FOR EVERYONE